INTERNATIONAL ACCLAIM FOR JAMES REDFIELD'S
THE CELESTINE PROPHECY

'It's magnificent, mind boggling, so powerful it makes you gasp out loud'

Insight Magazine

'*The Celestine Prophecy* has already reached cult status . . . it homes in on the deepest, most urgent search of our times, the search for meaning. For searchers who have been through everything from Anglicanism to Zen this is a book like no other'

Daily Telegraph

'This is an extraordinary and uplifting book'

Today

'If you want to read just one inspiring, adventurous and magical tale this year – make it this book'

New Spirit Magazine (New Zealand)

'*The Celestine Prophecy* is a wonderfully insightful book . . . it's really enriching, showing a dimension of life one isn't ordinarily in touch with'

Bestselling author, Patricia Cornwell

'If you haven't heard of *The Celestine Prophecy* then you soon will . . . a spiritual and transformative odyssey . . . it has taken America by storm'

Mind Body Soul Magazine

'*The Celestine Prophecy* has been without doubt, the most talked about book everywhere I've been in North America over the past year'

Lynne Franks, *Evening Standard*

'If you've ever wondered what the formula is for an "inspirational" bestseller, with promising potential for cult status, look no further'

Guardian

*

Also by James Redfield

THE CELESTINE PROPHECY
THE TENTH INSIGHT
THE TENTH INSIGHT: AN EXPERIENTIAL GUIDE
THE CELESTINE PROPHECY: A POCKET GUIDE TO THE
NINE INSIGHTS
A POCKET GUIDE TO THE TENTH INSIGHT

Also by Carol Adrienne

THE NUMEROLOGY KIT
YOUR CHILD'S DESTINY

THE CELESTINE PROPHECY
AN EXPERIENTIAL GUIDE

JAMES REDFIELD
AND CAROL ADRIENNE

BANTAM BOOKS
TORONTO · NEW YORK · LONDON · SYDNEY · AUCKLAND

THE CELESTINE PROPHECY: AN EXPERIENTIAL GUIDE
A BANTAM BOOK : 0 553 50370 7

First publication in Great Britain

PRINTING HISTORY
Bantam edition published 1995
Bantam edition reprinted 1995 (four times)
Bantam edition reprinted 1996 (twice)
Bantam edition reprinted 1997

Bantam Books are published by Transworld Publishers Ltd,
61–63 Uxbridge Road, London W5 5SA,
in Australia by Transworld Publishers (Australia) Pty Ltd,
15–25 Helles Avenue, Moorebank, NSW 2170,
and in New Zealand by Transworld Publishers (NZ) Ltd,
3 William Pickering Drive, Albany, Auckland.

Printed and bound in Great Britain by
Cox & Wyman Ltd, Reading, Berkshire.

We wish to dedicate this book to our children:

Kelly and Megan Redfield
Sigrid Emerson and Gunther Rohrer

and all the people who resonate with
The Celestine Prophecy

Contents

Acknowledgments

First we would like to thank everyone who read *The Celestine Prophecy* and passed the book along to friends. Without your enthusiasm and readiness to learn more this book would not have come into being.

Special thanks to Candice Fuhrman for bringing the authors together and sparking this joint project. We also want to express deep gratitude to Joann Davis for her support, advice, and editing.

Thanks must also go to Penney Peirce and Ellen Looyen, who both insisted that Carol Adrienne read *The Celestine Prophecy*. We greatly appreciate all those who contributed time, energy, and ideas in our workshops in Sausalito and Mount Shasta, California: in particular, Donna Hale, Larry Leigon, Donna Stoneham, Paula Pagano, Annie Rohrbach, Bob Harlow, and all of those whose stories illustrate key points of the book. Especially we would like to honor the contribution of Salle Merrill-Redfield, who acted as intuitive guide and advisor to the project.

We would also like to express gratitude for all the writers and thinkers who have influenced our work and contributed so much to the evolution of consciousness.

Preface

Soon after the publication of *The Celestine Prophecy*, many readers began to ask for more information and to suggest the writing of a study guide. My first response was to hesitate. After all, I consider the novel an "adventure parable," an attempt to relate a story that illustrates the new spiritual awareness many of us see emerging on our planet. And I wasn't sure a guide was appropriate. Our new worldview is not just a set of intellectual facts to be debated pro and con. It is much more intuitive and experiential than that. In fact, it can be argued that those who take a strictly intellectual approach to this subject will be the last to "get it."

The Paradigm shift that is occurring in our time is best thought of as a new common sense, or as what Joseph Campbell called a "new mythology." It may be the result of decades of intellectual description, but at the point where the description becomes lived, our new view is based on experience, not theory. We are getting in touch with something we knew but didn't realize we knew, as we recognize our half-conscious ability to follow hunches, take advantage of coincidental opportunities, and sense a higher spiritual guidance active in our lives. It is not so much a change in philosophy as a shift in how we sense and approach life.

Still, there is a difference between hearing about this new approach to life and having the perceptions necessary to adopt it. I firmly believe that this level of experience is humanity's destiny, but it is not real for any of us until we discover it individually and map it out in our own terms. Hence, such awareness seems best communicated by story and parable, by the sharing of biographical events, and by the contagion of one person seeing a higher truth in the life of another, and then coming to that same experience alone.

You can see, then, my ambivalence toward a study guide. I felt such a project would have to provide a strict definition of ideas and perceptions best left to the reader's own interpretation. Yet, thanks to the input of Carol Adrienne and others, I came to understand that a study guide didn't have to fit that mold. We could in essence elaborate on the ideas set forth in *The Celestine Prophecy* in a manner consistent with the spirit of the novel: by providing more information, but encouraging the reader to investigate these elaborations in self-directed ways. This is what we have tried to do in this companion book. What you will find is additional subject matter and some options from which to choose as you explore it. Some of these ideas are intended as background, others are given merely as interesting tangents. All, we hope, will help to clarify the experience conveyed in the original book.

This guide is designed both for individual readers and for those seeking group discussion. A designated group leader or facilitator is unnecessary. Consistent with the Eighth Insight, group members can each lead at various times, determined intuitively and through consensus. If you come upon someone who is charging money to teach *Celestine* concepts, my advice is that you use the same discretion you would employ when buying anything else from a stranger. There is no *Celestine* school from which accredited trainers graduate and never will be, and we endorse no one who teaches workshops on the subject, although many fine people seem called to do this.

Much of this book's energy, writing style, and group technique comes from Carol Adrienne, who seems to have a special talent for communicating the *Celestine* point of view. Without her initial vision of this guide, as well as her determination in thinking it through, the book wouldn't have happened. Our wish is that this guide will contribute to what is already an energized dialogue on the experience of spirituality.

Remember, the Insights are coming to all of us at the same time, but implementing them is a person-to-person process. The emergence of a fuller spiritual awareness on Planet Earth is occurring only because of individuals like you, who step back and decide life really is more mysterious than any of us thought, and who then break through the habits of skepticism and denial . . . to find their own mission and their own intuitive way of uplifting the world.

JAMES REDFIELD
August 10, 1994

The Nine Insights

1
A Critical Mass

A new spiritual awakening is occurring in human culture, an awakening brought about by a critical mass of individuals who experience their lives as a spiritual unfolding, a journey in which we are led forward by mysterious coincidences.

2
The Longer Now

This awakening represents the creation of a new, more complete worldview, which replaces a five-hundred-year-old preoccupation with secular survival and comfort. While this technological preoccupation was an important step, our awakening to life coincidences is opening us up to the real purpose of human life on this planet and the real nature of our universe.

3
A Matter of Energy

We now experience that we live not in a material universe, but in a universe of dynamic energy. Everything extant is a field of sacred energy that we can sense and intuit. Moreover, we humans can project our energy by focusing our attention in the desired direction ("where attention goes, energy flows"), influencing other energy systems and increasing the pace of coincidences in our lives.

4
The Struggle for Power

Too often humans cut themselves off from the greater source of this energy and so feel weak and insecure. To gain energy we tend to manipulate or force others to give us attention and thus energy. When we successfully dominate others in this way, we feel more powerful, but they are left weakened and often fight back. Competition for scarce human energy is the cause of all conflict between people.

5
The Message of the Mystics

Insecurity and violence end when we experience an inner connection with divine energy within, a connection described by the mystics of all traditions. A sense of lightness—buoyancy—and the constant sensation of love are measures of this connection. If these measures are present, the connection is real. If not, it is only pretended.

6
Clearing the Past

The more we stay connected, the more we are acutely aware of those times when we lose connection, usually when we are under stress. In these times, we can see our own particular way of stealing energy from others. Once our manipulations are brought to personal awareness, our connection becomes more constant and then we can discover our own growth path in life, and our spiritual mission, the personal way we can contribute to the world.

7
Engaging the Flow

Knowing our personal mission further enhances the flow of mysterious coincidences as we are guided toward our destinies. First we have a question, then dreams, daydreams, and intuitions lead us toward the answers, which usually are synchronistically provided by the wisdom of another human being.

8
The Interpersonal Ethic

We can increase the frequency of guiding coincidences by uplifting every person that comes into our lives. Care must be taken not to lose our inner connection in romantic relationships. Uplifting others is especially effective in groups where each member can feel the energy of all the others. With children it is extremely important to their early security and growth. By seeing the beauty in every face we lift others into their wisest self and increase the chances of hearing a synchronistic message.

9
The Emerging Culture

As we all evolve toward the best completion of our spiritual missions, the technological means of survival will be fully automated as humans focus instead on synchronistic growth. Such growth will move humans into ever-higher energy states, ultimately transforming our bodies into spiritual form and uniting this dimension of existence with the afterlife dimension, ending the cycle of birth and death.

CHAPTER 1

A Critical Mass:
The Coincidences That
Shape Our Lives

The Mystery Begins

In The Celestine Prophecy *the main character has an unexpected meeting with an old friend just at the moment in his life when he is feeling disenchanted and thinking about changing directions. Charlene, newly arrived from a trip to Peru, where an ancient Manuscript has been discovered, is able to shed some light on the cause of his restlessness.*

Our character, who remains nameless, is introduced to the First Insight: becoming conscious of the coincidences working in his life. Skeptical of the idea of a Manuscript explaining the secret of human existence, he is nevertheless intrigued by the mystery.

That night, after returning home, he has a dream about the nature of coincidences and how they always involve the appearance of a person with information. Buoyed by his increasing interest, he books a flight to Peru.

THE FIRST INSIGHT

Slowly, with little fanfare, a global transformation is taking place. As described in the ancient teachings of the Manuscript found in the Celestine ruins, the first sign that we are awakening to this deep inner call is a profound sense of restlessness. This restlessness may be described as dissatisfaction (even after reaching goals), vague uneasiness, or a sense that something is missing. Once in a while a chance event surprises and intrigues us. It's as if some higher purpose is being revealed, and for a moment we feel connected to a mystery that nevertheless eludes our grasp.

The combination of inner searching ("There must be more to life") and an occasional cosmic jostle ("Wow! What a strange coincidence. I wonder what that meant?") is a powerful process. Mysterious and exciting, coincidences are purposeful in moving us forward in our destiny. They make us feel more alive, as if there is some greater plan at work.

As more and more of us (a critical mass) become conscious of this mysterious movement of the universe in our individual lives, the more quickly will we discover the nature of human existence. If we open our minds and hearts, we will be part of the evolution of a new spirituality.

What Is Coincidence?

The First Insight in *The Celestine Prophecy* tends to capture our attention and fire our imagination because it taps into what our mythic reality has always taught—that there is a Golden Key, a magical stranger, a meaningful dream, or an unexpected clue that appears to guide us effortlessly to the treasure or opportunity that we seek. Swiss psychologist Carl Jung called it the archetype of "magical effect" and claimed that it was a universal trait in humans. Recognizing the important role that coincidence plays in moving our lives along takes us back to the instincts of the alert, poised hunter praying for the emergence of quarry, and the deeply attuned receptive state of a powerful shaman or medicine woman. Coincidences are the stuff of stories by firelight, and laughing memories at weddings, and tales of inordinate success and sublime irony. Life stories are studded by the mysterious by-products of chance meetings, missed trains, books opening to a significant passage, ajar doors, overheard conversations, a meeting of the eyes across a crowded room. Most of literature and theater wouldn't exist without such premises as two people meeting accidentally in a corridor or while waiting to board the ferry to Hong Kong. Much of the sometimes higgledy-piggledy nature of employment résumés can be explained by the effect of coincidental job opportunities that were not part of a career plan.

For example, Elisabeth Kübler-Ross, the famous expert on death and dying, describes in *Women of Power* (by Laurel King) a turning point while working in a residency with Dr. Sydney Margolin: ". . . one day, while I was putting together a polygraph machine, he came in and said he had to go somewhere and I would have to take over his lectures. This was like replacing God! I died a thousand deaths. . . . He said [the lecture] had to be about psychiatry, but I could pick any subject. I went to the library to see if there was anything written on death and dying because I thought the students really needed to know about it." Perhaps her choice of subject was unknowingly shaped by her early experiences in war relief in Europe, from which she still carries the images of those who perished in the death camps. Or perhaps this was a point of divine intervention. Whatever guided her choice of subject that day, Kübler-Ross's initial lecture on death and dying started a chain of events that changed the direction of her life and opened up what turned out to be a life's mission.

The First Insight has us start at the beginning, at that very point of convergence where life's mystery stares back at us, outside our logical expectations and experience. Becoming conscious of the reality of coincidences and aware of their message and meaning is the first step to evolving consciously and more quickly.

When was the last time you experienced something out of the ordinary? Perhaps this morning you were thinking

> . . . for me there is only the traveling on the paths that have a heart, on any path that may have a heart. There I travel, and the only worthwhile challenge for me is to traverse its full length . . . looking, looking, breathlessly.
>
> CARLOS CASTANEDA,
> *The Teachings of Don Juan*[1]

about someone and then got a phone call from that person. How many times have you said, "I was just thinking about you"? Was there a significant message from this person? Did you consider *why this coincidence might have happened? What followed it?* We tend to take for granted many of the subtle, ordinary chance occurrences, and often it is only the really startling events that make us shake our head in wonderment.

As the Manuscript predicted, the notion of seeing coincidences as more than superficially interesting began to emerge as psychology revealed the existence of the unconscious. At about the same time that Einstein was discovering that space and time are relative to a point of reference and not absolute concepts, another great pioneer, Swiss psychologist Carl Jung, was giving serious study to the idea of "meaningful coincidences," and his work has sparked significant inquiries in the past three decades. He called this phenomenon *synchronicity* and believed that it is as natural a connecting principle as cause and effect. With synchronicity, however, we are not able to immediately see the causal link. Nevertheless, coincidence seems to be a primary way that the universe evolves, and many of us have felt this effect in our own lives. Recognizing the importance of coincidence lays the groundwork for the remaining Insights, which inform us that the universe responds to our consciousness and expectations—creating the chance opportunities to move us along. With the awareness of coincidence, we are attuning ourselves to the mystery of the underlying principle of order in the universe. As Jung said, "Synchronicity suggests that there is an interconnection or unity of causally unrelated events,"[2] and thus postulates a unitary aspect of being.

People sometimes wonder if a coincidence is a random event that serves to awaken them, or if it is a response to an unconscious question. Before one has grasped the full extent of the First Insight, a coincidence seems to be an amusing or interesting diversion from "real life." Once we have understood that evolution often moves forward by leaps of transcausal events, the First Insight allows us to look more seriously for the hidden answer or meaning. By the time we have learned to keep our current questions in the forefront of awareness, and to ask the *right* questions, then we know that a coincidence is a response to the archetypal movement toward growth deep within the psyche.

Jung, fascinated by the phenomenon he observed repeatedly in patients, named it synchronicity. According to Ira Progoff, who interpreted and popularized much of Jung's thinking on the subject, synchronicity might seem to happen as follows:

Imagine two women, Claire and Danielle, who have agreed to meet to discuss a workshop on intuition. Claire invites Danielle to come to her house at ten in the morning. Claire, on her own path of cause and effect, gets up, takes a shower, makes coffee, puts out pencil and paper, and waits for Danielle to knock on the door.

Danielle, on her own path of cause and effect, gets up, dresses, gets in the car, follows Claire's directions, parks, and knocks on Claire's door. So far, they are on parallel tracks where there is a past, present, and future for each of them.

In the course of their planning session, the phone rings. It's Bill, who says he just read a great book on psychic healing and wanted to tell Claire all about it. "How odd you called. Danielle is here, and we're just planning our workshop on intuition," exclaims Claire, feeling energized with the mysterious interplay of events. Bill, who also knows

Danielle, tells Claire to say hi to her and hangs up. Danielle, eyes wide, remarks to Claire, "How weird. Just as you got up to answer the phone, Bill's face came into my mind." Both women feel excited by the mysterious coincidence.

According to Jung's theories, Danielle's and Claire's life paths were two vertical tracks of events through which Bill's call traversed across time, or horizontally. Bill's call became meaningful because the women had been activated by a common inner archetype—in this case, perhaps, the archetype of the teacher gathering information, since their intent was to plan their workshop.

In Jung's thinking, at the moment of coincidental events, there appears to be a change in the balance of psychic energy present in the unconscious and the conscious areas. Like balancing on a seesaw, the coincidence lowers for an instant the attention of the conscious psychic energy, pushing the unconscious material up from the primal depths. This psychic movement is perhaps similar to a galvanizing shock, making Claire and Danielle feel as if something exciting had happened. They suddenly feel more alive.

Of course, the beauty of synchronicity is that it is a gift of the universal flow of energy. We don't need a rational explanation in order to be moved by it. However, once we have felt the connection, we might want to play with it a little further to see what it is trying to promote. For example, Danielle, Claire, and Bill might get together with the conscious intent of discovering why the energy suddenly coalesced in this triangle. Do they have further work to do together? Is there a connection as yet undiscovered?

Alan Vaughan, author of *Incredible Coincidence*, a delightful collection of real-life coincidences, comments:

> The synchronistic events of everyday life are no different in form from the startling, dramatic occurrences that excite our wonder and make us say, "What an incredible coincidence!" The main difference lies in their subtlety, the ways in which minor

events of life are shaped and patterned. We often shrug them off as chance, but a moment's reflection makes us realize that the role of chance in our lives extends even to small, personal, and meaningful events . . . everyday coincidences show the artfulness of our unconscious minds in creating our lives. The least we can do is admire it. The most we can do is to give that creative expression our full support.[3]

Coincidences as Answers to Prayers

Synchronicities seem to occur when we need them most. It might well be that a state of flux, uncertainty, confusion, frustration, and chaos expands the opportunity for chance to play a starring role. As the First Insight says, our inner restlessness is a sign that something is afoot, and if we could but see behind the scenes, we might be surprised by the amount of "furniture rearranging" that is going on. How many times have you experienced the old adage that "It's always darkest before dawn"? What stories do you have to tell about the all-but-forgotten loan that is repaid on the day the rent is due with no money in the bank account—or some similar account of answered prayer?

Coincidences come into being most readily when we are in a highly expectant state. Most esoteric literature advises that a combination of emotional charge and vivid imagining stimulates the ability to attract into our lives that which we desire—in some form or other. Even the scientific parapsychological experiments conducted at Duke University in the 1950s demonstrated, without doubt, that the most important factors for success in the ESP tests were "enthusiasm," "high interest in producing accurate guesses, especially at the beginning of the day," and a general sense of "hopeful expectancy."

Donna Hale, a psychotherapist in Sausalito, California,

tells this story. A few years ago she had decided that she wanted to live on Corinthian Island, an exclusive part of Marin County, California. One of her friends laughed at her idea as impractical, since the area was so expensive. Fueled by a desire to prove to this friend that she could indeed find a place to live there, she kept looking for an apartment.

One day she saw an ad for a house in the exact neighborhood she wanted, and made an appointment to see it the next day. Even though she was delighted to find that it had all the characteristics that she wanted, the rent was still more than she wanted to pay. She remembers standing in the blinding light coming in from the bay window, deeply pondering whether to take the house or not, when all of a sudden she saw and heard a seal barking in the water outside. In that instant she remembered a fragment of a dream from the previous night in which five barking seals were splashing in the ocean. She was so amazed by the coincidence of the present scene with the dream that she took it as a sign to go ahead and take the house. Shortly after moving in, her business increased and she was easily able to pay the higher rent.

Coincidence, then, is beyond reckoning or will, is elegant, enigmatic, and sometimes funny. Coincidence is the mechanism of growth, the *how of evolution*. It can mysteriously open up new opportunities through which we transcend outdated self-limiting ideas, and experience the direct evidence that life is much more than materialistic survival or mere intellectual reliance on faith. Life is spiritually dynamic.

USING THE FIRST INSIGHT AND INCREASING ITS BENEFIT

- Be aware that your life has a purpose, and events happen for a reason.
- Begin the process of finding meaning behind each life event.

- Acknowledge restless energy as a sign of needed change and deeper awareness. Listen to your body.
- Realize that what you pay attention to will expand.
- Notice when you feel a signal to talk with someone who might be able to help with your current questions. Where does your attention go? What did you notice today?
- Trust your process. Live by letting yourself be guided, not by a forced set of goals. Know that you *are* fulfilling your life's destiny.
- Start a personal journal for recording synchronistic events. Writing in a journal is a good way to clarify your thoughts.

SUMMARY OF THE FIRST INSIGHT

The First Insight is the insight of awakening. We look out on our lives and realize that more is occurring than we thought. Beyond our everyday routines and challenges we can detect the mysterious influence of the divine: "meaningful coincidences" that seem to be sending us messages and leading us in a particular direction. At first we only glimpse these coincidences as we race by, hardly paying attention. But eventually we begin to slow down and to look more closely at these events. Open and alert, we are more able to detect the next synchronistic event. Coincidences seem to ebb and flow, sometimes rushing forward in quick succession, other times leaving us becalmed. Yet we know that we have discovered the soul process that guides our lives forward. The remaining Insights clarify how to increase the frequency of this mysterious synchronicity and discover the ultimate destiny toward which we are being led.

Further Reading

In addition to the excellent books listed in the notes for this chapter, we suggest:

How to Make ESP Work for You. Harold Sherman. Fawcett, 1986.

Synchronicity: Science, Myth, and the Trickster. Allan Combs and Mark Holland. Athena Books/Paragon House, 1990.

Emergence: The Rebirth of the Sacred. David Spangler. Delta/Merloyd Lawrence, 1984.

Transformation: A Guide to the Inevitable Changes in Humankind. George Leonard. J. P. Tarcher, 1987.

As Above So Below: Paths to Spiritual Renewal in Daily Life. Ronald S. Miller et al. J. P. Tarcher, 1992.

INDIVIDUAL AND GROUP STUDY

Personal experience of the insights can be enhanced by focusing more attention on them in your own life. You are invited to use the following exercises for individual study by yourself or with a friend, or in conjunction with a study group. Formats for group sessions follow the Individual Study sections in each chapter of this study guide.

We have formatted two group sessions for the First Insight. Feel free to add to, change, or delete exercises. For example, some people might want more time for informal discussion, and others might want to use the sessions as presented. The best use of your study group is to build a community where you can expand your thinking, get to know each other, and foster a sense of fun. These exercises are meant to get you started, and we encourage you to be creative.

INDIVIDUAL STUDY OF THE FIRST INSIGHT

For those of you who are not working in a study group, the exercises below can be explored on your own or with a friend, and they can also be completed in addition to group work. Since the First Insight of *The Celestine Prophecy* teaches us to become aware of coincidences, we suggest that you be open to attracting the perfect partner with whom to study—someone who has either read the book already or is open to reading and studying with you. Working in partnership may increase the depth of your study . . . and be more fun!

EXERCISE 1. Journal Work—Past Coincidences

Purpose: By taking special notice of coincidences in the past, you strengthen your ability to make more sense of them in the future.

Step 1: Answer the nine questions on pages 19–20 about Home, Work, and Relationship.

Step 2: Review your answers by yourself or with a friend, looking for similarities in how things generally come to you. What was the similarity, if any, between meeting a significant relationship and getting a job or a new apartment? Were you able to notice signs when they appeared? Did you act on your hunches? Are you used to taking small risks such as talking to someone with whom you've made eye contact?

EXERCISE 2. Daily Observation

External Cues

Begin to notice any external signs that seem to be beckoning you in a certain direction. For example, Bill told us that he noticed during one week that he and his boss wore the same color tie every single day (and they were different colors each day). This coincidence seemed to indicate to him that he must somehow be "in sync" with his boss. Even though he was a little embarrassed to tell anyone this observation, he decided to take this coincidence as a sign to approach his boss about a new project he wanted to do. "The first thing my boss said to me was, 'Bill, your timing couldn't have been better. I have been thinking along those same lines.' "

External cues can be something like following up on a lost message that suddenly turns up on your desk, seeing a new piece of information in the newspaper that relates to an emerging interest or career direction, a detour, any change of plans. Ask yourself, What information is coming my way? What do I need to pay attention to here? Not everything has a special message for you, but by becoming more open to these "little doorways" you increase your sense of adventure.

Internal Cues

Intuition is our inner sense of perception. With external cues we are hearing, seeing, touching, or being guided by something outside ourselves (or so it seems). With internal cues, we have to pay attention to our inner senses. Our inner senses usually give us very accurate feedback if we learn to really listen. For example, if you are feeling a sense of heaviness or foreboding, you might need to slow down in order to delay a decision or to gain more time or information. So many times we push through our feelings and deny or dismiss cues, and wind up making decisions that are counterproductive. A good rule of thumb is not to make important decisions when you're angry, hurried, frustrated, tired, or in any other negative state of mind. If you are interviewing for jobs, and an office environment immediately makes you feel out of sorts, fearful, or apathetic, this is probably a sign of future dissatisfaction.

Begin to notice over the next few days what internal cues arise in different situations, such as tightening in the neck or stomach, clenching the jaws, loss of energy, shallow breathing, tapping fingers, crossed arms or legs, or irritation with sounds. Ask yourself, "What's really going on now? What am I picking up?"

STUDY GROUP FOR THE FIRST INSIGHT

Session 1

2 hours 30 minutes

Session Purpose: This first session will allow people to get to know one another and focus on how coincidences affect their lives.

Preparation: Bring blank 3 by 5 cards (enough for two or three per person) for use in Exercise 2.

Introduction

Purpose: The introduction allows everyone to get acquainted, get comfortable, and express why they came to the study group.

Time: 15–20 minutes

Directions:
  Step 1: People might want to tell how they came to read *The Celestine Prophecy.* If your group is larger than

thirty, you might divide in half in order to save time. Ideally it's best if everyone has a chance to hear everyone's introduction.

Step 2: After everyone has expressed his or her reasons for joining the group, it is often helpful to make a summary statement about the purpose of the group that all can agree on. For example, "The purpose of this study group is to support each other in working the principles in the novel so that we can accelerate our evolution."

Step 3: Joining this group has already shown that you are experiencing a desire for growth. There is a reason that you have all been drawn together. In the spirit of fun and openness, be open to allowing individual and group purposes to unfold. Remember to respect the confidentiality of everyone who shares in the group.

EXERCISE 1. Discussing the Meaning of the First Insight

Purpose: A brief discussion of how each member understands the First Insight might be helpful in bringing in new perspectives and enlarging each member's perception.

Time: 15–20 minutes

Directions: You might want to start by having someone read aloud the recap of the First Insight on pages 1 and 2 of this study guide. Next, invite everyone to share how they understood the Insight when they first read the novel. After everyone has had a chance to speak, continue with the next exercise.

EXERCISE 2. Warm-up: Positive First Impressions

Purpose: The purpose of this exercise is to see how much we intuitively appraise others in first impressions. This is an enjoyable exercise and raises the energy level as well as builds trust and familiarity as your group begins.

Time: 30 minutes

Directions:

Step 1: If there are sixteen participants or more, assemble into groups of four. If the group is smaller, divide into threes. Hand out a couple of 3 by 5 cards for each person to keep. Suggest that someone in the group keep track of time so that everyone has a chance to participate.

Step 2: In order to break the ice and let people reveal a little about their personality, share with each other what was funny or synchronistic about how each of you got to the meeting today. (*Limit this to a couple of minutes per person.*)

Step 3: Have one person volunteer to start the exercise. This person turns his or her chair around and sits with his or her back to the others.

Step 4: Everyone now begins to say what positive qualities they see in that person. As the other members begin to call out positive impressions, the person listens and writes down the attributes on the 3 by 5 cards, without commenting. Be funny and original as long as the comments are positive. Throw in some ideas of what you think that person would be good at—even without knowing him. (*Take about 5 minutes per person or until the energy gets low.*)

Step 5: After everyone has received their positive first impressions, reconvene into the whole group and share for a few minutes how this exercise felt. (Save your Positive Impressions cards for a day when you

need upliftment!) Continue with Exercise 3—Sharing
Current Questions.

Exercise 3. Sharing Current Questions/Themes

Purpose: The purpose of this exercise is to explore (a) what
higher common needs brought people into this specific three-
or four-person group; (b) if there were any signals such as
eye contact or a sense of familiarity that triggered joining
the group; (c) if there are any coincidences between the lives
of each member; and (d) the practice of giving full attention
to each speaker.

Time: 30–40 minutes

Directions:
  Step 1: Each person briefly shares what his main life
    theme is right now. Problems? Needs? Life circum-
    stances? As each person talks, all the others will focus
    attention on him or her. (*Take about 3 minutes per per-
    son.*)
  Step 2: After everybody has spoken, discuss briefly why
    you think you are sitting with the people in your
    group. Have one person list all the questions or
    themes for that group.
  Step 3: Did any people experience subtle signals for
    joining the four-person group, such as spontaneous
    eye contact or a sense of familiarity?
  Step 4: When everyone has finished this exercise (or
    sooner if time is growing short), reconvene into the
    main group and share what common themes you
    found in your group. How did people select the group
    or person to work with?

This is a good time to have everyone introduce themselves
a little more fully to the entire group. For example, everyone

might tell their name, where they live, and what they do. (If the group is larger than thirty, you can divide it into manageable segments according to time available.) It will be interesting to see what similarities exist among members. For example, in one group in Sausalito, California, fourteen out of sixteen people were self-employed or sole proprietors.

Closing

Time: 20–30 minutes

Requests for support: You might want to end your session with a request to receive information and support that will help with current needs.

Step 1: Take turns verbalizing what you would like to have support for in the coming week. Use positive language such as "I'd like to feel full of energy next week," rather than "I'd like to get

---

People in one study group in Sausalito, California, commented on how they chose their groups:

"I thought I recognized her, and I didn't. She thought she recognized me and she didn't! But it turned out we had exactly the same issues. I couldn't have picked a better group if I'd tried to."

"I was just pulled to that end of the room."

"Our group had such a flow. We kept interrupting each other, but it was because we felt so engaged with each other."

"There were so many common interests in our group. There was immediate networking that went on."

"Our group all had big upheavals in our lives. The things that people said about me were things I'm trying to put out in the world. Someone said [in the Positive First Impressions], 'You look like you want to make a difference in the world.' I was so grateful for that."

"There was a quick look that had passed between me and one of the people sitting on the couch."

rid of this awful cold." Keep the focus on what you want, rather than what you don't want. For example, one person asked, "I'd really like to remain calm and centered while I move my office next week."

Step 2. After each request is made aloud, affirm the request and send loving energy toward the person and his or her situation.

For Next Session

During the coming week, watch for coincidences, signs, and dreams, jot them in your journal, and take your journal to the next meeting.

STUDY GROUP FOR THE FIRST INSIGHT

Session 2

2 hours 30 minutes

Session Purpose: To explore the flow of the coincidences in our lives

Introduction

Start the meeting by giving everyone a chance to share any coincidences that happened over the past week. Were any insights gained from the work done in the last meeting? What kind of support was received in answer to the requests of last week? Sharing positive feedback strengthens the whole group.

Exercise 1. Increasing Sensitivity to Coincidences

Purpose: The purpose of this exercise is to acknowledge past coincidences and become more aware of their effect on our lives. As we bring our attention to what has happened in the past, we are also stimulating an intention for higher consciousness to produce more coincidences.

Time: 2 hours (30 minutes for each partner) plus discussion

Directions:

Step 1: Choose a partner with whom to work.

Step 2: One person will read aloud each of the following questions and the other will answer. When answering, look for possible coincidences in these past events. (*About 30 minutes per person.*)

Home

1. Were there any particular coincidences or signs connected with getting your current living space (significant house numbers, encounters with neighbors, delays in negotiations, mixed-up phone calls, special street names, or any other odd detail)?

Work

2. How did you get your present job? Think back to how you found out about it, to whom you talked, and what messages you might have received.
3. What were your first impressions of the workplace?
4. Did you notice any signs that might have portended something that later occurred?
5. Was there something you wish you had listened to before taking this job?

Relationship
6. Describe how you met your most important relationship. What led up to your being in that place at that time?
7. Did the person you meet remind you of anyone else?
8. What was your first impression of this person? Has that impression been a true one?
9. Did you notice any signs (a dream after meeting this person, an odd coincidence, a delay, a mixup)?

Step 3: Do you see any patterns in how things come to you? What was the similarity, if any, between meeting your significant relationship and getting a job or a new apartment? Pay particular attention to questions 1, 4, and 9. Paying attention to the so-called omens around major turning points is one important way to harvest the maximum information from coincidences and increase your precognitive ability as future coincidences occur.

Step 4: Reconvene into your large group and share what you found in the exercise. For example, what kinds of coincidences were involved in finding homes, jobs, partners? In what way did the coincidences influence people?

In one group, Laurie Friedman, who owns a firm specializing in natural disaster management, told the story of a pivotal moment that confirmed her tentative decision to get a degree in public administration: "I had just moved to Eugene, Oregon, and needed a job. I went to the library and looked at some college catalogs. The only program that seemed open at the time was in the School of Public Affairs at the University of Oregon. I walked over to the school and put in an application. Within a week I was accepted in the master's program, but I still needed money. I went back to the office to put in an application for a teaching fellowship, and was told to apply for a student loan. I was at the Wells Fargo loan application desk filling out the papers when the phone rang, and the loan officer said, 'That was Dean Hill from the school of Public Affairs. He said to forget the loan. They're going to give you a graduate teaching fellowship.' " Laurie now looks back on the road that led to her current successful business and sees how certain events were presented to her. "Even though I wasn't ever sure where things were ultimately going, I do feel I was guided. I somehow just kept paying attention and following through, and it's worked out really well."

Closing

Requests for support (see page 17 for details).

Before Next Session
Continue to be alert for coincidences, signs, and dreams and write them in your journal.

CHAPTER 2

The Longer Now:
Expanding the Historical
Context

In flight to Peru, our character meets history professor Dobson. Coincidentally, Dobson is already familiar with the Second Insight and expounds on the importance of understanding what's been happening in Western thought for the past one thousand years as we complete this millennium and continue forward.

THE SECOND INSIGHT

The Context for Coincidence. The Second Insight places our awareness of "meaningful coincidence" within a longer historical framework. It answers the following questions: Are our perceptions of these life coincidences important in history, or are they merely a quirk or fad of our particular time, interesting to us but inconsequential to the future? Will our interest in the way the spiritual dimension seems to impact us and lead us forward (synchronistically) simply fade as human society evolves? The Second Insight involves stepping back and pondering the longer chain of events that clarifies what our new perceptions mean.

The Loss of the Medieval Worldview. From our vantage point here in the waning years of the twentieth century—poised as we are at the end of one millennium and the dawning of another—we are in a perfect position to see precisely our historical lineage. As the Manuscript in the book suggests, we are breaking free from the preoccupations of the past five hundred years—preoccupations that began at the end of the Middle Ages—in the reaction of reformers against the excessive influence of the medieval church.

The Split of Science and Spirituality. Citing political corruption and the church's dogmatic adherence to scientifically disproved facts, Renaissance reformers sought to remove the intellectual shackles of a cosmology they believed to be replete with speculation and superstition. In this battle with the medieval church, a tacit agreement was finally reached. Science could have the freedom to explore worldly phenomena without interference, if it refrained from investigating aspects of the universe considered the domain of religion: humanity's relationship to God, angels, miracles, or any other supernatural phenomena. Hence, early science gladly focused on the outside physical world. Discoveries came quickly. We began to map out and name the aspects of nature we found around us, careful to speak of these phenomena in concrete terms and physical causes. At the same time, new technologies were invented and energy sources were developed. The Industrial Revolution came as a by-product, enhancing the production of goods, lifting more and more people into a new secular security.

A Secular Worldview. By the beginning of the eighteenth century, the church wielded much less influence. A new worldview based on scientific materialism began to replace the old church-ruled ideas concerning life. It was a time of great optimism. With science as our exploring tool, we felt we could ultimately discover everything about humanity's existential situation, including whether there was a God, and if so, our relationship to this God. This would take time, of course, and for now we would have to be content with turning our focus on conquering the perils of life, on giving ourselves and our children a new secular security to replace the spiritual security that vanished when the medieval church was discredited. A new call to action motivated the time. Even if we had lost our certainty about God, mankind could face life and the hard realities of the universe relying on knowledge and ingenuity. With hard work and cunning, using our developing technology, we now were free to take life into our own hands. We could exploit the resources we found on this planet and make ourselves more secure. We had lost the certainty of our place in the universe the medieval church had provided, but we could replace it with a faith in science and a new work ethic around the idea of "progress."

Here, we can see the psychological preoccupation that infused the modern age. Throughout the eighteenth, nineteenth, and twentieth centuries this new, modern worldview expanded and instituted itself in our collective psyche. The more we mapped and named the physical phenomena in the universe, the more we could feel the world in which we lived was explained, predictable, secure, even ordinary and mundane. But in order to sustain this illusion we had to constantly screen and psychologically repress anything that reminded us of the mystery of life. The agreement to avoid religious phenomena grew into an outright taboo. Even attending church became a mere social occasion. The pews were still filled on Sunday, but mostly as a statement of intellectual belief and a way to avoid any consideration of the spiritual during the rest of the week. By the middle of the twentieth century, the universe had been almost totally secularized, reduced to its material components. But in order to create this illusion of a secure, explained world, we had to narrow our awareness of life, assume a kind of technological tunnel vision from which we dismissed out of hand any notion of the miraculous. To feel secure, we had to keep ourselves preoccupied, even obsessed, with the technological conquest of the world.

Waking Up to the Mystery. Then we began to wake up. The reasons are many. By the 1950s, the science of physics itself began to revise the very materialistic view it had instituted. The universe was known to be not materialistic at all, but an interwoven pattern of energy systems where time could speed up and slow down, where the same elementary particle can appear in two places at the same time, and where space is curved and finite but still unending and maybe multidimensional. Further, the technological manipulation of this space/time/energy fabric had resulted in the creation of massive weapons, now capable of ending life on earth.

At about the same time, other sciences began to rock our worldview, revealing the environmental damage resulting from the exploitation of the earth's resources. Pollution was steadily poisoning our biological life support systems. Clearly we were destroying the very world we hoped to improve with our progress.

In the 1960s we seemed to awaken enough to intuit en masse that Western culture had ignored the higher dimensions of human life. Material security had grown to a point where we could begin to address relevant social problems: inequality and prejudice among the races and between men and women, the problems of pollution and war. It was a time of great idealism, but also of conflict between those who wanted society to change and those preferring the status quo. By the end of the decade, we seemed to realize that if we were to truly open up and turn our focus to our unexplored potential as human beings, it was not a matter of one group telling another it must change, trying to *force* social evolution. It was a matter of each person looking within, transforming within, and then, by collective effect, transforming society.

Inner Explorations. This seems to have been the awareness that propelled the introspective self-analysis that characterized much of the 1970s. It was the decade that saw a great expansion of human-potential-oriented exploration. Humanistic psychology, the development of twelve-step addiction programs, and the first research into the relationship of stress and attitudes to the onset of disease, all made significant impact on the public mind. In addition, a wide interest in Eastern religion and thought emerged in the West. Yoga, the martial arts, and meditation all grew in popularity.

The target of our explorations and therapy seemed to be the materialistic preoccupation itself. Focusing solely on the technological, economic side of life had closed off a broad spectrum of experience. A full appreciation of beauty was overshadowed by a venal, utilitarian view wherein a tree, for instance, was appreciated not for its intrinsic beauty, but for its worth in lumber. Our own emotions of sorrow, love, loss, empathy, were dulled or repressed altogether. In this decade it suddenly became acceptable to see a therapist, to process the often difficult socialization of childhood, to somehow find a part of ourselves lost or perhaps never experienced. But in our long introspection we seemed in the end to reach another revelation. We realized we could process our inner lives forever and nothing might change—for what we most longed for, what we most hoped to regain, was the transcendental experience, an inner connection to the divine.

It is this awareness that propelled us back toward the spiritual in the 1980s. In traditional churches it took form as a move toward substance and away from church as social gathering. Outside the traditional religions, this awareness manifested as individually discovered spiritual approaches, usually combinations of particular religious truths, and often synthesized with the mystical descriptions of various visionaries of the East—loosely called the New Age movement. The 1980s proved to be a broad experimental sampling of various spiritual approaches: Eastern religions, rebirthing, fire walking, vision questing, channeling, out-of-body experiences, crystal energies, psychic development, UFO watching, pilgrimage to sacred sites, meditation of every description, paganism, aura reading, and card drawing, to name a few. All were looked at and investigated while we searched for the actual spiritual experience. Some were found to be silly, some helpful, but this active experimentation, this sorting, has now left us in a unique position as we look at our situation in the 1990s.

Creating a New Worldview. Freed from our five-hundred-year-long secular preoccupation, we are now pulling together a consensus about our higher spiritual nature. Propelling the shift in consciousness is the process of clearing and opening ourselves psychologically and the exploration of a variety of spiritual paths. Synthesizing what we valued in the psycho-spiritual realm with what we had discovered in the scientific realm, we are awakening to nothing less than a new, more relevant, more truthful reality.

The Second Insight, then, solidifies our perception of mysterious coincidences as the central feature of a whole new way of approaching life.

Connecting to the Spiritual Energy

As the Manuscript teaches, in order to evolve we must first reconnect with what we are surviving for as a human race. For the entire culture to thrive, a critical number of people must open to the idea of allowing intuition to guide them back to a connection with the spiritual.

The Second Insight, therefore, is the macrocosmic view of our group consciousness in which we have been preoccupied

> Our planet has been revealed in a new light, not as a static or cyclical world, but as an arena in which graduation upon graduation of species have occurred for several hundred million years. This stupendous advance suggests that humans might develop further. Evolution to date is a supreme inescapable gesture, pointing toward a mysterious future for living forms. . . . We harbor transformative capacities. . . . It is not unreasonable to think that, in spite of our many liabilities, further progress, even a new kind of evolution, might be available to us.
>
> Michael Murphy,
> *The Future of the Body*[1]

with competing, controlling, and conquering. The fruits of this belief system are what we are living with today. In essence, what we thought was what we got.

Crossroads

We are at an extremely exciting juncture with a vast array of choices never before seen. This period of cross-fertilization between the scientific advances in physics and telecommunications with the emerging strains of spirituality, ecology, alternative healing, and psychology is already preparing us for the future. Now our task, both culturally and individually, is to continue to choose more expansive, more life-enhancing priorities. Your own willingness to take time to study *The Celestine Prophecy* is part of the evolutionary process. *The amount of consciousness you bring to the collective mind is part of your contribution.*

> Only when complemented by a surrender to a "higher" or more inclusive order can the effort of the personal will bear wholesome fruit.
>
> PHILIP NOVAK[2]

Personal Time Line—from Macrocosmic to Microcosmic

This macrocosmic view of history presented by the Second Insight can be experienced in the microcosm of each of our lives. History is the story of our lives through time, and your present life reflects our collective life. Jung, in speaking about spiritual themes in dreams said, "One must always remember that every man, in a sense, represents the whole of humanity and its history. What was possible in the history of mankind at large is also possible on a small scale in every individual. What mankind has needed may eventually be needed by the individual too. . . ."[3] Therefore, applying the

Second Insight to our own life story helps us to understand some of the restlessness and searching for meaning that we are experiencing.

In order to see larger patterns at work in your life, you might want to think back over the major sections of your life and write down what your main lessons have been. This is a very helpful procedure for revealing how your beliefs, values, and expectations change. The Second Insight shows that many of us are beginning to realize that our common destiny is to live life from a more spiritual point of view. Apply this Insight to your own history and see what you find. At the end of this section, exercises are given for doing a personal time line for both individual and group study.

Current Preoccupations

Every thought, decision, and action we make each day creates our continuing reality. We are acutely aware of this when we set concrete goals such as "I'm going to lose ten pounds before the holidays" or "I'm starting a savings account for a vacation." With specific goals like these, we eventually see that we have either succeeded, failed, or fallen short of our intention. A more visible level of preoccupation will be those thoughts that you have on a daily basis, especially when you wake up in the morning and go to sleep at night. It's been estimated that we have about 90,000 thoughts a day, the majority of them negative!

Core Beliefs

Subtle and ever-present, core beliefs are invisible determining factors in our lives. These thoughts imperceptibly organize our internal energy field and determine our continuing reality. At the hidden foundation of our everyday thoughts about the laundry, picking up the children, and wanting more money are basic assumptions that we rarely question. These common assumptions learned from our culture are such beliefs as "I am a separate individual who must compete for my livelihood," or "I'm aging," or "The world of matter is what really counts." This deep level of preoccupation must first be brought into awareness before it can be expanded or changed. This idea of the power of core beliefs to mold our everyday life and attract synchronicity is the foundation of what we call new-paradigm thinking. A paradigm is a model or ideal pattern of thought or action. Our new model of life, then, shows how our beliefs create much of what happens to us.

Joseph Campbell, the great scholar of mythology, describes the evolutionary process of going beyond the known in what he calls "the left-hand path." In myths, which carry the living paradigms of all cultures, the Hero traditionally chooses the left-hand path as the place where he will encounter new information and discover the truth. The right-hand path is the current dilemma, the status quo, the place where all the problems are. In order to transform the dilemma, new material must be enlisted. Thus, the myths awaken within us the archetype of the journey toward transformation. We are never without the hope of discovery and recovery.

As the Second Insight points out, the new paradigm or new thinking began appearing in the decade of the 1960s through the medium of the Human Potential movement. New thinking has emerged in many fields, demonstrating the truth of the unity of body and mind. Evidence of the rising popularity and acceptance of this new thought is such best-selling books as *Ageless Body, Timeless Mind*, by physician Deepak Chopra. Chopra highlights some of the fundamental points that distinguish new and old thinking. For example, he compares the old basic assumption:

> There is an objective world independent of the observer, and our bodies are an aspect of this objective world.

with the new-paradigm concept:

> The physical world, including our bodies, is a response of the observer. We create our bodies as we create the experience of our world.[4]

In spite of the wealth of metaphysical literature that has always taught that we create our reality, this is an astounding thought to those of us who feel frustrated by our lives, our jobs, the state of our finances or health. As our character found in *The Celestine Prophecy*, the very size and potency of plants were affected by the positive energy sent to them by the researchers. Every day there is a growing body of medical and scientific research to corroborate the truth that reality is an outgrowth of mental intention. This one assumption alone gives us back our power, and promises hope for the future.

Another core assumption from our previous thinking, which Chopra debunks, is:

> Human awareness can be completely explained as the product of biochemistry.

New information has come in to show us that:

> Perception . . . is a learned phenomenon. The world you live in, including the experience of your body, is completely dictated by how you learned to perceive it. If you change your perception, you change the experience of your body and your world.[5]

In this study guide, we hope to help you rethink some of your past assumptions so that you can perceive a greater lesson or purpose behind all of your achievements, failures, or challenges. By adopting a positive, curious, conscious, adventuring attitude, your world can begin to look as you would like it to look.

A third assumption of the old paradigm, again from Chopra, is:

> Our perception of the world is automatic and gives us an accurate picture of how things really are.

One of the most exciting of the new-paradigm assumptions is that:

> Although each person seems separate and independent, all of us are connected to patterns of intelligence that govern the whole cosmos. Our bodies are part of a universal body, our minds an aspect of a universal mind.[6]

This idea is the foundation of the First Insight, which teaches that we can begin to evolve consciously by noticing the coincidental events that are purposeful to our growth. We are not alone. The answers to our questions come to us through an intelligence greater than our conscious mind, if we but trust in this process.

Listening for Basic Assumptions

We have presented only a few of the many new ideas that are coming forth now about redefining the world. The truth of these ideas can be experienced directly by you. For example, begin to listen for statements that people make about life. How do you see them buying into the old ideas of scarcity, competition, and all the "problems out there"? As you talk with friends, practice becoming a detached observer for a few minutes. What do you hear yourself and your friends saying about life?

Keep in mind that it is not helpful to rebuke others for their limiting attitudes. We evolve at our own pace. There is no need to create a new jargon or foster any separatism between those who are "enlightened" and those who are still searching or suffering. The simple process of observation, reflection, and acceptance will create a different energy for yourself *and others*. However, if there is a time when you sense that you could make a difference, let the moment guide you. Follow your intuition.

SUMMARY OF THE SECOND INSIGHT

The Second Insight is the awareness that our perception of mysterious life coincidences is a significant historical occurrence. After the collapse of the medieval worldview, we lost the security that came from the church's explanation of the universe. Therefore, five hundred years ago we collectively decided to focus on mastering nature, on using our science and technology to settle into the world. We set out to create a secular security to replace the spiritual one we had lost. To feel more secure, we systematically pushed away and denied the mysterious aspects of life on this planet. We crafted the illusion that we lived in a universe that was entirely explainable and predictable, and where chance events had no meaning. To maintain the illusion, we tended to deny any evidence to the contrary, to restrict scientific research into paranormal events, and to adopt an attitude of absolute skepticism. Exploring the mystical dimensions of life became almost taboo.

Gradually, however, an awakening has begun. Our awakening is nothing less than breaking free from the modern age's secular preoccupation, and opening our minds to a new, more truthful view of the world.

Further Reading

In addition to the excellent books listed in the notes for this chapter we suggest:

Life against Death: The Psychoanalytical Meaning of History. Norman O. Brown. Wesleyan University Press, 1985.

Global Mind Change: The Promise of the Last Years of the Twentieth Century. Willis Harmon. Sigo Press, 1991.

The Structure of Scientific Revolutions. Thomas S. Kuhn. University of Chicago Press, 1962.

The Power of Myth. Joseph Campbell with Bill Moyers. Doubleday, 1988.

At the Edge of History and Passages about Earth. William I. Thompson. Lindisfarne Press, 1990.

INDIVIDUAL STUDY OF THE SECOND INSIGHT

EXERCISE 1. My Past Preoccupations

Purpose: To help you become conscious of recurring themes in your life, and possible underlying belief systems

Directions: In the following list circle your three most important preoccupations and write one paragraph in your journal about their effect on your life. How have these themes *added* to your life? How have they *hampered* your life? From now on become aware of their presence in your life and notice how they are related to what you call your problems.

PAST PREOCCUPATIONS

independence	addictions
intellectual accomplishment	overspending
self-criticism	underearning

security

physical image

resistance to authority

lack of love

emotional dramas

anger

fear

guilt

control

perfectionism

gaining approval

revenge

conformity

other(s)

family entanglements

EXERCISE 2. More Preoccupying Ideas

Directions:

Step 1: Complete the seven unfinished sentences below. What did you learn about your beliefs and values by looking at your preoccupying thoughts?

Step 2: You might want to write some thoughts about this exercise in your journal. Notice if you have any dreams after writing about your preoccupations.

I'd like to change

1.

2.

3.

I'd like more

1.

2.

3.

I keep thinking

1.

2.

3.

In six months I'd like

1.

2.

3.

The most important things in my life right now are

1.

2.

3.

The qualities in the people I admire most are

1.

2.

3.

I'd be delighted if my life included

1.

2.

3.

EXERCISE 3. Where in My Life Am I Just Going through the Motions?

Write a paragraph or two in your journal about the parts of your life where you feel stuck or as if you are "just going through the motions." Really describe your feelings in detail. The more you can bring these feelings into awareness, the more you will open the doors for answers, opportunities, and insights.

EXERCISE 4. Finding New-Paradigm Alternatives to Your Old Preoccupations

Review the new-thinking parallels for your old preoccupations listed below:

OLD	NEW
independence	interdependence
intellectual accomplishment	wisdom
self-criticism	acknowledgment of strengths
security	adaptability
resistance to authority	sharing leadership
emotional dramas	self-actualization
fear	love
control	trust
gaining approval	self-trust
conformity	creativity
family entanglements	honest commitments
addictions	self-security
overspending	healing deprivation

OLD	NEW
underearning	being paid what you are worth
physical image	intrinsic worth
lack of love	divine love within
anger	empowerment
guilt	love with wisdom
perfectionism	self-acceptance
revenge	forgiveness

Look at what you circled on the list in Exercise 1 as major preoccupations in the past. Make a note of the correlating *new*-paradigm idea. Take each new attribute and write it down in your journal. As the mood strikes you, write how you could begin to attract more of this attribute into your life. For example, if you have always fixated on physical image as the most important way to feel good about yourself, how could you become more aware of the inner worth of yourself and others? You don't have to know the answers at this moment. If any of these ideas is ready to become more of a reality, you will probably have a stronger feeling of excitement around it. You might want to write an affirmation for yourself for one or two of the new ideas. For example, if you have been preoccupied with fear or self-doubt, you might affirm: "I trust myself to make good decisions."

EXERCISE 5. Constructing and Analyzing Your Personal Time Line

Purpose: This exercise gives an overview of the events in your life up to the present and helps you find meaning or purpose for what has happened so far.

Directions: Even though you can do this exercise on your own, it's helpful to have another person go over your life events with you and perhaps identify a purpose or meaning you had not considered.

Step 1: Fill out the Personal Time Line in Exercise 1, Group Session 4, page 47.

Step 2: Simplify the events into major turning points or lessons that you learned and write them in chronological order below. On the line starting with Birth, jot down key events, people, or actions that took place.

Step 3: In your journal, write a short paragraph describing your life from birth up to the present. Now look at the events you've described and separate them into "lessons learned." What pattern emerges?

Optional: Just for fun, take a guess at what appears to be the *logical* next step for you right now. Now make an innovative suggestion for your next step, one that is completely outrageous! Write out your forecasts and date the entries. What would have to happen in order for the suggested next step to occur?

EXERCISE 6. How to Get Answers to Your Questions

Step 1: In your journal write down the areas you most want to know about in your life right now (your *current* life question).

Step 2: Take a moment to notice the structure of your question. It might shed some light about what answer you are expecting. For example, a question such as "I want to know if Jane is going to come back to me" might indicate that the questioner is feeling powerless, is not clear on why Jane left, or is unwilling to open up communication, etc. Be as specific as you can in your questions, as this will help you gain insight about yourself and the situation.

Step 3: Be alert to some kind of message or intuition,

daydream or night dream within the next seventy-two hours. Jotting down any coincidences or answers to your current questions helps increase your sense of "hopeful expectancy," encouraging guidance from your higher self.

One woman wrote in her journal, "I need to buy a new car. I need help making this decision. What's the best way to proceed?" The next day she had a sense that she should call her brother, but didn't know why. In the course of the conversation, he mentioned that his next-door neighbor was selling an almost new car that had belonged to his sister-in-law, who had recently died. It was one of the models that she had been considering.

EXERCISE 7. Centering and Energizing Meditation

Before you leave the house each day, stop and take three deep breaths. Close your eyes for a second and remember back to a place of serene beauty that you feel especially close to. Breathe in the beauty of that place. Keep breathing in slowly and gently until you feel yourself starting to smile. Notice how expanded your energy has become. Now state your question to yourself and surround it with this expanded energy. Try to maintain a connection to this loving feeling all day long.

> One person told us, "I bought a little pocket notebook to carry around with me. During the day, when I got really frustrated with something, I wrote it down in my notebook. Underneath it I wrote, 'Help. I need an answer on this right away!' and then I circled that. It made me feel better, and I relaxed, knowing that sooner or later, I'd get some kind of message."

EXERCISE 8. **Have an Adventure**

Step 1: This exercise can be done on your own, or, to increase the fun and possibility of synchronicity, make a date with someone to do something that is new or fun for both of you.

Step 2: On the day of your adventure, spend a few minutes reminding yourself of your current life question and be in an expectant mood for possible answers. Take a small notebook in case messages come in. Notice what your intuition prompts you to do. Be spontaneous and let go of the need to control. Be bold!

STUDY GROUP FOR THE SECOND INSIGHT

Session 3

2 hours 30 minutes

Session Purpose: Awakening to our historical roots and analyzing our personal preoccupations

EXERCISE 1. **Discussion on the Second Insight: History of Beliefs**

Purpose: To discuss the historical attitudes from the Middle Ages to the present and see how we relate this information in our own life

Time: 15–20 minutes

Directions: Start the discussion by asking such questions as "How did the ideas of security and materialism influence you and your family?" "How or when did you begin to question traditional religious views?" "Who were your heroes when you were growing up?" "What effect did the 1960s, 1970s, and 1980s have on you?"

Exercise 2. My Past Preoccupations

Purpose: This exercise will help you become conscious of recurring themes in your life and of possible underlying belief systems.

Time: 15–20 minutes

Directions: In the following list check the areas you feel have been of primary importance to you up till now:

Past Preoccupations

____independence
____intellectual accomplishment
____self-criticism
____security
____resistance to authority
____emotional dramas
____fear
____control
____gaining approval
____conformity
____family entanglements

____addictions
____overspending
____underearning
____physical image
____lack of love
____anger
____guilt
____perfectionism
____revenge
____other(s)

Now circle the three areas that have influenced you the most. How have these themes *added* to your life? How have they *hampered* your life? From now on become aware of their presence in your life, and notice how they are related to what you call your problems.

EXERCISE 3. More Preoccupying Ideas

Step 1: Give at least three answers (write more if you can) to the unfinished sentences below:

I'd like to change

1.

2.

3.

I'd like more

1.

2.

3.

I keep thinking

1.

2.

3.

In six months I'd like

1.

2.

3.

The most important things in my life right now are

1.

2.

3.

The qualities in the people I admire most are

1.

2.

3.

I'd be delighted if my life included

1.

2.

3.

Step 2: Break up into groups of two, three, or four to exchange your lists, and share ideas. *Be open to information that others may have for you in achieving some of your goals or desires.*

Step 3: Reconvene in your large group and share what happened in the smaller groups. Did anyone furnish a message or provide any information? What did you learn about your beliefs and values by looking at your preoccupying thoughts? You might want to write some thoughts about this exercise in your journal at home. Notice if you have any dreams after this session.

EXERCISE 4. Where in My Life Am I Just Going through the Motions?

Purpose: To have a dialogue with yourself about where you are feeling stuck or where you have not admitted that something needs to change

Directions: Write your thoughts in your journal. You can share them with a partner in the group if the group determines this is something everyone wants to do.

EXERCISE 5. Finding New-Paradigm Alternatives to Your Old Preoccupations

Look at what you checked in Exercise 2 as major preoccupations of yours in the past. Make a note of the correlating *new*-paradigm idea below. Take each new attribute and write it down in your journal. As the mood strikes you, write how you could begin to attract more of this attribute into your life. For example, if you feel independence has been learned fairly well, how could you bring more interdependence into your life? You don't have to know the answers at this moment. If any of these ideas is ready to become more of a reality, you will probably have a stronger feeling of excitement around it.

OLD	NEW
independence	interdependence
intellectual accomplishment	wisdom
self-criticism	acknowledgment of strengths
security	adaptability
resistance to authority	sharing leadership
emotional dramas	self-actualization
fear	love
control	trust

OLD	NEW
gaining approval	self-trust
conformity	creativity
family entanglements	honest commitments
addictions	self-security
overspending	healing deprivation
underearning	being paid what you are worth
physical image	intrinsic worth
lack of love	divine love within
anger	empowerment
guilt	love with wisdom
perfectionism	self-acceptance
revenge	forgiveness

You might want to write an affirmation for yourself for one or two of the new ideas: "I know that physical image is but one part of myself and others. I am able to see within for their intrinsic worth as well as my own."

Closing

Requests for support. Sending loving energy.

STUDY GROUP FOR THE SECOND INSIGHT

Session 4

2 hours 30 minutes

Session Purpose: Constructing your personal time line of events

Introduction

Open the meeting by asking people to share any new insights that occurred to them or to report any coincidences or messages they received during the week. When the energy of the group seems to indicate completion, move on to the next exercise.

Exercise 1. Constructing and Analyzing Your Personal Time Line

Purpose: Your time line may (a) give you a chance to view your life more objectively; (b) reveal a pattern; (c) reveal a sequence of coincidences; (d) forecast the next development; or (e) hint at a life purpose. This information will be used again in Chapter 6.

Time: 1 hour 40 minutes. This gives you approximately 15 minutes for individual work, 45 minutes for partner work, and 40 minutes for group discussion. Note: Time lines are powerful tools; for in-depth work you might want to devote the entire meeting to it for as many meetings as it takes to examine each member's life.

Part I. Constructing the Time Line

Time: 15–20 minutes

Directions:
  Step 1: Jot down on the lines below significant events in your life from birth to the present. This is the "raw material" from which you may be able to glean a pattern. (If you don't have enough time to complete this work in the group, try to finish it during the week.)

Birth _____

_____

_____ present

Step 2: Simplify the events of your life with a short title that describes the main activity or process you felt occurred in that time period. For example, if you moved several times from birth to age sixteen, you might sum up that period by writing: Age 0 to 16: "Many moves. Learned to be flexible." Age 17 to 20: "Turned to academic achievement. Made good grades in school in X subject." Age 20 to 25: "Felt lost. A significant person influenced me." Age 26 to 38: "A period of responsibility."

Step 3: Write down your key events, negative or positive lessons, turning points, and key people.

Step 4: When everyone has finished, stop working individually and begin working with a partner.

Part II. Analyzing Your Time Line

Time: 45 minutes

Directions:

Step 1: Choose a partner with whom to work. Take turns working on your time lines. Discuss your list of turning points, achievements, and key people. You might find patterns or purpose by reviewing these questions:

a. What were turning points?

b. Do you see a repeating pattern of experience, achievement, or lesson?

c. What feels complete for you? What feels unfinished?

   d. What were things that energized you? What would
      you avoid repeating?
   e. How have your values changed?
   f. What, if any, were the positive intentions of the
      negative events?
   g. What would you say you have been "in training"
      for?
   h. What does the purpose of your life seem to be *so
      far*?

Step 2: Using the information you have learned from
your analysis, complete these statements:

I can see that my life has been focused heavily on

_____,

_____, and

_____.

I have been "in training" for _____

_____

_____ all my life.

The positive intention behind the negative events of

my life might have been _____.

What stands out to me is _____

_____.

The purpose of my life so far seems to have been to

_____.

For example, Deborah, a thirty-six-year-old mother of three children and freelance editor, wrote down the following life events:

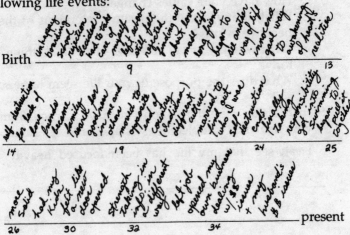

Next, Deborah wrote down her key events, negative and positive lessons, turning points, and key people:

1. severe sadness, lack of love
2. self-destruction with drugs
3. reformation
4. rebirth
5. now building

Next, she checked the areas of primary importance in her life so far:

✓ independence   ✓ addictions
___ intellectual accomplishment   ___ overspending

✔ self-criticism	——underearning
——security	——physical image
——resistance to authority	✔ lack of love
——emotional dramas	——anger
——fear	——guilt
——control	——perfectionism
✔ gaining approval	——revenge
✔ conformity	——other(s)
——family entanglements	

Deborah saw several themes that had been important lessons, but she felt that conformity, emotional dramas, and independence stood out the most for her. Using those three points, she wrote:

I can see that my life has been focused heavily

on _gaining enough independence, not_

needing to conform to something I , and

didn't believe in transforming old hurts .

Using the information she had gathered, she wrote:

I have been "in training" for _standing on my_

own two feet all my life.

The positive intention behind the negative events of my

life might have been _to encourage me to leave the_

"family nest" and grow in my own direction .

What stands out to me is ___ *how much courage I've shown* ___.

The purpose of my life so far seems to have been to *gain clarity and strength to become stable myself and maybe help other women*.

Part III. Sharing Your Analysis of the Time Line

Time: 40 minutes

Directions: Everyone can now come back together to share what they found in their time lines. *This allows the larger group energy to help each person find meaning in events and to perhaps find a relevant message for themselves.* Someone might wish to write some of the key points on a large sheet of paper or poster board. Encourage comments from everyone.

Further Study: People might want to write down in their journals any new thoughts about their time-line progression during the next week. New pieces of information might surface through coincidences or dreams. Be sure to share your insights with your group next week. This will help to increase the general energy flow.

EXERCISE 2. How to Get Answers to Your Questions

Purpose: The purpose of this exercise is to ask specific questions so that your higher self can send you a coincidence, message, intuition, daydream, or dream to help guide you.

Time: 15 minutes

Directions:

Step 1: Work with a partner. Take turns coming up with a question you would like to have answered now.

Step 2: Take a moment to notice the structure of your question. It might shed some light about what answer you are expecting. For example, a question such as "I want to know if my child is in the right school" might hint that you already have an intuition that he is not at the right school, or the question might show that you are looking for all the answers to come from a change of school, when your child may need further attention at home as well. Be as specific as you can in your questions, as this will help you gain insight about yourself and the situation.

Step 3: Be alert to some kind of message or intuition, daydream, or night dream within the next seventy-two hours. Jotting down any coincidences or answers to your current questions helps increase your sense of "hopeful expectancy, encouraging guidance from your higher self."

Exercise 3. Centering and Energizing Meditation

Purpose: To bring your current life question into the energizing vibration of love

Time: 15 minutes

Directions:

Step 1: You can center yourself with eyes closed in a short period of quiet reflection or someone can lead the following relaxation meditation:

CENTERING MEDITATION

Take two or three deep breaths, allowing the air to come into your body to soften and relax it . . . Breathe in slowly and hold the breath for a couple of seconds and then release it . . . Beginning with your feet, take a mental survey of your body and notice which parts of yourself are tense and tight and which parts are soft and relaxed . . . How do your feet feel? . . . Mentally travel up to your legs . . . Now up to your torso . . . Notice how your arms and hands feel . . . Now focus on your shoulders and neck . . . If there is any tension, gently breathe into these areas to release the muscles . . . Notice the feelings in your head and face and gently relax those muscles . . . Now go down your back and spine, noticing how they feel . . . Pay attention to every part of your body . . . Slowly take a deep breath and allow the air coming into your body to relax and release any tension you may have felt . . . Now visualize a beautiful white light above your head . . . Feel that light begin to surround your body . . . Allow your body to fill up with the light and use it to nourish your organs and tissue . . . Your body acts like a sponge and absorbs all the light it can . . . Every cell of your body is being bathed by the light . . . You are becoming a glowing being of light . . . Take a deep breath and feel the peace and love as your body completely relaxes.

After everyone is relaxed, continue to Step 2.

Step 2: Someone can lead the group by saying: Now remember your most recent experience of well-being . . . Remember the feeling of joy that you had, and the warm feelings of loving energy, happiness, and well-being. [Give a few minutes for everyone to find this feeling.] Feel that well-being in every cell of your body . . . Surround yourself with warm, light, energy . . . Feel love course through your veins, filling your entire being with serenity and joy. Increase the feeling . . . Increase it once again, so that you fill the entire room with this feeling of love, light, warmth, and joy. [Allow everyone to feel this in silence for a minute or so.]

Step 3: Now bring into this feeling the question you would most like to have answered today . . . If you want to know how to find a new relationship, bring that question into the warm, light-filled feeling of love and joy . . . If you want to know how to have better health, bring that question into this warm, light-filled feeling of joy. Surround your question with love and light in any way you can imagine . . . Increase the feeling of love . . . [Give them a moment or two of silence.]

Step 4: Now see your question turn into the actuality of what you desire . . . Feel in your heart that you *do* have a new relationship, or that you *do* have better health . . . Now express your gratitude for being led to whatever it is you need . . . Increase that feeling of gratitude as much as you can. Feel the actuality of your desire, whether it is a satisfying life work . . . or a relationship . . . or better health . . . or more prosperity . . . Bathe yourself in this loving, joyful vibration.

Step 5: Now gently release all concern for what you want. Accept that you are now drawing it, or something better, to you . . . the universal intelligence is now handling the details . . . Release all thought and concern of what you have requested . . . Continue to feel the warm, light, joyful energy. At the count of three you will return to the meeting full of energy One . . . two . . . three. Open your eyes.

Step 6: Ask people to share how the exercise felt to them.

EXERCISE 4. Have an Adventure

Step 1: Before leaving the group, make a date with someone in the group to do something that is new or fun for both of you before the next session.

Step 2: On the day of your adventure, spend a few minutes telling each other about your current life question and any possible answers you have already received. Take a small notebook in case messages come in. Notice what your intuition prompts you to do. Be spontaneous and expectant (but with no control/agenda).

Step 3: If you happen to be out of town during the following week, do one thing wherever you are that is fun and new for you. Sometimes it's a good idea to get a phone number from someone in the group and find out the best time to call. This is a short check-in call to talk about whether or not you have received any answers to your life questions, and to report on your adventure plans.

Closing

Requests for support. Sending loving energy.

USING THE SECOND INSIGHT AND INCREASING ITS BENEFIT

- Be aware that you have chosen to live at this crucial time in history.
- Ask support from your higher self to give you clear messages.
- Recognize the amount of time you spend trying to control events or people.
- Choose enjoyable activities. Do less out of a sense of obligation (which is different from responsibility). Choose one activity that you are willing and able to let go of right now with a clear conscience. Having fun and creating more open time raises your energy level and increases your chances for coincidences.
- Acknowledge any support you receive with gratitude.

STUDY GROUP FOR THE SECOND INSIGHT

Session 5

2 hours 30 minutes

Session Purpose: To continue to discuss individual insights about your personal time line, and to share what happened on the day of adventure and see what issues or information were revealed

Beginning Meditation

With or without music, start with a meditation for relaxation and alignment of energy (see page 53).

EXERCISE 1. Sharing the Adventure

Purpose: Everyone will have a chance to talk about how his or her day of adventure went. The purpose of the sharing is to give and receive insights about what happened on the adventure and how it helped illuminate a question you are currently asking.

Time: 2 hours

Directions: If your group is fifteen or fewer, you might want to stay together in one group. Start by having one person talk about how she or he selected a partner last week for the adventure, and how they decided where to go and why. After the first partner has finished, the second partner will have a chance to tell it from his or her experience.

In order to look for the significance in any of the events of the day, it might be helpful to discuss the day with these questions in mind:

a. How did you select your partner?
b. How enthusiastic were you about doing this exercise?
c. How did your expectations before the adventure affect your day? Did the day follow your expectations?
d. What similarities do you see between your usual preoccupations and the events or feelings you had on your adventure?
e. What were the positive outcomes of the day?
f. What did you learn?
g. Does anyone in the group pick up any insights as the story of the day is being told?

In one group a woman named Ellen told the story of her experience: "Well, when I heard *adventure*, I thought, sky-diving, hot-air ballooning. But when Robert asked me to be his partner on the adventure day, he suggested a hiking trail that I walk three times a week. The idea seemed boring to me, but I went along with it. I knew I was going into it with a negative attitude.

"We were going to have lunch first. When I arrived at the cafe where we had agreed to meet, I saw a Rolls-Royce parked in the lot, and I thought, 'Now, why couldn't I be going out in that!' Well, you guessed it. It was his car. The whole day turned out to be different than I thought, and it was really quite interesting to hear about his life experiences."

Ellen told her study group that her current question before her day of adventure had been, "How can I best sustain my relationship with my new boyfriend?" Interestingly, her new man was also named Robert and had similar interests to her adventure partner. It wasn't until a couple of days later that she realized how much she had learned from the day of adventure with Robert. She began to see how the negative expectations she carried into that day were a familiar pattern of negativity that also applied to the new relationship. She *had* received answers—with a bonus of practice time on a platonic interaction.

Another student named Denise was telling her study

group about an encounter she had the previous week with a friend with whom she was having an extremely hard time. They had been fighting, things were going from bad to worse, accusations were flying. On the way to an art opening all sorts of delays prevented Denise from being on time, which further infuriated her friend. One of these delays, which she casually mentioned, was having to stop for a funeral procession.

Someone in the group asked Denise to consider for a moment the funeral procession that crossed her path. Could this be a significant symbol, since Denise herself, in the previous week, had been struck by the value of the "deaths" she had had on her time line? Death, she had said, seemed to be an important aspect of transformation—something had to die or change before new life could be begun. Suddenly the metaphor created by the funeral procession awakened Denise to the idea that something was dying in her life and needed to be buried or transformed. This realization allowed her to recognize the control drama patterns with her friend (which began with her mother), and she decided to end her relationship with the difficult friend.

Closing

Requests for support. Sending energy to each person.

Further Study

You might want to reread *The Celestine Prophecy* and see if your understanding of the Insights has changed since the first reading.

For Next Session

- Ask one or two volunteers to bring to the next meeting some objects of beauty—perhaps a bouquet of flowers, a small plant, a bowl of fruit, or other natural item of special appeal.
- Bring oranges and napkins for each member.

CHAPTER 3

A Matter of Energy

Traveling with Wil through the majestic mountains of Peru, our character arrives at the Viciente Lodge, an estate of incredible beauty surrounded by exotic plants and ancient oaks. He finds himself surprisingly energized. Encountering several researchers exploring the energy fields of plants, he begins to learn about the Third Insight. Practicing what he learns about seeing energy by focusing on the beauty of nature, he sees, just for a moment, the energy field surrounding a plant and how it can be affected by consciousness. The idea that perhaps we can make certain events come faster or slower depending on how we think intrigues our character. Skepticism gives way to genuine interest and curiosity.

THE THIRD INSIGHT

The Universe Is Pure Energy. The Third Insight informs us that everything in the universe is made up of energy, and this energy creates all the forms and substances of what we call our reality. One big ocean of vibration, this energy coalesces into the myriad forms of existence, whether it be a rock, a wave, a flower, a coat in your closet, or yourself. Existence is made of the same basic substance, and it is always in action—being born, unfolding, transforming, and shifting.

We Are Cocreators through Our Thoughts. The Third Insight reveals that all things are literally one and therefore interconnected. Because all energy is interconnected, it is malleable to human consciousness through the action of intention. Incredibly, it responds to our expectations. Our radiating thoughts and feelings cause our energy to flow out into the world and affect other energy systems.

Beauty Raises Our Energy. The Third Insight encourages us to own the reality of this universal energy by observing it in nature and with people. In the beginning, the easiest way to get closer to seeing energy is to cultivate our appreciation of beauty. When we become aware of the unique and beautiful qualities of nature or a person, we have, in effect, raised our vibration on the continuum of consciousness. After putting ourselves into resonance with the beauty of an object or person, the next level of perception will be to see the energy in that which we find beautiful.

Becoming Aware of Energy Raises Our Vibration. Awareness of universal energy is the foundation for ultimately engaging its flow and becoming a cocreator with it. Once we *know* that we are part of a living system of heretofore invisible energy, a core belief will have shifted and we will exist at a higher vibration. When our mind reads the words on the page, and our heart recognizes those words with a "Yes, of course!" then we are beginning to integrate this Insight. For some people, there might be a quickening of events and synchronicities, and for others, perhaps, a newfound hope, clarity, or confidence. Some of us might have to go through a painful reorganization before we can rebuild. Even though things might not change in our lives as rapidly as we want them to, they will change.

Try visualizing states of mind as different frequency bands. As you bring in the higher vibrations of energy, such as awareness, gratitude, beauty, integrity, joy, and trust, you are actually harmonizing more closely with the universal energy. Everyday life becomes infused with your ability to stay connected through awareness, and even though there will be times when you experience stress, you will be more likely to stay connected to the heartbeat of your spiritual guidance. When you are taking care of yourself, paying your rent, sharing with others, you are building a strong base that will support you in times of doubt. Every insight and connection you make with others who are also growing takes you to a higher level. Each shift makes the next one easier.

Cellular Consciousness

What does a philodendron plant have in common with a cup of yogurt? In 1973 a book, *The Secret Life of Plants*, fascinated readers all over the world with stories of experimental research showing that plants possess amazing powers. Among these powers was the ability to detect what humans were thinking—even from miles away (we will explore this in a minute). Although the search for a basic substance of life has gone on since the ancient Greeks, a new field of bioenergetics began in earnest in the 1960s, bringing to light the existence of invisible, intelligently communicating energy.

One fateful day in 1966, an American expert on polygraph examination (the lie detector test), Cleve Backster, playfully hooked up his galvanometer to his office philodendron plant. To see what kind of reaction, if any, he might record, he decided to dunk its leaves in the hot coffee he happened to be holding in his hand. Since there was no reaction, he began to think of a more serious threat to the plant. The instant that he thought of burning the leaf with a match, the galvanometer went wild. The reactions that he saw on his machine that evening led to hundreds more experiments that yielded proof that plants have the ability to "think." Plants, normally attuned to each other, seem to monitor the movements of humans and animals in the environment down to the cellular level. For example, in one experiment where a researcher purposely destroyed one of two plants, the surviving plant was able to correctly identify the culprit among six other people. In a demonstration of the plant's ability to detect even subtler acts of violence, it also reacted when a researcher was preparing to eat a cup of yogurt. As he stirred some jam into the yogurt, the preservative in the jam caused the death of some of the live yogurt bacilli. This cellular death was picked up by the plant.[1]

Serious inquiry has since begun to bridge the fields of science and metaphysics. One investigator in the 1970s, research chemist Marcel Vogel, worked extensively with plants and their sensitivity to humans and their ability to register human thoughts and emotions. In one lecture he stated:

> It is fact: man can and does communicate with plant life. Plants are . . . extremely sensitive instruments for measuring man's emotions. They radiate energy forces beneficial to man. One can feel these forces! They feed into one's own force field, which in turn feeds back energy to the plant. . . . The American Indians were keenly aware of these faculties. When in need, they would go into the woods. With their arms extended, they would place their backs to a pine tree in order to replenish themselves with its power.[2]

Apparently, life retains memory and sentience—the ability to perceive—even at the molecular level. Experiments at the cellular level by Backster and cytologist Dr. Howard Miller showed that

> sperm cells turned out to be surprisingly canny in that they seemed to be capable of identifying and reacting to the presence of their own donor, ignoring the presence of other males. Such observations seem to imply that some sort of total memory may

go down to the single cell. . . . Sentience . . . does not seem to stop at the cellular level. It may go down to the molecular, the atomic and even the subatomic. All sorts of things which have been conventionally considered to be inanimate may have to be re-evaluated.[3]

Even though we might not be consciously aware of these minuscule connections, we are beginning to realize that we live within an intelligence greater than our own. Life, the eternal flow of living energy, is the outgrowth of our intention and attention and *is designed to meet our needs* through the blueprint within our cellular DNA. With the power of awareness we activate our field, attracting, in due time, what we need.

Developing at Your Own Pace

In the novel our character frequently makes such comments as "I didn't quite grasp what Dobson was getting at"; "I'm not sure what that means"; "I was still confused"; or "I felt as if the story continued but I couldn't quite grasp it." You might have had similar feelings, too, as you read *The Celestine Prophecy*, once, twice, or even several times. You might have a tendency to want to get all the Insights down, to understand them, use them, and move quickly toward a new life. Rather than trying to solidify, codify, or hang on to your excitement about the Insights, accept that you are learning and integrating these ideas at your own pace.

For example, the Third Insight tells us that we will learn to see the invisible energies around plants and people. Some of us do see this field, and many more will see it in the near future. For some it will be easier than others. The important thing with the Third Insight is to accept the reality of universal energy.

In *The Adventure of Self-Discovery* Dr. Stanislav Grof writes:

A very common experience in the holotropic [breathing] mode is to see energy fields of various colors around other people that correspond to the traditional descriptions of auras. Occasionally, these are associated with spontaneous specific insights into the health condition of the people involved. I have personally observed phenomena of this kind, not only in subjects in unusual states of consciousness, but also in accomplished psychics who can use their capacity to see auras in a reliable way in their everyday life. The extraordinary ability of one of these psychics, Jack Schwartz, to read the medical history of his clients and diagnose current diseases has been repeatedly tested and documented by medical researchers with impressive credentials.[4]

You might literally see energy, or you might sense it in other ways. Some people interpret energy as an inner knowing, and they might express it as: "I feel great power in that tree. I can feel its roots reaching for the center of the earth. I sense its wisdom, and its age." Or: "The tree feels like a blessing, a shelter, a teacher." Others, more attuned to the sound vibrations, might say, "I love hearing the creaking of the branches, and I hear the leaves whispering encouragement to me."

If you cannot *see* the en-

> . . . the body radiates several forms of energy that can be measured by the instruments of Western science. Each of us is surrounded by an aura, if you will, of radiant heat; this heat may be perceived several inches from the skin by a sensitive hand, and from much greater distances by thermistor and infrared sensors. . . . We exist as intermingling fields . . . we possess many ways of sensing one another at a distance.
>
> GEORGE LEONARD,
> *The Ultimate Athlete*[5]

ergy fields in nature, don't worry. One woman said, "I got to the Third Insight and put down the book. I went downstairs to stare at my cat. She is so beautiful, I thought I could see her energy. As much as I focused on her beauty, I still couldn't see the field!" Continue your experiments if you wish, but don't assume that you are not evolving because you are not yet able to actually see the energy.

The heart awakens over time. In order for our own insights to grow into wisdom, they need fertile ground in which to place their roots, and time to deepen.

Fertile Ground

A quiet mind is a fine place for us to begin. In *The Celestine Prophecy* the beautiful old estate of Viciente Lodge provided a refuge where our character felt refreshed. In that supportive environment he was able to respond to some of the suggestions for seeing energy, communing with the giant oaks, and appreciating the beauty. If he were speeding down a freeway through the heart of a metropolitan area, it would have been more difficult to accomplish these tasks. When our intention is clear, even if it doesn't seem like a particularly spiritual desire, the result usually exceeds the expectation. If you are eager to apply the Insights to your life, ask yourself, "How can I improve my contact with natural beauty?"

Stability developed through nourishing daily habits is fertile ground for deepening our spiritual roots. Paradoxically, there are other times when our greatest fertility is found in adversity and challenge, where our seedling ideas are tested for strength. As one observer remarked about his desire for instant spiritual understanding, "I guess I always want to grab the blossom, without putting in the time developing the roots." Let your understanding of the Insights develop gradually if that's the way it happens. If you desire greater spiritual fulfillment, you might ask yourself, "Am I taking good care of myself in everyday life?"

Radiating Energy Affects Everyone

In India there is a belief that if there is one holy person in a village, the whole village reaps the benefit of his or her enlightenment. Dr. Patrick Tribble of Albany, California, tells how he observed the effect of one person's energy on others:

"I was lucky enough to meet painter Elizabeth Brunner, who had been friends with several world leaders such as Gandhi and Nehru. I went to her house once when she was in her eighties and was amazed to see that she had an aura that extended about four hundred feet beyond her physical body. I watched visitors come to her, and just by being in her presence they became immediately loving and kind— even if they were greedy types. Such was her dedication to God."

Many of you read *The Celestine Prophecy* and felt great energy and excitement. You might have felt as if the Insights were somehow familiar to you. The degree to which you resonate with the Insights shows that you have already been making preparations for the shift in consciousness. Remember, it might take some time to integrate your understanding of the Insights with your existing framework of beliefs.

If you are feeling a desire to make a deeper contribution to others through your life and work, you are already radiating out a level of support that assists the growth of new thinking. Your contribution is *being you* as fully as you can be. You are a radiant being. Ask yourself, "Do I respect and like who I am?"

Energy Fields

Earlier in this century, photographs of a mysterious luminescence emanating from leaves, inanimate objects, and the fingertips of humans gave us the visual validation of what mystics had always referred to as the aura. For instance, Kirlian photography, named after the Russian couple who invented the process, is believed by many people to show this energy field. In the 1970s further research by one of the world's experts on crystals, William A. Tiller at Stanford University, led to the speculation that "the radiation or energy coming out of a leaf or a human fingertip actually might be coming from whatever is present *prior to the formation of solid matter* . . . this . . . may be another level of substance, producing a hologram, a coherent energy pattern of a leaf which is a force-field for organizing matter to building itself into this kind of physical network."[6]

> Research, involving over seventeen hundred experiments, demonstrates that the DNA in living cells can communicate with other nearby cells through the transmission of energy in the form of light. These results indicate that cells can communicate with one another independently of biochemistry and of organ systems such as the circulatory system, nervous system, or immune system.
>
> LEONARD LASKOW, *Healing with Love*[7]

As each decade of the twentieth century ends, the scientific search for proof of the ineffable continues. Even though these esoteric research projects remain in the periphery of most of our lives, it's possible that their discoveries reach us through the collective unconscious (our telecommunications system), as if sending little voice mail messages to us. These unconscious shifts in understanding create the fertile ground wherein the Insights of the Manuscript can take root.

Energy Responds to Our Expectations

Information seems to come when we need it. Perhaps more precisely, information is a constant stream, and our intention starts a sorting process for relevancy to the need. Like the Bold function key on the computer, intention selects out what we need to know.

As we shift to a higher vibration, messages tend to flow in more quickly. When we are using our gifts and abilities with right intention, things come to us.

If you are not experiencing that flow right now, shift your intention to being shown the way back to your path. Expect that during the day you will encounter people who have messages relevant to your needs. As you sharpen your awareness of this phenomenon it tends to build.

Think back to a project that you really liked doing. Was there an ease to the flow of energy? How did things start to fall into place? Did friends mention relevant sources of information or books? Usually the flow toward completion happens by a combination of conscious intent and unconscious attraction.

Let's say you decided to create a more beautiful area on your outdoor deck for your meditations. You decide that plants in pots would look nice. You remember you have a friend with a green thumb, and so you specifically ask for assistance: "Say, Barbara, do you know any good books on how to garden with containers?" She gets enthusiastic about your project, too, and now you can vividly imagine magenta bougainvillea and trellises of pink and yellow sweet peas. Expectation rises. Your awareness of different kinds of plants becomes activated as you drive through neighborhoods with yards that had seemed insignificant before. As you drive past a nursery, your eye instantly spots an array of Mexican pottery way back in the yard. Last month you probably never even noticed the nursery on that corner because your mind had not yet formulated a need for it. Then, oddly enough, your neighbors move away, leaving you with their herbal planter box. For your birthday, two friends give you geraniums and a potted lemon tree. Eventually, there comes a time, perhaps at sunset, when you look around and realize that your dream of an abundance of plants and blooms surrounding your meditation chair has become a reality.

The life you have at this moment is the completed picture of your current thoughts, beliefs, and past responses.

Looking for Messages in the Events of the Day

We never quite know how universal energy will appear with a message for us. For example, a woman we know received news that she was to be the new head of the psychiatric ward after working at a hospital for only six months. She had been promoted over someone else who had been there longer than she, and she was having a momentary anxiety attack over her ability to take on this new responsibility. Just at that moment, a colleague from her previous employment called to chat and said she had been thinking of her. "I really never told you how much I valued your input in designing our program last year. You created a whole new attitude when you were here. We really miss you!"

She could have chosen to see this call as just a friendly chat, or she could have noticed that it was a sign of encouragement that she was on the right path, not to worry.

As an experiment, carry your journal or a small notebook with you all day for three days and write down all important messages or lessons you pick up from daily encounters in person or on the phone. You might be surprised at the pattern that emerges.

Pitfalls That Cause Energy Loss

Even though you might have learned to accentuate the positive in your attitudes and even begun to use more conscious positive language, you still might experience energy drains that seemingly slow your evolution. Anger, fear, resentment, aloofness, skepticism, and victimhood, not to mention sheer fatigue, are all common life occurrences for most of us. At first, as you open to a higher awareness of your life, you might begin to experience these states more often or more intensely.

Several times in the novel, our character begins to droop, feels confused, has trouble making a decision, or reacts to his surroundings with fear, anxiety, and distrust. These are all signs that his energy had dropped. We all go through these periods. What to do?

Getting in Touch with Your Energy Just the Way It Is

If you are experiencing low energy and need a boost, first get in touch with your body to identify just exactly what you are feeling. In most cases, it helps to write down your feelings in your journal. One woman told us, "The other day at work I had the most anxious feeling. I had no idea what was going on. I was filling in at someone else's desk and couldn't leave right then. I didn't have my journal, so I just wrote on the back of an envelope.

"I realized that I was really overreacting to the fear that I didn't know how to operate the telephone system at this desk very well, and I felt like I could easily get overwhelmed if more than two calls came in at once. The deeper fear behind the panic was that I'm new at this job and scared of making mistakes and getting fired. Anyway, I prayed that the phones wouldn't ring all at once, and they didn't! It seems like even tiny prayers get answered more for me lately."

Keep Breathing

No matter where we are we have our breath. Many times we can calm ourselves quickly by simply paying attention to our breath for a few minutes.

If you are feeling drained, try sitting quietly and imagine a sturdy cord extending from the base of your spine downward into the earth. Imagine drawing some of the powerful earth energy up your cord into the center of your chest. Then imagine opening the top of your head to allow a silver cord to extend upward into the sky. Let healing, refreshing energy flow down your cord into the center of your chest connecting with the earth energy. Soon you should experience a shift in energy.

At other times you will be overamped with energy—for example, in a heated argument. If you want to calm down, you might take yourself to another room or neutral quiet place and sit with eyes closed. Again it may help to visualize a sturdy cord connected to the end of your spinal cord and extending downward into the earth. Let your excess energy drain off down that cord and return to the earth energy.

Eastern masters have perfected the ability to cultivate energy with the breath, and there are many good books on such ancient practices as pranayama and chi kung. You might want to practice these. See our suggested reading list on page 128.

In either case of being over- or undercharged, a brief five- or ten-minute walk can also do wonders.

Bringing in Light

A simple exercise that you can do to energize yourself or help solve a problem is to imagine surrounding yourself with light. This is especially good to do on breaks from work or anywhere that you don't want to call attention to yourself. Close your eyes briefly (or rest your closed eyes on the palms of your hands). Imagine a great shower of light bathing over you, enveloping you in radiance. Bask in this inner sunbath. Feel the warmth and brilliance of the light. Imagine the room you are sitting in to be flooded with this light. Take a few minutes to intensify the image. Experiment a few times a day for a week and see if you notice any changes in yourself or those around you. They're getting the light and energy, too, whether they know it or not!

SUMMARY OF THE THIRD INSIGHT

The Third Insight describes our new view of the universe as energy dynamic. As we look out on the world around us, no longer can we think of everything as composed of material substance. From the many findings of modern physics and the growing synthesis with the wisdom of the East, we are coming to know the universe as a vast field of energy, a quantum world in which all phenomena are interconnected and responsive. From the wisdom of Eastern thought, we know that we ourselves have access to this universal energy. We can project it outward with our thoughts and intentions, influencing our reality and the reality of others.

Further Reading

The Tao of Physics: An Exploration of the Parallels between Modern Physics and Eastern Mysticism. Fritjof Capra. Shambhala Publications, 1991.

Hyperspace: A Scientific Odyssey through Parallel Universes, Time Warps, and the Tenth Dimension. Michlo Kaku. Oxford University Press, 1994.

Secrets of Ancient and Sacred Places: The World's Mysterious Heritage. Paul Devereux. Blandford, 1992.

The Findhorn Garden. Findhorn Community. Harper & Row, 1976.

Sacred Places: A Journey Into the Holiest Lands. Sarah Osmen. St. Martin's, 1991.

The Sacred Earth. Courtney Milne. Viking, 1991.

INDIVIDUAL STUDY OF THE THIRD INSIGHT

Increasing Appreciation of Beauty

For the next month or two, make a point of visiting a park, church or temple (especially when it's empty and quiet), or an art museum. How do you feel there?

One evening a week take a leisurely walk down a street that has particularly beautiful front gardens. Continue the quiet mood without any television that evening. How do you feel the next day? Contrast these experiences with the energy you feel when you're at a supermarket or gas station.

Make a point of connecting with something beautiful in nature each day. Look at a flower up close.

Connecting with Energy

Seeing Energy in Nature

How long has it been since you went into a forest or even a park? Maybe you live by a river, lake, or the ocean but "never have time" to go there. Make a date with yourself for some period of refreshment in nature.

When you are in nature, you can try the experiment mentioned in the novel. Sit down somewhere comfortably and focus your attention on the beauty of the forms of a special tree or plant. Does one plant seem more beautiful than another?

If you want to try to see the radiant band of light around a tree or plant, the best times of day are probably dawn and sunset. Soften the focus of your eyes as you gaze at the outer edges of the plant. Sit quietly and see this living being in all its grandeur. Breathe in the beauty and fill your being with it. Let your body expand with all the beauty you feel. Imagine you are connected to the plant. Feel the living energy of it. Continue absorbing the energy, keeping your focus soft until you detect a bluish band of light. If you don't actually see it, pretend you see it for a moment.

Seeing the Energy in Your Hands

To see the energy field in your own hands try the following exercise. Sit comfortably in a position where you have blue sky in front of you. Touch the tips of your index fingers together. Keep the blue sky in the background. Now separate the tips about an inch and look at the area directly between them. Take your eyes out of focus a little and move the tips closer, then further apart. Place your gaze on the area between your fingers. Let your fingertips become slightly blurry. You should be able to see something like strands of smoke or mist stretching between the tips.

You can also hold your palms or forearms very closely together and see the streaks of energy between them.

Seeing Energy around People or Plants

It is easier to see energy fields if you soft-focus the details of a form or face. In a room, keep light dim, and place your person or object against a fully light or fully dark background. Try looking at the outline of a friend against the sky to see the radiating band of light surrounding his or her body. In either case, squint your eyes to blur your vision slightly.

Feeling the Energy in Your Hands

Briskly rub the palms of your hands together for one or two minutes. Cup your two palms facing each other and feel the tingling sensation in the space between them. Slightly increase and decrease the space between your palms. Imagine you have a ball of radiant light in this space. Feel its presence and density as you move your hands slightly. You can place this energy by focusing awareness somewhere in your body and let it energize or heal you.

Building Energy at Home

Once you start to become aware of the various energy shifts in your body, you will be more likely to choose to increase your vitality in the way that feels appropriate for the moment. Raising energy need not be complicated or cost anything. Energy increases when you are fully present, living neither in the past nor in the future. The most important ingredient is focused awareness in the moment. Try some of the following:

- Consciously breathing energy into all parts of your body
- Doing fifteen minutes of yoga stretching
- Listening to a favorite environmental tape of natural sounds or drumming music
- Appreciating the beauty in a bouquet of fresh flowers
- Gardening

- Taking time to admire a view from your home or neighborhood
- Meditating to quiet the mind and then bathing yourself in inner light
- Dancing

Increasing Energy at Work

- Get centered. Imagine being connected to the energy from the earth and from the sky. Bathe yourself in inner light.
- Keep personally meaningful objects such as posters, photos, and positive affirmations or spiritual quotations on your desk.
- Take a walk at lunch. Focus on seeing the beauty in passersby, a fountain, a piece of sculpture, or a park.
- Take a five-minute stretch break every couple of hours.
- Water a plant very slowly and listen to the sound of the water.
- Keep fresh flowers on your desk and breathe in their beauty for a few minutes.
- Play an environmental tape of natural sounds if appropriate in your place of work.

> When your intention is to transfer loving energy there is no way you can fail . . . because in the subtle realms intention is action.
>
> LEONARD LASKOW,
> *Healing with Love*[8]

STUDY GROUP FOR THE THIRD INSIGHT

Session 6

2 hours 30 minutes

Session Purpose: To see how others understand the Third Insight, and to work with energy

Preparation: Have someone bring an object of beauty—perhaps a bouquet of flowers, a small plant, a bowl of fruit, or other natural item of special appeal.

Introduction

Allow a few minutes for members to share any insights, coincidences, or unfinished thoughts from last week. Keep the energy focused on sharing specific points about the Insights.

EXERCISE 1. Discussion of the Third Insight

Purpose: To discover the kinds of beliefs we now hold about this Insight, and to hear how others understand it

Time: 30 minutes

Directions: Have someone read aloud the synopsis of the Third Insight on page 60 of this chapter (up to "Cellular Consciousness") and then use some of the following topics for discussion:

- What stood out for people when they read this chapter in the novel?
- How many people are skeptical of this idea? Why? How many easily accepted this chapter? Why?
- Has anyone been able to see energy? How did they do it?
- Did people see these energy fields when they were children?
- In what ways do people in the group raise their energy at home? At work?

- How many people take walks in nature?
- What books and resources can people share about the nature of energy and how to work with it?

When the discussion seems to be complete, you may go on to the next exercise.

Note: The following appreciation exercise can be enhanced with a background of evocative music or an environmental tape such as the sounds of a brook, birdsong, or the ocean.

EXERCISE 2. Practicing Appreciation of Beauty

Purpose: (a) To practice how to be mindful of what is in front of us; (b) to connect with beauty and raise our consciousness to a higher level, thus enhancing our connection to spiritual energy; (c) to stimulate the ability to see energy; (d) to notice how we project qualities of ourselves into outside objects

Time: Approximately 5–10 minutes for observation, 10 minutes for journal writing, and 20 minutes for sharing experiences

Directions:
Step 1: Put one of the items of beauty that were brought to the meeting in the center of your group so that everyone can see it clearly.
Step 2: Have a volunteer guide the group through the meditation by reading the following steps as the meditation is in progress. Begin by doing the brief relaxation meditation on page 53 to align the energies of the group.
Step 3: Following the relaxation, gently bring your full awareness to whatever object you have selected to appreciate.
Step 4: Become aware of the elegance of the shape, the intensity of the color, the light on the surface, and

the specific presence of the item. What makes this item unique?

Step 5: Drink in the essence of this object. Breathe in its best qualities as if you could absorb those qualities into yourself.

Step 6: Look at tiny details and notice how each contributes to the whole. Now look at the entire object and sense its grandeur even though it might be small and subtle. Practice going from the small to the large view. Now try to see the object as huge, as filling the room in front of you. Bring it back to normal size.

Step 7: Blur the focus of your vision slightly and try to see a glow around the object. Can you sense a radiation of any kind from this object?

Step 8: Finally ask yourself, "How am I like this object?"

Step 9: After a few minutes of observing the object, let your energy tell you when you are finished. Take a moment to write down the *most important things* you noticed about the object. Also write your answer to the question "How am I like this object?"

Step 10: All members of the group should have a chance to share their observations, feelings, and writing about the object. *Notice that the part of the object's beauty that stands out to each person reflects back qualities he or she already possesses.*

EXERCISE 3. A Conscious Eating Experience

Purpose: To become aware of how food can provide more than just nutrients, and to slow down and notice the simple experiences of life and what they might bring to you

Time: About 5 minutes eating and 10 minutes sharing the experience

Directions:
  Step 1: Pass out an orange and napkin to each person.
  Step 2: Eat your orange and notice its smell, texture, flavor, energy, and the sounds of eating it. Fill yourself up with the energy of this fruit.
  Step 3: Share what you learned from this experience.

EXERCISE 4. Mutual Appreciation

Purpose: To practice seeing the beauty and energy of another person

Time: About 10 minutes

Directions: You might play quiet music for this process and dim the light slightly. Members will sit in pairs facing one another, so that at least one of them has a darker background behind him. Remain silent during the process. Someone should signal when about 7 or 8 minutes have elapsed, so that people have time to gently disengage from the process.
  Step 1: Begin to focus on the uniqueness of the other person. Appreciate his or her being. See his or her beauty.
  Step 2: Imagine sending light energy from yourself to this person, bathing him or her in a warm glow of radiant energy.
  Step 3: Focus on this person's unique qualities and continue to see him or her as a beautiful, radiant being.
  Step 4: After about 7 or 8 minutes, gently disengage from the other person and thank each other.
  Step 5: Ask people to describe what happened during this experience.

Closing

Requests for support. Sending energy to each person.

Further Study
   People might wish to do the Individual Study to practice seeing energy in plants or with people.

USING THE THIRD INSIGHT
AND INCREASING ITS BENEFIT

- Spend some time in a natural setting this week.
- Practice focusing on a tree or a plant at least once this week, and imagine a band of light around it.
- See if you can beautify your environment in small ways.
- Notice energy shifts each day, and practice building energy consciously at least once.
- Practice seeing the beauty in your friends, family, and coworkers.

CHAPTER 4

The Struggle for Power

Leaving behind the secluded beauty of Viciente Lodge, our character and Wil travel deep into the mountains, continuing their journey to the highest peaks. "Stay alert," says Wil, "because the coincidences will now occur regularly and you must watch events closely." As if on cue, the two stop for the night and witness a volatile scene between family members at dinner. As our adventurer ponders the idea that energy flows between people, he and Wil unexpectedly encounter a psychologist who is studying human conflict. Experiencing the movement of energy firsthand, our character is by turns captivated by Marjorie, the researcher from Viciente, and interrogated by Jensen, an archaeologist also pursuing the Manuscript. As he comes under the influence of Jensen, he becomes confused and rattled about what to do next. Wil appears just in time to keep him on his search for the rest of the Manuscript.

THE FOURTH INSIGHT

The Fourth Insight tells us that humans compete for energy with each other. We do this unconsciously in every encounter. By observing our own and others' interactions, we can become conscious of this competition and begin to understand the underlying nature of human conflict. As we become more aware we will also come to realize that energy gained in this way doesn't last very long. Further awareness brings us to the realization that the true energy we seek comes from a universal source. We don't need to secure it from another person.

We begin to release these habits as we increase awareness of our tendency to control, undermine, second-guess, and please others.

The Struggle for Power

Our struggle for power might start as early as the first bellowing cries we make announcing our entry into the world. Our survival instinct is accompanied by the psychological and spiritual needs for security, intimacy, financial well-being, a sense of belonging, recognition, and control over our lives. Trying to keep our needs in some kind of balance underlies everything we try to accomplish in the outer world. When one need is lacking we tend to focus all our energy to get that need met.

> The need for control and the addictive quest for dominance is a universal quest aimed at avoiding the inner void. Because of its scope, and because it forms the underpinnings of all unhealthy addictions, it has won itself the label as the Master Addiction.
>
> PHILIP KAVANAUGH,
> *Magnificent Addiction*[1]

Early Childhood

The "having to be in control," in order to maintain energy, is a situation that begins in childhood. As children we depend on adult caretakers for our survival and we develop very specific ways to get energy from our family system. Getting enough love to feel secure and enough recognition to help us build an identity is crucial to our development. Anne Frank, who wrote with such perception about her family life in *Anne Frank: The Diary of a Young Girl*, expressed her feelings about the balance of power between herself, her sister, Margot, and their father:

> With Daddy it's different. If he holds Margot up as an example, approves of what she does, praises and caresses her, then something gnaws at me inside, because I adore Daddy. He is the one I look up to. I don't love anyone in the world but him. He doesn't notice that he treats Margot differently from me. Now Margot is just the prettiest, sweetest, most beautiful girl in the world. But all the same I feel I have some right to be taken seriously too. I have always been the dunce, the ne'er-do-well of the family. I've always had to pay double for my deeds, first with the scolding and then again because of the way my feelings are hurt. Now I'm not satisfied with this apparent favoritism any more. I want something from Daddy that he is not able to give me. . . . It is only that I long for Daddy's real love: not only as his child, but for me—Anne, myself.[2]

Anne's words speak to all of us who have experienced sibling rivalry, competition, failure to please the one we love, and the feeling of invisibility. The withering remnants of early pain, belittlements, abuse, neglect, fear, abandonment, and guilt are the birthplace of our struggle for control. We pack these along with our grown-up bodies and diplomas as we turn into adults, and ultimately these early experiences spark the formation of particular styles of winning energy (these "control dramas" will be discussed in Chapter 6).

Everyday Life Is the Interchange of Energy

As the Third and Fourth Insights make clear, the exchange of energy happens so constantly and ubiquitously that we are barely aware of it—until our energy is perceptively drained or increased. One model for interchange of energy was brilliantly described in the 1960s by Eric Berne, M.D., in a system called *transactional analysis*.

Analyzing transactions between people, Berne and others identified how each of us vies for attention. In transactional terms, positive feelings or attention are called *strokes*. As we mature, positive attention (or strokes) helps us build a sense that we are okay, that we are worthwhile and important in the scheme of things. In the same way that we learn our native tongue, we pick up the language of social interchange. These devices are our habitual way to give and receive energy without having to think too much about it, and we tend to become stuck in the particular techniques that were effective in our early families. Berne wrote:

> Positions are taken and become fixed surprisingly early, from the second or even the first year to the seventh year of life . . . it is not difficult to deduce from an individual's position the kind of childhood he must have had. Unless something or somebody intervenes, he spends the rest of his life stabilizing his position and dealing with situations that threaten it: by avoiding them, warding off certain elements or manipulating them provocatively so that they are transformed from threats into justifications.[3]

Losing the Bid for Attention

In early life we have few ego defenses to understand or ward off the effects of being ignored, ridiculed, and criticized. As we grow, the accumulated negative encounters affect our self-evaluation and expectations from the world. We have a deficit, and a natural desire to make up for it by getting energy from others.

For example, perhaps you can remember a time when you were in a group where the conversation was going at a lively pace. You had been waiting for an opportunity to leap in and tell a story, when finally there was a lull. Just at the moment you spoke the first words of your story, the conversation resumed as if you weren't even there. Did you turn to someone closer to you to try to mask your embarrassed start? In that instant you lost energy. In order to regain it, you had to hook that person into your energy and get his or her attention away from the general conversation. Could you see how this person's eyes focused attentively on you, or perhaps looked back to the others to see if the group conversation was more interesting? How did you feel if this person turned his or her attention to the group, thereby making you twice ignored, first by the group and second by the individual? How did the energy flow feel to you as you realized no one really heard you? You probably felt somewhat discounted or maybe even invisible. Perhaps it reinforced your natural tendency to play it safe and be aloof and quiet, or perhaps you responded in a more aggressive way, demanding recognition. Depending on your self-esteem at that moment, you either shrugged it off, blamed yourself for lack of assertiveness, or resented others for their lack of sensitivity.

Becoming aware of how we discount *ourselves* helps us take responsibility for our part in a negative energy exchange.

> Individuation begins when we look inside ourselves for answers, when we stop blaming others for our feelings and begin relating to our emotions and intuition as our teachers.
>
> PHILIP KAVANAUGH,
> *Magnificent Addiction*[4]

Ego States

As we shall see with the Sixth Insight, fixed ego positions foster a recurrent dramatic style called a *control drama*. The positions describe three important attitudes. These attitudes, described in Berne's best-selling book *Games People Play*, are defined as the Parent, Child, and Adult ego states. The Parent ego state corresponds to the more aggressive "Intimidator" and "Interrogator" control dramas. The Child ego state corresponds to the more passive "Poor Me" and "Aloof" dramas. The Adult state, once it is expanded to include connection with the higher self, corresponds to the heightened state of synchronistic growth. Being aware of these ego states is useful in understanding how complex our interactions may be.

The Parent Ego State

According to Berne, the Parent ego state is composed of the behaviors, attitudes, and values you saw in your parents or other adults. When you communicate from this ego state, you might sound critical, judgmental, rigid, righteous, or overly protective and rescuing. You want to *feel* in control, so you try to control others.

In a power struggle, you might find that your critical inner Parent is busy at work making the other person wrong. Your behavior might closely resemble that of your parents, or reflect their values. For example, if you are in a power struggle with your spouse and your Parent ego state is active, you hear yourself saying, "There you go again. You always leave the cupboard doors open. Why can't you get more organized?" You might even wince inwardly, thinking, "God, I sound just like my father!" In the Parent ego states, key words like "always" or "you never" alert you that old, *past* patterns are being used in the *present*. When you hear yourself go on about other people's transgressions, it might be helpful to step back and notice what is happening within you. Do you have a need to control to win energy?

The Child Ego State

Berne defines the Child ego state as that familiar part of us that feels as we did as an infant or very young child. We manipulate from a position of weakness, guilt, or irresponsibility. This is an ego position that wants what it wants *now*, but always assumes that this need must be filled by others by making others feel responsible for it.

The Adult Ego State

The third state that transactional analysis defined is the Adult ego state. When we use our abilities to gather information from a variety of sources, consider options, and make choices based on current information, we are functioning from an Adult ego state. We are in the here and now. We are aware of our feelings, and we know that we have choices. We are willing to take risks based on the best information we have at the time. We might take into consideration what others have to say, but we trust ourselves to make the final decision. We are able to hear different opinions without feeling threatened or falling into a rigid position where we feel we are winning or losing. We stay in touch with our feelings and express ourselves as accurately as we can, knowing that more will be revealed as we open to events. The Adult state is the ego's readiness to connect with the faculties of intuition and inner guidance.

Power Struggles and Ego States

Irrational power struggles always occur when we find ourselves losing energy because of someone's manipulation of our attention, and we fight back to control the situation.

In order to begin to unhook ourselves from the need to control, the best thing we can do is focus on our feelings in the moment that we feel caught or anxious. We need not analyze other people or try to change them. All we need do is ask, "What am I feeling right now? What do I need here?" Once you have contacted your inner self and gut-level feelings, you can move into an adult mode—agreeing to disagree, not needing to win—then shift your attention to tapping into the universal source of energy.

> . . . the surest way to make ourselves crazy is to get involved in other people's business, and the quickest way to become sane and happy is to tend to our own affairs.
>
> MELODY BEATTIE,
> *Codependent No More*[5]

Begin to become aware of your daily interactions and see if you tend to communicate from your Parent, Child, or Adult voice.

Notice the difference in energy flow between your peers and those above and below you in the hierarchy at your workplace. How authentic are you being? Do you edit or block your energy flow with anyone? With whom do you stay in your Adult ego state most of the time?

Games People Play

When certain patterns are used repetitively, they become like games between people. Dr. Berne has shown that the variation for bids for attention is almost endless. In these games we see the tug-of-war as described by the Fourth Insight. Even without an in-depth analysis of the rules of these games, their names aptly describe situations that we have all encountered with our families, friends, and coworkers. For example, a classic "Interrogator/aloof" game is "Why Don't You—Yes But." In this exchange, the person playing the "Yes But" role listens but finds something wrong with every statement offered by the other, keeping the energy flowing toward him by resisting all suggestions of a solution to a stated problem. When the "Yes But" person has drained the problem-solver of any further solutions, he or she has the option of moving on to someone else or replaying the game later or with a different problem.

A popular "Poor Me" game defined by Berne is "Look How Hard I've Tried." This one is played from the Child ego state and reinforces helplessness and lack of accountability. The person keeps the energy coming in his direction by doing just enough token action to keep others, perhaps in an employment setting, from writing him off entirely.

"If It Weren't for You" is a game that can be played in many arenas—marital, teenage, alcoholic, and career. It specifically keeps the flow of energy exquisitely controlled so that people buy into the assignment of blame and send energy. At the root of this interchange is the phobic fear of risk or change which is masked by accusing the other of getting in the way. For example, Gloria, a fifty-six-year-old, blamed her husband's health for keeping her at home, but deep down she was terrified of having to compete on the job market.

When People Voluntarily Give Us Their Energy and Power

In *The Celestine Prophecy* our main character unexpectedly meets up again with Marjorie, one of the researchers from the Viciente Lodge. Conversing together in a cafe, he finds himself talking animatedly and at length with her. The energy she is pouring into him makes him feel expanded and alive. At this point in his development, the encounter serves to demonstrate how energy flows between people. Later in the book, he is warned that unless two people stay centered, accepting another's energy but not depending on it, an addictive relationship develops.

Awareness of how we vie for energy is the first step toward reclaiming our own power. Balance begins to be restored when we stop tapping into others for our energetic charge, and look inside ourselves for our connection to spirit.

Releasing the Need for Control

Coincidentally, as this chapter was being written, we interviewed an actor the week after he was hired for a new television pilot. He had just finished reading *The Celestine Prophecy* and was happy to share what he learned about letting go of control.

"In an audition I am always painfully aware of how my energy is affected by other people," he said. "It is so easy to give your energy away. Any unkind remark or even a look from somebody can make you fall apart. It's such a place of judgment—about the other actors, the casting people, and most of all yourself." But he told us that this time was different.

"Well, I had just read *The Celestine Prophecy*, and I decided that I was going to go to this audition with a different approach. Usually, I go in and try to muster up my confidence and force myself to be courageous. It always feels kind of forced and scary, like I'm second-guessing myself.

"This time I decided I was just going to let it unfold and see what happened. I decided to be in a state of peaceful oneness, not let anything affect me good or bad, just be there for myself."

We asked him if he had always been interested in metaphysical or spiritual ideas.

"Not at all. I was a total skeptic, but someone gave me the book, and after I read it, I changed my whole perception about how I wanted to do this audition." How did it work?

"Well, I felt very open. I just took everything in. I looked at it as a mystery that's going to unravel, rather than some daunting experience that ends up as a disappointment. I just wanted to do the best job I could. It was one of the best auditions of my life, and I had the job before I got home."

He said, "I really experienced everything differently because I didn't feel any of those judgments coming at me. I feel like my peaceful oneness created that same feeling with other people. I saw that very clearly—that what goes out of me comes back. I can change my perspective quicker now by, say, observing a tree on the sidewalk. When I really see the beauty of that tree, I begin to notice how great everything is around me, and I get back into a better frame of mind."

Once we stop depending on control as our only way to make things happen, our lives miraculously open up. Letting the universe guide us puts the mystery back into our life and makes us feel truly alive. Although each resistance and feeling of struggle is not necessarily "bad," because it can offer us the opportunity to see what we need to change, there is a more exciting way to live.

One of the leading metaphysical writers about transformation is Shakti Gawain. In her book *Living in the Light* she says about her own journey:

> Eventually I lost interest in trying to control my life, to make things happen in a way that I thought I wanted them to be. I began to practice surrendering to the universe and finding out what "it" wanted me to do. I discovered that in the long run it really wasn't that different. The universe always seems to want me to have everything I want, and it seems to know how to guide me in creating it better than I would know how to do so myself. The emphasis is different though. Instead of figuring out what

I want, setting goals, and trying to control what happens to me, I began to practice tuning in receptively to my intuition and acting on what it told me without always understanding why I was doing what I was doing. It was a feeling of letting go of control, surrendering, and allowing the higher power to be in charge.[6]

The purpose of the Fourth Insight is to help us recognize our need to control energy in interactions with others in order to feel a psychological lift. After you become aware of this tendency, you might find that you wish to "make a change" in how you relate. It is human nature to want to *do* something. However, the key point in your evolution is to increase consciousness about yourself and the universe. If you expect radical shifts or suddenly harmonious relationships and you continue to get stuck in competition for energy, don't assume you aren't "getting it." *What you need to become aware of will be presented to you.* If you feel frustrated at seemingly slow progress, realize that all your new insights need time to become integrated with your whole belief system.

SUMMARY OF THE FOURTH INSIGHT

The Fourth Insight is the awareness that humans have often cut themselves off from an inner connection with this mystical energy. As a result we have tended to feel weak and insecure, and we have often sought to build ourselves up by securing energy from other human beings. We do this by seeking to manipulate or dominate the other's attention. If we can force the attention of another, then we feel a boost from the other's energy, making us stronger, but leaving that person weakened. Often others fight back against this usurping of their strength, creating a power struggle. All conflict in the world stems from this battle over human energy.

Further Reading

In addition to the excellent books listed in the notes for this chapter we suggest:

Games People Play. Eric Berne, M.D. Ballantine, 1964.

Who Gets Sick? Blaine Justice. Jeremy P. Tarcher, 1988.

Spiritual Emergency: When Personal Transformation Becomes a Crisis. Stanislav and Christina Grof. Jeremy P. Tarcher, 1989.

The Politics of Experience. R. D. Laing. Pantheon, 1983.

The Family Patterns Workbook. Carolyn Foster. Jeremy P. Tarcher/Perigee Books, 1993.

Getting Love Right: Learning the Choices of Healthy Intimacy. Terence T. Gorski. Fireside/Parkside, 1993.

Enduring Grace. Carol Lee Flinders. HarperCollins, 1993.

Autobiography of a Yogi. Paramahansa Yogananda. Self-realization Fellowship, 1993.

Altered State of Consciousness. Charles Tart. Psychological Processes, Inc., 1992.

INDIVIDUAL STUDY OF THE FOURTH INSIGHT

The following exercises are offered only as suggestions to further increase your awareness. As you study and practice what you study, your vibration becomes higher. You will attract exactly the situations that offer you the most learning. Whenever you work on an exercise in this book, notice closely what happens to you in the seventy-two hours following your process work. You might get a golden opportunity to see a pattern you want to change.

EXERCISE 1. Discovery of Self-Imposed Obstacles

Purpose: To discover how you perpetuate unnecessary struggles to gain energy

Directions: Next time you have a specific situation that feels like a power struggle, consider how you might be justifying your position or preventing resolution. In your journal answer the questions in this exercise.

You might also want to have a friend work with you, asking each question. Hearing yourself answer aloud with no comments from your friend is a powerful experience.

Have your friend ask you each question without responding to your answers until you have answered everything. Have her jot quick notes about your answers on a separate piece of paper or in your journal. Then, if you want feedback, ask her what stood out in your answers.

Part I. Discovering Self-Imposed Obstacles

1. Locking yourself into a position that feels like a power struggle
 a. Describe the situation briefly.
 b. What are your feelings about the situation?
 c. What are you trying to accomplish?
 d. How would you *like* to feel in this situation?
 e. What are your most important needs in this situation?
 f. How do you interact with the other person from your inner Parent or Child voice?
 g. Have you locked yourself into a position?

2. **Being righteous**
   a. How have you categorized the other person and kept looking for ways to reinforce this judgment?

3. **Making everything black or white**
   a. How are you limiting options by looking only for a certain outcome?
   b. What are three more options?

4. **Focusing on the feeling of scarcity**
   a. What are you afraid of?

5. **Projecting your issues onto another**
   a. How is this struggle showing you what you need to become aware of?
   b. Do you interpret the other person's actions through the filter of your own fears?
   c. Does he or she reflect some part of your own unwanted anger, hatred, sexual feelings, or judgments?

6. **Using perfectionism or confusion as an excuse for staying stuck**
   a. Are you unwilling to move ahead until everything is "perfect" or because *you* are not "perfect" yet?
   b. Are you claiming to be confused instead of recognizing what you really want or need to do?

7. **Focusing on the struggle instead of looking for resolution**
   a. Are you investing energy in this power struggle instead of taking responsibility and acting on your own issues?

8. **Focusing on problems to keep energy coming to you**
   a. Are you focusing on this problem to keep yourself under the illusion of having something to control?
   b. What is the payoff for you to stay focused on this problem?

9. **Letting underlying fears run your life**
   a. What is the worst outcome in this situation?
   b. What is an even worse outcome than (a)?
   c. What do you fear is even worse than (b)?
   d. Is your worst fear realistic in this situation?

  e. Finish this statement with your response to (c): "This
     situation is being run by my fear of . . ."

Part II. Transforming Self-Imposed Obstacles

  a. What do you want from the other that you could do
     for yourself?
  b. What could you do differently?
  c. What is an action that you would be willing to do to
     turn this situation around *for yourself*?
  d. How would you like the universe to support you in
     resolving this situation?

EXERCISE 2. Six Intentions That Help You Stay Connected to Universal Energy

Purpose: The following list of intentions might help you integrate the Insights of *The Celestine Prophecy* into your relationships.

Directions: Become familiar with the following concepts, and
practice them often during the day. It might be helpful to
write the six points on a 3 by 5 card and keep it at your
desk, in your purse, or daily planner for a few weeks. Begin
to pay attention to what happens in your relationships. If
you feel any changes, make a quick note in your journal.

I am increasing my awareness of energy.

  One of the best ways to start transforming your need to
control is to check in with yourself several times a day.
Practice staying conscious of the movement of energy in
your body: How does your stomach feel right now? When
did your neck start to ache?
  Become aware of the energy moving between you and

others. When do you feel drained? When do you feel energized?

I have a strong internal connection to my higher self.

The best thing you can do for yourself and others is to take time to connect with your higher self. Take a break from whatever you are doing every couple of hours and close your eyes. Reconnect with a scene from nature or a loving exchange you've recently experienced. Feel the sensation of love coming into your body. Feel yourself expanding.

My best decisions are made when I am connected to my inner wisdom.

Try not to make decisions when you are tired, hungry, angry, or under time pressure.

Once I have made a decision, I follow through with appropriate action.

If you have come to a decision, but have let some time pass without taking even a small step toward the new direction, you might feel very depressed or drained. Following through with action gives you energy for the next step.

If you operate from a drained state, you might miss the significance of coincidences. Remember that in the Fourth Insight Wil told the main character, "Stay alert. Pay close attention to everything that happens."

I take time to reflect on important decisions.

Often when you are engaged in a power struggle, you are swept along and might make a decision you later regret. If you feel pushed, rushed, or boxed in *for any reason*, take some time to get centered. Have a "rescue statement" ready to use so that you can retreat from a situation where you feel pressured. For example, Pamela, an accountant starting her own business, learned to say, "Gee, I'd really like to help you. I'm not sure how to do that right now. Let me think about it." Or "Sounds interesting. Let me call you after I've had some time to think about it." Stick with your statement.

I trust that my process is taking me to a higher level of living.

Every time you feel empowered, you exist at a higher vibration. Acknowledge any small steps that you take successfully. At this new level of energy, you will feel as though you are attaining your destiny. This feeling will attract more coincidences.

EXERCISE 3. Using New Behaviors

Purpose: To practice keeping your energy focused, yet free-flowing

Directions:
a. Choose one of the behaviors below. Describe in your journal how you could apply it to a current problem. *Or:*
b. Choose one behavior and practice it for a week. Do you feel increased energy and more open? Do new opportunities come your way?

BEHAVIORS TO KEEP YOUR ENERGY FOCUSED AND FREE

Stay present in the moment.
Be your authentic self—be real.
Pay attention to your feelings.
Listen actively—clarify what you hear.
Stay in your Adult ego state.
Focus on how you want to feel.
Tell the truth as you feel it.

Let go of attachment to only one outcome.
Let the mystery unravel.
Stay open.

Change happens not by trying to *make* yourself change, but by becoming conscious of what's *not* working.

SHAKTI GAWAIN,
Living in the Light[7]

Your life has a purpose that is in the process of being revealed to you. Keep your current questions in the forefront of your attention. Whenever you need to, ask for more clarification from the universe.

Meditation to Connect to Inner Wisdom

Step 1: Sit or lie down in a comfortable position where you won't be disturbed for 15 or 20 minutes. Bring your attention to your breathing and take a few deep breaths. Let your body relax and let your mind become quiet. Let go of each thought that arises. Continue to let thoughts flow past without holding on to any.

Step 2: Now bring your attention to the center of your being, wherever you feel it to be. Imagine that your inner wisdom resides in this place. In this deep, quiet place, you may bring any question or issue that you would like to know more about. Ask your inner wisdom, "What do I need to know here? What is this situation trying to show me?" Listen quietly for any message from your intuition. Remember any suggestions for actions to take. Whenever you feel complete, end your meditation.

Step 3: Take the actions your intuition indicated. If you are on track you will feel more aliveness and doors will open. Coincidence may increase.

STUDY GROUP FOR THE FOURTH INSIGHT

Session 7

2 hours 30 minutes

Session Purpose: To study the Fourth Insight and become more aware of how we compete for energy

Introduction

Time: 10–15 minutes

Directions: Start the meeting by having everyone briefly share coincidences or pertinent insights gained over the week.

EXERCISE 1. Discussion of the Fourth Insight

Purpose: To hear the range of understanding of how we compete for energy in everyday life, and to give members a chance to share experiences of losing energy or being confused

Time: 30 or 40 minutes or until the group agrees to move on. If energy and interest are high, let the topic continue for most of the evening.

Directions: Have someone read aloud the synopsis of the Fourth Insight on page 83 (up to the heading "Early Childhood"). Talk about how you understand this Insight or give examples of a recent interesting energy interchange. Whenever the group feels complete on this exercise, move on.

EXERCISE 2. Discussion of Family Attitudes

Purpose: To review your family dynamics and note how people used energy or tried to gain attention

Time: 15 minutes per person for each pair of partners and 15 minutes to share with the group, for a total of 45 minutes

Directions:

Step 1: Choose a partner and ask each other three or four (or more if you have time) of the following questions for 15 minutes per person:
- Who was in your family?
- Describe the general theme of your family (e.g., "everyone for himself" or "always cautious about the future" or "distrust of others," etc.).
- Who ran the family? Describe their energy.
- What did you think of your family when you were a child?
- What did you think of their values?
- How does your life reflect their values today?
- How does your life not reflect their values today?
- Did you have to fight for your individuality? How?
- What did your family like best about you? What did you tend to get into trouble for?

Step 2: After a half hour, everyone can reconvene with the big group and volunteers can share their experiences.

EXERCISE 3. Meditation to Connect to Inner Wisdom

Time: Approximately 15–20 minutes, depending on the time left in the meeting. If there is not enough time, suggest people practice this over the next week, as outlined above under Individual Study, page 95.

Directions: Have one person read aloud slowly the meditation on page 101 and have the rest of the group relax into it. People may share their experiences.

Closing

Requests for support. Sending loving energy.

For Next Session
   Read through the section on Individual Study in this chapter and select something to practice. Share your experiences and results next meeting.

STUDY GROUP FOR THE FOURTH INSIGHT

Session 8

2 hours 30 minutes

Session Purpose: To continue practicing awareness of the Fourth Insight

Introduction

Start the meeting with each person briefly saying how he or she feels at the moment and sharing any significant events from the week related to the Insights.

Review of Homework

People can talk about what they learned from using some of the new behaviors from the Individual Study. As your group sees and hears insights, coincidences, and personal stories from others, the energy will grow, and individual effects will be enhanced. If homework is given in the week previous, it's important to review how it went during the week. This helps reinforce the importance of staying aware.

EXERCISE 1. Meditation for Transforming Power Struggles

Purpose: To gain more clarity about a specific situation and begin to heal it

Time: Approximately 20–30 minutes for the meditation and 30 minutes for discussion or until the energy is complete. Note: *Take it slow and don't rush the questions.*

Directions:
   Step 1: Sit comfortably and close your eyes. Take a few deep breaths and concentrate on bringing your energy to the center of your being.
   Step 2: After a few minutes of relaxation, have a volunteer ask the following questions slowly, giving people time to answer them silently in their meditation:
   • Bring into your mind any problem you are having with someone.
   • How did you feel the last time you spoke or when you were having problems?
   • What do you feel is the main issue *for you*?
   • What do you want?
   • How would you like to feel about this issue or person?
   • How are you like this person?
   • What is the main thing that bothers you about him or her?
   • How are you like that in some way, even slightly?
   • What do you know to be true, but you have not said it?

- How have you been using a "parent" voice with this person?
- How have you felt like a child with this person?
- Imagine yourself speaking to the person from an adult perspective. What would you like to say?
- Now ask your inner wisdom what you need to know about this situation.
- Ask your inner wisdom to give you any kind of symbol to represent what this situation means to you. It can be anything, a picture, words, a color, a feeling—anything at all.
- Ask your inner wisdom what small step you need to take.
- Imagine you have taken the step. How does it make you feel?
- Now imagine a ball of light in the center of your being. Allow it to gently expand. Feel its radiance expand even more, filling all parts of your body. Imagine this radiant light even filling up the cells of your body.
- Next, send this light out to the person with whom you want to heal relations. Ask it to neutralize and heal the situation.
- Ask the light to invigorate you and bring you clarity.
- Feel yourself let go of the need to control any outcome. Remember, you are in the process of discovering a mystery.
- When you are complete, please bring your attention back to the room.
- Be sure to record any relevant information in your journals.

Step 3: Allow time for volunteers to express what came up in the meditation, particularly in response to having a symbol appear. It is useful for others to offer feedback about what the symbol seems to represent after the person has tried to do this first.

EXERCISE 2. A Profile of Your Strengths

Purpose: To practice becoming a whole person—acknowledging your strengths and unique qualities

Time: 10 minutes to write the answers, 10 minutes per person to describe to a partner, and 10 minutes to share experiences with the group, for a total of 40 minutes

Directions:
   Step 1: Write down three of your:
            best physical attributes
            best mental abilities
            best financial moves you ever made
            most unusual characteristics
            best general human attributes
            best social skills
            best business skills
            most important interests
            and your single most important value
               (e.g., health, love, freedom, creativity)
   Step 2: Choose a partner and read your lists to each other.
   Step 3: Keep your list where you can see it frequently.

Closing

Requests for support. Sending love and energy.

For Next Session
   • Continue to practice the new behaviors listed for Individual Study in this chapter.
   • Read the chapter "The Message of the Mystics" in *The Celestine Prophecy* as well as the next chapter of this study guide in preparation for discussion next time.
   • Ask someone to bring a tape recorder and meditation music to the next session.

CHAPTER 5

The Message of the Mystics

Wherein our adventurer and Marjorie face great danger as forces beyond their control threaten their lives. At the crossroads where they have coincidentally run into each other, soldiers tear through the area arresting or killing Jensen's followers. Our man watches helplessly as Marjorie is captured, and suddenly finds himself being hunted down. Splattered by the blood of another escaping man, he charges terror-stricken up the mountain. Convinced of his imminent death, he surrenders to his fate, and as his ego opens to higher-self energy, he enters a new world of expanded consciousness. Watching his pursuer inexplicably turn and walk down the mountain, he is filled with joy and wonder. On the highest peak of the mountain, he suddenly feels at one with everything—as if the world, the sun, and the sky were all part of his own body. In a vision he witnesses the entire story of evolution: matter moving into greater forms of complexity, creating the exact conditions for each of us, as individuals, to emerge. His next encounter connects him to Father Sanchez, a friendly priest who becomes an ally in his further development.

THE FIFTH INSIGHT

More People Will Experience Transcendent States. The Fifth Insight encourages us to *experience* firsthand the magnitude of the universe and our undeniable oneness with it. Doing so allows us to make a giant leap in understanding, even to glimpse the future. Within transcendent states, time, space, and natural laws are bypassed, and one experiences ineffable peace, love, and a feeling of truly being at home. The universe provides all we need—if we open to it. Until this century, the evolution of humanity—our physical size, the development of skills and technology, the structure of our societies, and our longer life span—took place unconsciously. The enormously profound shift in the twentieth century is that henceforth human evolution will occur *consciously*.

The Fifth Insight predicts that at this historical period more people will begin to attain nonordinary states of consciousness—not just a few practitioners of esoteric traditions. No longer are we satisfied to just talk about these states; we now want direct experience.

Creativity Rather Than Control. Linking with the universal source through intuition, we will be guided to live from a place of creativity rather than control. The Fifth Insight solves the dilemma of the competition for power outlined in the Fourth Insight. As growing numbers of us are connected to, and by, spiritual energy, struggles for power by individuals and societies will be outgrown. This process will happen at first by fits and starts as we learn new ways of being.

Surrender is the key that opens the door to no less than universal alignment. In the case of our adventurer, this oneness with all things is arrived at through an extreme condition of fear, panic, and certainty that he is going to die. He has surrendered control and is willing to accept whatever happens next.

Quite literally his journey up to this point culminates in

the death of his old consciousness and a rebirth into new possibilities.

The Fifth Insight encourages us to practice attaining this consciousness without waiting for divine intervention or a life crisis. Our task is to begin opening a little at a time and to begin the journey toward that ultimate state of union. To do this, we are told "to consciously fill up with energy because this energy brings on the coincidences, and the coincidences help us actualize the new level on a permanent basis."[1]

Raising the Vibration

We can increase our connection to this energy by practicing being open, using our sense of appreciation, and concentrating on the sensation of being filled up. In the words of Father Sanchez:

> Think about it: when something occurs beyond chance to lead us forward in our lives . . . we become more actualized people. We feel as though we are attaining what destiny is leading us to become. When this occurs, the level of energy that brought on the coincidences in the first place is instituted in us. We can be knocked out of it and lose energy when we are afraid, but this level serves as a new outer limit which can be regained quite easily. We have become a new person. We exist at a level of higher energy, at a level—get this—of higher vibration.[2]

As our character saw in the Third Insight, being in ancient forests and connecting with the powerful living energies of nature help us cross over into the higher vibrations. Some places increase energy more potently than others, and this depends on how our energy "shape" fits with the energy of the place.

Coming Down

The Fifth Insight shows us both the potential for the universal connection and the reasons we are unable to make or sustain that connection.

An important part of the Fifth Insight is demonstrated when our character "comes down from the mountain." Metaphorically he reenters the world of conflict—guns, soldiers on patrol, and relationships based on competition for energy (Marjorie proves to be his teacher in this as they begin to fall in love). Like a fledgling learning to fly, he has to learn to stay aloft in the new current of energy. Others might drain him and cause him to have self-doubts.

At One with the Universe

Take a look at the specific details of our character's moments on the mountaintop. What can be applied? "I felt this euphoric connection with everything, and this total kind of security and confidence. I was no longer tired. . . . I felt light and secure and connected . . . like the whole landscape was part of me."[3]

Searching for the best way to describe the overall feeling, he says, "I guess I felt a love for everything." His rapturous feeling parallels the ecstatic states of many Christian mystics and of near-death reports that describe becoming aware of the omnipresence of the divine in all living things.

> The important thing is not to think much but to love much; and so do that which best stirs you to love.
> SAINT TERESA OF AVILA, *Interior Castle*[4]

Accepting the Universal Energy of Love

As he begins to practice regaining this feeling by focusing on the beauty of a nearby tree, he becomes confused about how to do it. He protests to the priest who is helping him, "Love is something that just happens. I can't make myself love anything."[5]

The priest presses on with the lesson, clarifying the role of love. "You do not make yourself love. *You allow love to enter you.*"[6] To do this, he says, one must position the mind by remembering what love felt like in the past, and try to feel that love again.

Valiantly, our character tries again. Admiring the shape and presence of the tree, his appreciation for its beauty and uniqueness grows and grows until he can actually feel the emotion of love. Even though the tree is the focus of his attention, he has re-created a surrounding experience of love.

As our character concentrates on the beauty of the tree, the priest can see that he is accepting the energy by observing the increase in his energy field. So far our adventurer has achieved the ability to be open, to connect, to use his sense of appreciation, and to get the sensation of being filled up.

> The necessary condition for the existence of peace and joy is the awareness that peace and joy are available.
>
> THICH NHAT HANH,
> *Present Moment
> Wonderful Moment*[7]

Notice the dynamic of this event. Our character is not *forcing* the feeling of love, nor is he *creating* it artificially. The love is not going from him into the tree, the path we normally think love travels. Usually, we tend to think of love as a feeling that is generated within ourselves, going outward to the object of our love. With the Fifth Insight we learn that in order to tap into universal energy, we must *open* ourselves to it. Open, we can receive—energy, coincidences, and other gifts from universal intelligence.

Connecting to the Energy in Small Steps

As soon as our character begins to judge himself for not duplicating his experience on the mountain, his energy falls abruptly. The priest emphasizes that he must try to reconnect in small amounts.

Releasing his doubts and judgments, he once again opens himself. Appreciating the beauty of the tree, he opens a little further. The feeling of appreciation for the form of the tree grows. This time he is successful, and the priest observes the energy flowing into him, and *flowing back into the tree*. In the words of the priest, "When you appreciate the beauty and uniqueness of things, you receive energy. When you get to a level where you feel love, then you can send the energy back just by willing it so."[8]

In summary, an expanded state often begins to disintegrate when we try to interact with those in normal consciousness, or resume living in a competitive world. However, even if we fall back to what we perceive as ordinary awareness, the mystical experience has forever changed our idea of our limits. We now have an example of another way of being that will help us as we discipline ourselves to regain this consciousness.

Do you remember a time when you felt open, alive with appreciation for a scene in nature? Did you experience a sense of timelessness and connection to the earth? How long has it been since you've had an experience such as this? What has been keeping you from it? If your answer is that time and the necessities

> The closer you get to enlightenment the more often you see signs of your progress. You may spend years laying a foundation and then suddenly leap forward in many areas at once. It may take years for some people to make the decision to grow and to take their first steps, but the time between successive shifts will grow shorter and shorter.
> SANAYA ROMAN,
> *Spiritual Growth*[9]

Your accelerated growth means that you are making a new and deeper connection to your Higher Self. This can sometimes create a release of old patterns. Often when you take a leap forward the pattern that was holding you back the most may surface. Don't blame outside circumstances for the way you feel; look within and ask yourself what pattern or belief you are being shown. Ask your Higher Self for guidance about how you can release this pattern.

SANAYA ROMAN,
Spiritual Growth[11]

of life have prevented you from this important connection to nature, consider the advice of Father Sanchez: "Finding enough energy to maintain that state of love certainly helps the world, but it most directly helps us. It is the most hedonistic thing we can do."[10] Sanchez points out that we must rethink our definition of love as something we *do* to make the world a better place. The real work of evolution is done when we are in a state of connection to the universal energy *for ourselves*. In this feeling we exist at a higher vibration and, consequently, are more able to live our purpose. Together with others resonating at these levels, we automatically change the worldview.

Individually we contribute to evolution through a process of filling up with energy, moving ahead through coincidences, filling up again, and moving ahead again.

Closer Encounters with Evolution

Since the 1960s interest in the paranormal has burgeoned. As the Fifth Insight predicted, there has been a huge growth in the literature on phenomena such as extrasensory abilities, verifiable accounts of past lives, near-death and out-of-body experiences, and mystical experiences attained through spiritual practice. More people than ever before are willing to discuss their personal encounters with invisible, mysterious forces. Movies contribute to bringing these ideas into the mainstream by using such themes as reincarnation, ghosts, and the spiritual review after death.

Surprisingly, even sports offers fertile ground for the occurrence of nonordinary states. In the fascinating book *The Psychic Side of Sports*, coauthored by Esalen founder Michael Murphy and Rhea A. White, we eavesdrop on the amazing stories of some of the most accomplished athletes and adventurers in the world. The book's table of contents alone reads like a description of our character's experience: [mystical sensations of] acute well-being, peace, detachment, weightlessness, ecstasy, being in the present, instinctive action and surrender, mystery and awe, unity, altered perception of size and field and time, and exceptional energy. Since the intuitive spiritual world is all too often derailed into a marginal position in our culture, it is important to understand that changes in consciousness take place in *all* spheres of life.

In the following reports we hear athletes describe the same sensations as those reported by spiritual adepts, and by our character on his mountaintop.

Ecstasy—a Peak and a Foundation

In the Fifth Insight, our man's feeling of ecstasy on the mountain becomes a foundation for re-creating the connection. However, nonordinary states may also occur in everyday life. Peak experiences in sports, for example, can be used as starting points for building energy. When you wish to enter into a higher level of energy, remember back to when you experienced joy and ecstasy in a sport. Use this feeling to help tap into the universal energy in the incremental way suggested by the priests in the novel.

For example, Murphy and White quote such athletes as

quarterback Francis Tarkenton, who says that he played football for one reason: "I love it. Nothing in my life compares to the ecstasies I [got] from this game."[12] Skiers tell of "the magic moment when you are right on the mark, when everything falls into place and the only sensation you feel is the ecstasy of what you are doing. Skier, skiing, skied are one."[13] Mountain climbers have a natural leg up in the quest for spiritual highs: "The simplest climbs made me crazy with joy. The mountains were a sort of magic kingdom where by some spell I felt happiest."[14]

An account of a successful ascent of Annapurna by Maurice Herzog (with Pierre Lachenal) closely parallels our character's experience: "I felt as though I were plunging into something new and quite abnormal. I had the strangest and most vivid impressions, such as I had never before known in the mountains. There was something unnatural in the way I saw Lachenal and everything around us . . . all sense of exertion was gone, as though there were no longer any gravity. This diaphanous landscape, this quintessence of purity—these were not the mountains I knew: they were the mountains of my dreams."[15]

Swift and rhythmic movement, two key triggers for producing ecstatic states, are found in other activities such as jogging, flying, riding, and surfing. The ecstatic state is also attained in trance dancing, chanting, and drumming in shamanic practices and Eastern religions such as the Sufi tradition.

Weightlessness

The feeling of floating and being outside oneself is a common feature of a mystical experience and of an athletic peak experience. Many runners report that they often reach a point, after prolonged exertion, of wanting to float and fly. One long-distance runner, after six hundred miles of running, suddenly "had this *light* feeling, I felt as though I was going through space, treading on clouds."[16]

Long before Westerners were donning Nikes and sweat-bands and practicing for marathons, Tibetan monks were undergoing a special meditation training called *lung-gom-pa* that resulted in incredible feats of endurance and speed. After years of practice in the secret lore, these monks obtained an altered state of consciousness in which they could run for several consecutive days and nights over treacherous mountain terrain.

Unlike marathoners, who train physically, *lung-gom-pa* monks "train" for this type of trance running by entering meditation cubicles which are then sealed up. For periods of months or years, they live in silence, *with no physical training*, receiving only gifts of food through an opening about nine by ten inches. It is said that a monk's body after several years becomes so light and subtle that *he can exit through this opening*.

Surrendering

The mystical experience takes us out of the *need* for control. The oneness of mind, body, and spirit lies in surrender. In *The Joy of Sports* Michael Novak writes:

> This is one of the great inner secrets of sports. There is a certain point of unity within the self, and between the self and its world, a certain complicity and magnetic mating, a certain harmony, that conscious mind and will cannot direct. . . . Command by instinct is swifter, subtler, deeper, more accurate, more in touch with reality than command by conscious mind. The discovery takes one's breath away.[17]

As athletes share their experiences, our collective evolution is quickened and expanded. Basketball player Patsy Neal captures the spirit of the Fifth Insight in her book *Sport and Identity*, when she wrote (in 1972):

There are moments of glory that go beyond the human expectation, beyond the physical and emotional ability of the individual. Something unexplainable takes over and breathes life into the known life. One stands on the threshold of miracles that one cannot create voluntarily. . . . Call it a state of grace, or an act of faith . . . or an act of God. It is there, and the impossible becomes possible. . . . The athlete goes beyond herself; she transcends the natural. She touches a piece of heaven and becomes the recipient of power from an unknown source . . . the performance almost becomes a holy place— where a spiritual awakening seems to take place. The individual becomes swept up in the action around her—she almost floats through the performance, drawing on forces she has never previously been aware of.[18]

The Eastern Connection

A major contribution to spiritual awakening in the West has been made by those who began to study and practice Eastern philosophy via Zen meditation, hatha yoga, the martial arts, acupuncture, and other healing disciplines. As the Fifth Insight predicts, this influx of information about the mind/body connection has contributed significantly to expanding our perception of the world. Even splashy karate and kung fu movies serve to break down the barrier of the mind/body separation so ingrained in the West.

With the Eastern perspective of mind/body unity we gain a tremendous tool for accessing the unlimited range of universal energy (variously called *chi, ki,* or *prana*). Discipline and intention make this path available to all who wish to apply themselves.

Evolutionary Power Surges

In his spiritual awakening on the mountaintop, our character also experienced a rush of energy up his spine. This inherent energy, available to all of us, is called *Kundalini* in the Indian spiritual tradition. Represented by the image of a coiled snake lying dormant at the base of the spine, it is pure creative energy and is seen as *no less than the moving force of evolution*. When awakened, the energy rushes up the spinal cord, activating the energy centers of the body and releasing various emotional and physical sensations.

Carl Jung, who studied many forms of mysticism, believed it would take thousands of years before it would be commonplace in the West. According to psychiatrist Stanislav Grof, however, "Future development showed this estimate to be wrong. Whether this can be attributed to accelerated evolution, popularity and rapid spread of various forms of spiritual practice, pressure of the dangerous environmental crisis, or the facilitating effect of psychedelic drugs, it is quite clear that unmistakable signs of Kundalini awakening can be observed these days in thousands of Westerners."[19]

The marriage of the Eastern attunement with universal flow (being) and the Western ability to act on new information (doing) is a major aspect of the trend toward wholeness that is so central to an emerging spirituality. Together, harmony of thought and action takes us to new levels of evolution.

Dimensions of Consciousness

Our adventurer's experience on the mountain is part of the family of transcendent events ranging from merging spatial boundaries with other people, plants, and inorganic matter to transcending boundaries of linear time and space.

As we know, the pace of the evolution of consciousness

> [The new shamans] are not lonely, even if alone, for they have come to understand that we are never really isolated. Like Siberian shamans, they realize, "Everything that is, is alive!" Everywhere they are surrounded by life, by family.
>
> MICHAEL HARNER,
> *The Way of the Shaman*[20]

was facilitated by broad social unrest in the 1960s. Because we were so detached from the sacred view of life, interest in alternative perspectives and freedoms created a climate of revelation, renunciation of tradition, and a certain amount of social havoc. Travels into other dimensions of consciousness via drugs, for example, had no stabilizing context, unlike the indigenous cultures whose use of such substances was ritualized and spiritualized.

The search for the transcendent experience is one of the most powerful instincts in the human psyche. As the Fifth Insight reveals, the conscious desire for direct experience continues to grow in the last half of the century. Researchers have since developed alternative nondrug techniques using the breath, music, and body work to evoke transpersonal healing experiences. Sounding much like our character in the novel, one of Grof's students using breath work reported:

> . . . There was no question that I—the Earth—was a living organism, an intelligent being trying to understand myself, struggling to evolve to a higher level of awareness, and attempting to communicate with other cosmic beings. . . . I felt in my body the injury of the industrial insults of strip mining, urbanization, toxic and radioactive waste, and pollution of air and water. The strangest part of the session was that I was aware of rituals among various aboriginal peoples and experienced them as very healing and absolutely vital for myself. . . .

during my experience it was extremely convincing that doing rituals is important for the Earth.[21]

Transpersonal states such as these add to the growing awareness of our evolutionary crossroads. As these nonordinary states of awareness find wider acceptance and change our collective belief systems, they help transform human culture.

Tools for Transformation

Self-exploration through meditation and regression therapy, as well as research in parapsychology and out-of-body and near-death experiences, clarifies the nature of mystical experience. In addition, we are now seeing a dramatic increase of interest in shamanic practices. Indigenous peoples have always viewed nonordinary states of consciousness as an experiential connection to the cosmos during which guidance is received. Westerners who study this lore and work with native people are helping to keep these traditions alive. Researchers in the psychospiritual domain believe that we are poised for yet another explosion in understanding.

Evolving Consciously

The availability now of ancient techniques as well as other psychotherapeutic methods gives us the tools to work individually on our *personal* evolution.

We must cross, one by one, the barrier of our Western intellectual framework that labels nonordinary states as bizarre or even pathological. As more of us avail ourselves of these paths and share our experiences, we make it easier for others to go forward as well. Grof writes:

There are important realms of reality that are transcendental and transphenomenal. The impulse in human beings to connect with the spiritual domain is an extremely powerful and important force. It resembles, in its nature, sexuality, but is much more fundamental and compelling. Denial and repression of this transcendental impulse introduces a serious distortion into human life on both an individual and collective scale. Experiential self-exploration is an important tool for a spiritual and philosophical quest. It can mediate the connection with the transpersonal domain of one's own being and of existence.[22]

Spontaneous Illumination

While years may be spent in the pursuit of higher consciousness through a variety of spiritual practices, many people also have a completely spontaneous connection with the divine. For example, psychotherapist Donna Hale tells this story: "About eighteen years ago I was studying for a college exam, and after several hours I felt absolutely drained. I went outside in the garden to 'meditate.' As I sat down I was aware of the beauty of the flowers around me. Their simplicity and color really stood out I guess in contrast to all the words I had been reading. At that time, I didn't really know how to meditate, so I just closed my eyes with the intention of being still. Immediately I felt the sensa-

> Soul and mind instantly lost their physical bondage and streamed out. . . . My sense of identity was no longer narrowly confined to a body but embraced the circumambient atoms . . . a swelling glory within me began to envelop towns, continents, the earth, solar and stellar systems. . . .
> PARAMAHANSA YOGANANDA, *Autobiography of a Yogi*[23]

tion of something pouring over me, a clarity and peacefulness. I felt this tremendous buoyancy that seemed to elevate me to a state of ecstasy. When I opened my eyes after a few minutes, I felt as if there was no separation between me and all the things in my life. I felt that everything was working just as it was meant to be, and that I was connected to it. I felt like I knew everything. This feeling lasted about thirty minutes, and dissolved when I had to go back to studying." Hale remembers that it felt as if a door had somehow opened up, allowing her to touch the fabric of consciousness. "It's always kept me looking for it again."

Opening the Door

Many of us are asking the question. "How can I find my life's work? In what meaningful way can I contribute to the world?" Often, people see these questions in terms of career choices. While many will choose careers as practitioners and teachers in alternative fields, it is important to realize that our desire to "serve the planet" might best be approached by working on our own spiritual development and consciousness. Whether we change jobs might be less important than bringing a new spiritual awareness to the jobs we have. Our present situation might be the perfect place to practice our commitment to connect with our inner source. Without specifically setting about to change things, we can ready ourselves by devoting time to practices that assist our opening up to energy, such as meditation, the martial arts, yoga, therapeutic dance and movement, breathing exercises, and body work. Spending time in sacred sites and surrounding oneself with beauty and energy could be most important in clarifying a sense of personal mission.

Seed Experiences

In his second book, *Heading toward Omega: In Search of the Meaning of the Near-Death Experience*, Kenneth Ring develops a hypothesis consistent with the Fifth Insight. Studying the long-term effects of near-death experiences, he concludes that these experiences might assist the overall transformation of consciousness on the planet.

He believes that near-death experiences (NDE) are equivalent to seeds in the lives of those who have them, gradually flowering into deeper spiritual growth.

Striking in their similarities, these experiences are remarkable for the understanding of life and death that they reveal to the person. In crisis, the person typically becomes aware of the death of his body and subsequent entry into the indescribable light of joy and love. The significance of the NDE phenomenon is multidimensional. At one level, the NDE is the personal experience of death as an ecstatic encounter with loving beings of light, and possibly a reunion with departed loved ones. This rapturous aspect of the NDE is a reassuring and liberating phenomenon, and is well documented.

> Always know and remember that you are "more than your physical body.". . . This will provide instant perspective on any Earth . . . activity. The agony becomes tolerable, the ecstasy more profound. Locally induced fears evaporate. . . . Accidents may happen, but you cannot lose; you have had the experience of being human.
>
> ROBERT A. MONROE,
> *Ultimate Journey*[24]

At another level, however, the NDE serves as an important contribution in the advance of evolution. Ring's hypothesis is that near-death experiences not only change the lives of the survivors, but that their transformed consciousness may help to catalyze an acceleration of human spiritual evolution.

Perhaps the most significant change in consciousness is the awareness of survival of consciousness following physical death. A woman who almost died during the birth of her second child reported: ". . . the next thing I knew, I was in—I was standing in a mist and I knew *immediately* that I had died and I was so happy that I had died but I was still alive. And I cannot tell you how I *felt*. It was, 'Oh, God, I'm dead, but I'm here! I'm me!' . . . [I was] filled with nothing but these feelings of gratitude because I still existed and yet I knew perfectly well that I had died. . . . I remember I knew that everything, everywhere in the universe was OK, that the plan was perfect. That whatever was happening—the wars, famine, whatever—was OK."[25]

Later in the experience she described meeting a being whom she did not know. She was told, "There are no sins. Not in the way you think about them on earth. The only thing that matters here is how you think."[26]

A recurring theme in the NDE is the "life review," which makes an important imprint upon the survivor, contributing to a changed consciousness in the subsequent life. This detailed life review, while always given without judgment, drives home such points as the importance of being loving toward others—the importance of human relationships and love over material things. People are often shocked by seeing forgotten little episodes from their lives that reveal a thoughtless or hurtful action that did not seem important at the time. These reviews demonstrate how each person is sent to earth to learn certain lessons or to attempt to fulfil a particular purpose.

One man in Ring's book saw not detailed events, but every emotion he had ever felt, "and my eyes were showing me the basis of how that emotion affected my life. What my life had done so far to affect other people's lives using the feeling of pure love that was surrounding me as the point of comparison. . . . You know, I'd done a horrible job, using love as the point of comparison. . . . Lookin' at yourself from the point of how much love you have spread to other people is devastatin'. You will never get over it. I am six years away from that day [of his NDE] and I am not over it yet."[27]

These reports reveal how the beginnings of new spiritual awareness, carried by these survivors, will inevitably begin to permeate beyond their individual lives. In terms of the evolution of consciousness, these people are in the forefront.

Continued Flowering

Ring interviewed over 150 near-death survivors and concluded that among the primary characteristics they showed was an attitude of increased spirituality—not necessarily religious in nature. They were convinced that life continues after the material transition through death, and felt an inward closeness to God.

The importance of a spiritual awakening is not just the specific event of the blissful state. Its real significance is that it continues to function as the active organizing principle in one's evolution. Perhaps we might imagine these states as analogous to the birth of an interior faculty that helps one to send and receive energy, tuning into intuitive guidance. The long-term effects of NDEs and other mystical experiences tend to be an increase in psychic sensitivity and frequencies of synchronicities.

Gateways to Higher Consciousness

Higher consciousness is what distinguishes the mystical journey and is not always the result of spiritual discipline or meditative practice. As we have seen, it can be triggered by being close to death, experiencing a personal trauma, or even just by closing one's eyes for a moment of introspection. Characteristics common to these states are:

- seeing a dazzling light accompanied by a feeling of joy
- feeling absolutely secure and loved
- feeling ecstatic

- a feeling of lightness, buoyancy
- understanding intuitively how the universe works
- releasing all fear of death, seeing the continuum of life

As you practice direct connection to universal energy, the most important measures are a background feeling of love (not connected to any one object) and contact with your interior knowing or hunches. If you are truly connected, you will feel love. Otherwise you are not in contact with your source.

> "That which you drank," [Saint Germain] explained, "comes directly from the Universal Supply, pure and vivifying as Life Itself, in fact it is Life—Omnipresent Life—for it exists everywhere about us. It is subject to our conscious control and direction, willingly obedient, when we Love enough, because all the Universe obeys the behest of Love. Whatsoever I desire manifests itself, when I command in Love."
>
> GODFRE RAY KING,
> *Unveiled Mysteries*[28]

Our Changing Consciousness

The common changes that occur in the lives of those who have had mystical experiences may be summarized as:

- feeling connected to a higher source
- shifting interest from material accumulation
- enhanced appreciation of beauty and other people
- enhanced abilities, desire to learn
- enhanced extrasensory abilities
- sense of mission
- lack of self-consciousness
- ability to inspire others

SUMMARY OF THE FIFTH INSIGHT

The Fifth Insight is the experience of inner connection with divine energy. By exploring and pursuing our divinity within, we can personally make contact with a type of experience called *mystical*. In our search for this altered state, we distinguish between intellectual description of this awareness and the awareness itself. In this regard, we apply certain experiential measures which indicate we are in connection with universal energy. For instance, do we experience a lightness of body? Do we feel light on our feet, buoyant? Do we experience a vividness of perception such as enhanced colors, smells, tastes, sounds, a sense of beauty? Do we experience a sense of oneness, total security? And above all, do we experience the state of awareness called love? Not toward someone or something, but as a constant background sensation in our lives. No longer do we want to just talk about mystical awareness. We have the courage to apply these measures to really seek this connection with the divine. It is this connection with total energy that resolves all conflict. We no longer need energy from others.

Further Reading

In addition to the excellent books listed in the notes for this chapter we suggest:

The Aquarian Conspiracy: Personal and Social Transformation in the 1980's. Marilyn Ferguson. J. P. Tarcher, 1980.

Foundations of Tibetan Mysticism. Lama Anagarika Govinda. Chronica Botanica, IA., 1987.

Life after Life. Raymond Moody, Jr. Mockingbird Books, 1975.

Person/Planet. Theodore Roszak. Anchor Press/Doubleday, 1978.

History of Mysticism. S. Abhayananda. Atma Books, 1987.

The Book of the Vision Quest: Personal Transformation in the Wilderness. Steven Foster with Meredith Little. Prentice Hall Press, 1988.

Cultivating the Ch'i: The Secrets of Energy and Vitality. Stuart A. Olson. Dragon Door, 1993.

The Universe Story: A Celebration of the Unfolding of the Cosmos. Brian Swimme and Thomas Berry. HarperCollins, 1992.

Cosmic Consciousness. Richard M. Bucke. Viking Penguin, 1991.

The Way of Zen. Alan Watts. Random House, 1965.

Mysticism: Christian and Buddhist. D. T. Suzuki. Routledge Chapman & Hall, 1982.

INDIVIDUAL STUDY OF THE FIFTH INSIGHT

Morning Intention

A few minutes before you get out of bed, allow yourself to find the center within your body. Silently or aloud, state your intention for the day. For example, "Today I intend to have a good time at work and learn something new." Or "Today I intend to stay in the moment and be open to what the universe has to say."

With eyes closed, imagine a ball of light in the middle of your forehead. Allow it to expand throughout your whole body and into your world. As you send this light out into all areas of your life, feel the serenity of knowing that you are alive and on purpose.

Morning Sounds

If you live alone, this is easy to do when you arise. If you live with others, you might want to do this in the shower.

Upon waking, begin making any kind of sound that wants to come out of you. Don't worry if the first few sounds are rather "ugly" or guttural. Keep expressing sound and begin to follow it with your attention as it goes up and down. Gradually the sound will start to change, rising and clearing. Continue the clear sound for a few minutes. Notice how your day goes.

Breathing Practice

Remember that you exist in a universe of pure energy. At any time during the day, even in an important meeting, you have this energy completely available to you if you remain open.

Pay attention to your body frequently during the day and take opportunities to breathe consciously. In these moments draw in fresh air deeply into your whole body. Imagine the healing and energizing exchange of air taking place in your lungs and bloodstream. Imagine that you are inflating your body with the energy of the universe. Feel yourself open up and expand. Conscious breathing will center you no matter what is happening.

Evening Practice

After arriving home in the evening, take five minutes or more to listen to some rhythmic sounds such as drumming, chanting, or other nonvocal music that is stimulating but relaxing. Begin to move your body to the rhythm for a few minutes, letting all tension and daily concerns flow out of your body. If you have time, any kind of stretching exercise is an invaluable tension releaser to energize you for the rest of your evening. Start by doing this practice one day a week, adding days as you wish.

Bedtime Practice

Before going to sleep bring your attention to the center within your body. Acknowledge yourself for whatever small steps or things that you did today, and express gratitude for all that you received. If you need clarification on something, ask that clear information come through your dreams. This practice is best done on a daily basis.

Further Study

For those who wish to learn specific techniques for using breath to strengthen, heal, cleanse, and deter aging there are many good teachers and books on methods such as chi kung and pranayama. Explore which local classes in meditation or yoga are appropriate for you. Go to a good bookstore and browse in the sections on metaphysical and Eastern literature.

STUDY GROUP FOR THE FIFTH INSIGHT

Session 9

2 hours 30 minutes

Session Purpose: To exchange ideas about the Fifth Insight, and to discuss different ways to build energy

Preparation: Have someone bring a tape recorder and a variety of sound such as chanting, drumming, ethnic, environmental, or meditation music. Several members might want to contribute their favorite pieces.

Introduction

Ask a volunteer to read aloud the synopsis of the Fifth Insight in this book on pages 109–110 (up to the section "Raising the Vibration"). How do members of your group understand this information? Share your experiences.

EXERCISE 1. Meditation on the Mountaintop

Purpose: To experience going to a higher vibration as described in the Fifth Insight

Time: About 15 or 20 minutes for the meditation and 20 or 30 minutes for the discussion or until the group is ready to move on

Directions:
   Step 1: Ask everyone to get comfortable, and adjust the lighting to a fairly low level, but not completely dark. Start one of your tapes, preferably meditation or environmental, with a slow rhythm conducive to relaxation. A volunteer can proceed with Steps 2 to 4.
   Step 2: Tell everyone to close their eyes and become aware of their body.
   Step 3: Read the relaxation meditation on page 53.
   Step 4: Lead the meditation by saying: Now imagine yourself sitting on a mountaintop and look around at what you see. [Give people 2 or 3 minutes to do this.] What do you feel on this mountaintop? . . . What temperature is it? . . . What do you smell on this

mountaintop? . . . Now look out at the farthest horizon and feel how close it is to you . . . extend your consciousness out to the horizon . . . feel the roundness of the earth upon which you sit . . . feel the space around the earth . . . imagine the earth as a living, breathing organism, just like you . . . immerse yourself in the feeling of being suspended, floating, amid space that exists in all directions . . . feel yourself being held up by an inner buoyancy . . . imagine you are filled with helium which allows you to hover just above the ground . . . notice that you are in perfect athletic condition . . . feel your coordination and lightness . . . perceive that everything you see on the mountaintop is a part of you . . . now let your mind go back to your childhood . . . go back further to when you were in the womb . . . see yourself as part of the chain of being that has existed since the human race began . . . imagine this chain of being as a vibrating strand of energy . . . you are one piece of this vibrating strand of energy . . . imagine how this vibrating strand of energy is connected to all the energy in the universe . . . feel in your body how the energy moves and shifts in unexpected, coincidental events . . . now begin to bring your awareness back to the mountaintop . . . slowly bring your awareness back into the center of your physical body . . . prepare to bring your awareness back into normal reality . . . take a few deep breaths . . . and when you are ready, bring your awareness back to the room and open your eyes.

Step 5: Give people a minute to adjust and stretch and then ask for volunteers to share feelings, images, or information received from the meditation.

EXERCISE 2. Raising Energy

Purpose: To experience how different sounds affect the body

Time: Play each type of music for 2 or 3 minutes so that you can cover three to five types, but be flexible and tune into the energy of how people respond.

Preparation: Have several different types of music available to play for 2 or 3 minutes at a time. Choose fast and slow rhythms without lyrics (other than chanting). You might wish to play chanting, drumming, organ music, classical guitar, ethnic music, or New Age music. Continue to keep the light level low, but not dark.

Directions:
Step 1: Stand up and close your eyes.
Step 2: As each piece is played, move your body in place. Notice the different effects of each type of music.
Step 3: When you finish playing the music, share your impressions of the music. Energy should be high.

Further Study
You might wish to schedule another session using music, and include a discussion of any additional reading done on mystical states.
Another idea is to invite someone to your meeting who teaches a spiritual practice that members might like to explore for themselves such as yoga, meditation, aikido, tai chi, or chi kung.

Closing

Requests for support. Sending love and energy.

For Next Session
Read Chapter 6 before the next meeting and do the Parental Review exercise in the Individual Study section (pages 164–173).

CHAPTER 6

Clearing the Past:
Our Parental Lineage
and Control Dramas

As our character travels onward over narrowing, twisting mountain roads with Father Sanchez, he has time to ponder how he might control energy by being aloof. Speaking directly to this question, an incident with two people on the road clearly demonstrates a missed opportunity to advance on his path because of his unwillingness to reveal himself. Crestfallen, he asks his mentor what is the next step. He is told that he can discover and accelerate his life purpose by reflecting on the achievements, failures, and philosophy of his parents—but only if he stops indulging in his control drama. Appropriately, he meets Father Carl amid the ancient ruins of Machu Picchu. This priest guides our character through the process of clearing his own past. He begins to see that he has always been working on a life question that was formed in early childhood.

THE SIXTH INSIGHT

The Sixth Insight teaches that each of us is the next step in evolution along the lineage created by our two parents. Our higher purpose on earth can be found by recognizing what our parents accomplished and where they left off. By reconciling what they gave us with what they left for us to resolve, we can get a clear picture of who we are and what we are meant to do.

Why, then, are we not feeling fulfilled and fully actualized? The Sixth Insight tells us that we interfere with our evolution by getting stuck in trying to control energy by a process called a *control drama*. We literally stop the advancement of our destiny by using a repetitive childhood pattern of control, rather than allowing synchronicity to move us forward.

In general, there are two aggressive and two passive ways of controlling energy, which we learned in childhood. By identifying our specific control drama, we begin to free ourselves from this limiting behavior. Once we are aware of how we stop the flow of energy that naturally takes us to our higher purpose, we will begin to know our true selves.

Back to the Past

Until now our main character has been traveling on his path metaphorically blindfolded. He is seeking answers but doesn't really know what his questions are. He feels by turns restless, excited, confused, defensive, depleted, euphoric, and intrigued. He doesn't know where he's going, and he doesn't understand why he hasn't gotten there. Sound familiar?

So far he has learned from the First Insight that he keeps having coincidences that are meaningful, showing him that something mysterious is happening. From the Second, he realizes that his awareness is historically significant, and he wants to be part of the spiritual awakening. With the Third Insight, he becomes aware of the existence of the invisible energy of the universe that responds to how he thinks. From the Fourth Insight, he sees clearly that he and others get caught up in trying to get energy from each other, and wind up feeling depleted and dissatisfied. The Fifth Insight emerges when he spontaneously connects to universal energy on the mountaintop. From that peak, he reenters the mundane world and is ready to become a more active participant in the synchronistic unfolding of his destiny.

At this stage of the journey, he knows that he can consciously connect to universal energy and begin instituting his new level of awareness. He is ready to define his life question so that the mysterious action of the universe can accelerate. He is ready to release his need to control.

The Parental Review

Our character is now at the point of seeing what lineage he inherited from the lives of his two parents. He is told that his true spiritual identity will be seen if he looks at his entire life as one long story. He must look at the events of his life, from birth until the present, for the higher meaning of their purpose, and ask, "Why was I born to my particular family? What was the purpose of what happened?" Father Carl expresses it this way: "Each of us has to go back to our family experience . . . to review what happened. . . . Once we find this truth, it can energize our lives, for this truth tells us who we are, the path we are on, what we are doing."[1]

Setting the Stage in Early Childhood

An example of how specific family influences give birth to evolutionary movement can be seen in the life of Nobel Prize–winning author Albert Camus. At the time of his death in an automobile accident in 1960 he was working on a novel that was largely autobiographical. Recently published, this incomplete manuscript describes Camus's early childhood as dominated by the loss of his father, who was killed in World War I.

Camus grew up in an uncommunicative household with his mother and an uncle, who were both illiterate and nearly deaf. Out of this silent upbringing, he gave birth to books whose themes were alienation and whose style was starkly spare. Even the titles of his books, *L'Étranger* ("The Stranger"), *La Peste* ("The Plague"), and *La Chute* ("The Fall"), suggest the perspective of the outsider. Hating any form of ideology that oppressed people, he also did not support the leftist philosophies popular with the intellectuals of his time. In his Nobel acceptance speech, he spoke of his raging, rebellious urge "to speak out for the speechless." Camus, then, was able to transform his early difficult experiences into an artistic reflection of alienation for a whole society.

Case History. Another example of how parental influences create fertile conditions to advance their child's destiny comes from an intuitive trainer and counselor, Penney Peirce, who shared her parental review with us. Peirce, who believes she already had a purpose when she was born, feels that she chose her particular parents because they would create the right conditions to prepare her to manifest her purpose. "Both my parents left small towns and traveled all over the country. My grandfather was a minister, but my father never got into the spiritual side of life. He was brilliant and became an engineer, then a management consultant, but never got a higher degree, which he could easily have done. He was an organizer, interested in stability and structure, and a frustrated philosopher. My mother was also highly intelligent and became an architect and sculptor. She stood for the artistic life, but was a frustrated writer. Both of them had ambition, and wanted to build something lasting. All the traveling I did when I was young introduced me to every kind of situation—city life, farm life, different ethnicities—and today I have become a synthesizer of cross-cultural and multidimensional worldviews. I picked up the spiritual piece that my father rejected, and now consult with people about spirituality in business. My sister went for the academic piece that neither of my parents finished, and she has a Ph.D. My next step is to finish writing my book on the intuitive process."

Case History. One person studying the Sixth Insight described how he saw his two parental influences: "I've done a lot of therapy around my early childhood, but this was the first time I really had compassion for my parents as people. I had never looked at their lives before as a lesson that I could learn from, but what I saw astounded me. I can see how much I am like them, particularly my father, whom I have always judged so harshly. I'm an accountant, and I also lead programs at night on alcoholism education. My dream is to make an educational video about drug and alcohol recovery, but I keep getting cold feet and not doing anything about it. When I looked at my dad's life I saw that he was born with a silver spoon, and had every opportunity to accomplish anything he wanted to. But he came out [of the service] a major and died a janitor. When I was young I remember my mom standing at the ironing board and crying. She was bright and capable, but entirely frustrated and filled with fear.

"I'm really clear that I cannot afford *not* to move ahead with my project. Seeing the frustration they had is literally too high a price to pay, and if I don't try, I am guaranteed to fail. What I'm learning is that I can maintain my freedom and still be responsible, because being responsible feels good to me, not because I'm doing it to please someone else. Doing this exercise really changed my judgments on my parents. Even more importantly, I'm much more excited about taking some new risks than I am fearful."

Case History. Larry L. is a California businessman who started his own beverage company. Born and raised in Texas, Larry struggled with the idea of coincidence and surrendering control: "I did the parental review exercise with some reluctance because, to be frank, I've had a lot of therapy and thought I had understood my childhood influences pretty well. But in doing this exercise I saw something that

> *Breathing in, I calm my body.*
> *Breathing out, I smile.*
> *Dwelling in the present*
> *moment,*
> *I know this is a wonderful*
> *moment!*
>   THICH NHAT HANH,
>   *Present Moment*
>   *Wonderful Moment*[2]

is really a big shift for me. I went into it with the idea of looking for the good intention behind my parents' influences. I felt my parents were the spirits closest to me and that they somehow had to have prepared me for what I needed to do in my life. They are loving, successful people, but absolutely determined to control everything in their lives. My whole lesson from them was summed up by the statement 'You've got to get control of yourself.' Naturally, I spent my whole life trying to be out of control. I think I somehow needed their extreme example of fear in order to get me to learn to trust the universe more. I even grew up feeling that nature was something scary. I'm much more at home in a subway than in the woods. I can see now that my so-called choices in life were really reactions to that upbringing.

"I have always prided myself on a sort of skeptical, pessimistic point of view, so for me to see the silver lining in my early scenario is quite a shift. I have so much more compassion for them, I feel like something has really been healed in me that I didn't even know was there.

"I had already done some work about my core question and concluded that I'm here to do what has not been done before. I guess this new information about practicing trust is the next piece I needed to know."

Internal Shifts

Each of the people in our examples underwent a shift in perspective. They were able to see their history in a different way, which allowed them to bring themselves into alignment. Their stories demonstrate that internal paradigm shifts are possible. Through such individual shifts in outlook, our cultural worldview changes accordingly.

Life Question

Our character is told in the novel, "You are here because this is where you need to be to continue the evolution. Your whole life has been a long road leading directly to this moment."[4] Like our character in the book, you have come to the point where you are ready to evolve consciously. Stop reading for a few moments and think about this statement in terms of yourself.

> . . . [Buddha] taught that social institutions co-arise with us. They are not independent structures separate from our inner lives, like some backdrop to our personal dramas, against which we can display our virtues of courage and compassion. . . . As institutionalized forms of our ignorance, fears, and greed, they acquire their own dynamics. Self and society are both real, and mutually causative.
>
> JOANNA MACY,
> *World as Lover,*
> *World as Self*[3]

Think back to how you came to read *The Celestine Prophecy* and other similar books on spirituality and self-development. Can you see that your whole life has led you to this moment of reading this page? How is your study of the Insights helping you to continue your life evolution? All your achievements, interests, frustrations, and stages of growth were preparing you to be here, now, exploring the Insights.

> My mother played the piano almost continuously when she was pregnant with me. . . . I can't imagine what my life would have been like if my parents had not encouraged me to study music.
>
> GLENN GOULD, pianist[5]

In the Individual Study

section below, you will have a chance to examine in detail your own parental influences. After you have integrated your view of their lives and how they affected you, continue the analysis of your own life that you started in Chapter 2 with your personal time line. Studying both your parental influences and your own history should help reveal the life question that you have been working on.

What Are Control Dramas?

Remember that the Fourth Insight tells us that human beings compete for energy. We do so in order to feel a psychological lift. We believe that we must get attention, love, recognition, support, approval—all forms of energy—from others. We adopt a way to pull the energy in our direction by the kind of interactions we had as children with our parents.

One of the first steps we must take to evolve consciously is to clear away our past attitudes, fears, misinformation, and behavior for controlling the flow of energy. Early in life we unconsciously adapted ourselves to our environment. How our parents treated us, and how we felt around them, was our training ground for learning to control the energy flowing to us. In *The Celestine Prophecy* we are told:

> Each of us must go back into our past, back into our early family life, and see how this habit was formed. Seeing its inception keeps our way of controlling in consciousness. Remember, most of our family members were operating in a drama themselves, trying to pull energy out of us as children. This is why we had to form a control drama in the first place. We had to have a strategy to win energy back. It is always in relation to our family members that we develop our particular drama. However, once we recognize the energy dynamics in our families, we can go past these control strategies and see what was really happening.[6]

There are four main classifications of energy manipulations spoken of in the Manuscript, and they operate on a continuum. Some people use more than one in different circumstances, but most of us have one dominant control drama that we tend to repeat, depending on which one worked well on the members of our early family.

Control Drama Classifications

Intimidator

Intimidators get everyone to pay attention to them by force of loudness, physical strength, threats, unexpected outbursts. They keep everyone on edge for fear of triggering off embarrassing comments, anger, and, in extreme cases, rage. Energy comes toward them because of the fear and suspicion of the "next event." Intimidators always have the stage. They make you feel afraid or anxious.

Basically egocentric, their behavior may range from ordering others around, talking continuously, being authoritarian, being inflexible and sarcastic, to being violent. Intimidators are probably the most cut off from universal energy. They initially engage others by creating an aura of power.

Each of the four control dramas creates a specific energy dynamic called a *matching drama*. For example, the matching drama that is created by an Intimidator is primarily the Poor Me—an extremely *passive* energy dynamic. The Poor Me, feeling that the Intimidator is robbing him or her of energy on a frightening scale, tries to stop the threatening interchange by assuming a cringing, helpless attitude: "Look what you're doing to me. Don't hurt me, I'm too weak." The Poor Me is attempting to make the Intimidator feel guilty in order to stop the attack and regain a flow of energy. The other possibility for a matching drama is the Counter-Intimidator. This drama will occur if the Poor Me attitude does not work, or, more likely, if the personality of the other person is also aggressive. Then this person will fight back with the original Intimidator. If one of your parents was an Intimidator, chances are one of his or her parents was an Intimidator or a passive Poor Me.

Interrogator

Interrogators are less physically threatening, but break down spirit and will by mentally questioning all activities and motivations. Hostile critics, they look for ways to make others wrong. The more they dwell on your faults and mistakes, the more you will watch them and react to their every move. As you strive to prove yourself or answer to them, the more energy you send their way. Everything you say will probably be used against you at some time. You feel as if you are being constantly monitored.

Hypervigilant, their behavior may range from being cynical, skeptical, sarcastic, needling, perfectionistic, self-righteous, to viciously manipulative. They initially engage others with their wit, infallible logic, facts, and intellect.

As parents, Interrogators create Aloof children and sometimes Poor Me's. Both types want to escape the probing of the Interrogator. Aloofs want to escape having to answer (and be drained of their energy) to the constant scrutiny and needling of the Interrogator.

Aloof

Aloof people are caught up in their own internal world of unresolved struggles, fears, and self-doubt. They believe unconsciously that if they appear mysterious or detached, others will come to draw them out. Often lonely, they keep their distance for fear of others imposing their will or questioning their decisions (as their Interrogator parents did).

Thinking they have to do everything on their own, they don't ask for help. They need a "lot of space" and often avoid being pinned down by commitments. As children they were not often allowed to satisfy their need for independence or acknowledged for their own identity.

Prone to move toward the Poor Me side of the continuum, they don't realize that their own aloofness might be the cause of their not having what they want (e.g., money, love, self-esteem), or for their feelings of stagnation or confusion. They often see their main problem as a lack of something (money, friends, social contacts, education).

Their behavior ranges from disinterested, unavailable, uncooperative, to condescending, rejecting, contrary, and sneaky.

Skilled at detachment as a defense, they tend to cut off their own energy with such phrases as "I'm different from others," "No one really understands what I'm trying to do," "I'm confused," "I don't want to play their game," "If only I had . . ." Opportunities slip away while they overanalyze everything. With any hint of conflict or confrontation, the Aloof becomes vague and can literally disappear (screening telephone calls or not keeping appointments). They initially engage through their mysterious, hard-to-get persona.

Aloofs usually create Interrogators, but can also get into dramas with Intimidators or Poor Me's because they are in the center of the continuum.

Poor Me or Victim

Poor Me's don't ever feel they have enough power to confront the world in an active way, so they elicit sympathy, pulling energy toward them. When using the silent treatment, they may slide toward the Aloof mode, but as a Poor Me, they make sure that the silence does not go unnoticed.

Always pessimistic, Poor Me's pull attention to themselves by worried facial expressions, sighing, trembling, crying, staring into the distance, answering questions slowly, and retelling poignant dramas and crises. They like to go last in line and defer to others. Their favorite two words are "Yes, but . . ."

Poor Me's initially seduce by their vulnerability and need for help. However, they are not really interested in solutions because then they would lose their source of energy. They might also exhibit overaccommodating behavior which eventually leads them into feeling taken advantage of and reinforces their Poor Me method of gaining energy. As accommodators they have little ability to set boundaries and limits, and behavior ranges from convincing, defending, making excuses, repeatedly explaining, telling too much, to trying to solve problems that are not their business. They open themselves to being objectified, perhaps through their beauty or sexual favors, and then resent being taken for granted.

Poor Me's sustain their victim stance by attracting people who intimidate them. In the extreme cycles of domestic violence, an Intimidator will involve the Poor Me in increasingly violent episodes of abuse toward the Poor Me until a climax is reached. After the climax, the Intimidator retreats and apologizes, thus sending energy that seduces the Poor Me back into the cycle.

Reference Chart of Control Drama Positions

AGGRESSIVE

OUTER BEHAVIOR	INNER STRUGGLE

Intimidator

Denial, not listening	Fear of being controlled.
Anger	Fear of not enough.

OUTER BEHAVIOR	INNER STRUGGLE
Get it any way I can	Someone else will get it first.
Arrogance	No one notices me.
Me first	No one cares.
Control	I have to do it alone.
Rage	No one ever took care of me.
Violence	I'm dead.
Makes others feel:	*Matching Drama:*
Afraid	Poor Me: "Don't hurt me, I'm not threatening."
Angry	Intimidator: "You can't hurt me. I'll fight back."
Vengeful	Interrogator: "You're not as powerful as you appear to be. What's your weak point?"
Negated	Aloof: "I will not confront you."

Interrogator

Who do you think you are?	No acknowledgment as a child.
Where are you going?	People leave me and I'm afraid.
Why didn't you . . . ?	I want proof of your love.
Why don't you . . . ?	You're going to leave me.
I told you so.	You need me. I need you.

OUTER BEHAVIOR	INNER STRUGGLE
Makes others feel:	*Matching Drama:*
Monitored	Aloof: "You don't know what I'm thinking."
Negated	Aloof: "You are more powerful than I am. You count more than I do."
Wrong	Martyr/Poor Me: "Someday you'll see my true worth."

PASSIVE

OUTER BEHAVIOR	INNER STRUGGLE

Aloof

I'm not ready to . . .	I'm not sure I can survive.
I need more (money, education, time)	I don't trust myself; I'm afraid.
I don't know, I'm not sure. Maybe.	I'll be trapped and I won't be able to perform.
I'll let you know.	I don't know what I feel.
Makes others feel:	*Matching Drama:*
Uncertain	Interrogator: "Are you mad at me?"
Suspicious	Interrogator: "What did I do wrong?"

Poor Me

I'm tired.	I do so much, no one sees me.

OUTER BEHAVIOR	INNER STRUGGLE
That's just the way I am.	I don't know how to get energy any other way.
I'm doing the best I can.	If I change, you won't love me.
I'm fine.	You don't really care about me.
Let me do it.	You need me. I need you.
Don't worry about me.	I need recognition.
Makes others feel: Guilty	*Matching Drama:* Intimidator: "You want to control me." Interrogator: "You are so self-centered."

It's often easier to see these dramas in others. For example, a woman who recently read *The Celestine Prophecy* told us, "I saw a control drama in the making yesterday when I was in a shoe store. A mother had come in looking for shoes with her nine-year-old daughter. The bored little girl asked, 'Mom. Mom. What color shoes are you gonna buy?' Intent on searching the shoe racks, the mother did not respond to the question. In a whinier tone, again the question came, 'Mom. Mom. What color shoes are you gonna buy?' Still the mother did not respond." The woman said to us, "Before knowing about control dramas, I would just have seen that little girl as a pest, too, being a mother myself. Yesterday I felt like telling the mother, 'Say, did you realize your aloof manner is creating a little interrogator?' "

Control Dramas Are Fear Based

Each of the modes for controlling energy is rooted in the original fear that if one loses the connection to the parent, he or she will not be able to survive. When we were children, our parents *were* the source of our survival, and when we needed energy to feel secure, we used one of the dramas that seemed to work.

With the knowledge that there is a universal source of energy available to all, we need no longer stay in our old pattern of control and survival. Transforming the fear-based drama by connecting to our inner source, we exist at a higher vibration. When brought into awareness, the control dramas may potentially change to positive attributes.

One woman, a thirty-one-year-old single mother who currently works as a receptionist, wants more out of life. She has a dream, and her question is, "How could I become financially independent enough to live anywhere I wanted to in the country and teach others how to be self-sufficient?" In doing her parental analysis she discovered the following beliefs from both parents:

- "Sometimes you just have to do things you don't want to."
- "Wait to live."
- "Plan for the tragedies."
- "There's not enough time to do everything."
- "Never a moment's rest."
- "You got a good thing there. You'd better stay."

Her parents, while hardworking, good-intentioned people, had no passion or joy in life. She looked at her question about becoming financially independent and living anywhere she wanted and realized that the beliefs instilled by her parents were not going to lead her to her dream. While she realized it is important to be strategic, their lives were perfect feedback that excessive caution did not lead to a self-fulfilled life. She also realized that she was saying the same thing to herself about staying in her present job because it was "a good thing." In addition, she was putting her life on hold ("wait to live") pending the receipt of a legal settlement. In subtle ways she was reflecting those early beliefs of her parents.

You might want to consider the following questions:

• What made your mother afraid? What behavior did she exhibit?
• What made your father afraid? What behavior did he exhibit?
• What makes you afraid? How do you act? How are you similar to your parents?

Transforming Control Dramas

Once we become centered internally, our control dramas come into awareness, and these old habits can evolve into positive strengths.

Intimidator/Leader. When connected to the true source of power, an Intimidator will find more self-esteem when he uses his leadership qualities. Assertive without being domineering, confident without being arrogant, he has more chance for enjoying challenges and gaining the cooperation of others.

One sixty-year-old management consultant once owned and operated a manufacturing company. Self-described as a "bastard on wheels," he almost never lost an argument and relished his illusion of power and intimidation. Bankruptcy and divorce proved humbling experiences and showed him how out of balance his life had become. Today he is an executive coach, helping people see why they make certain decisions and helping them get in touch with their true power. Knowing what his feelings are and how they can guide him with integrity has freed him from his self-imposed exile.

Interrogator/Advocate. The Interrogator, transformed, channels the predilection for questioning into research, using more well-rounded interpersonal skills as a teacher, counselor, or advocate.

A forty-five-year-old woman who was part of a senior management team in a multinational financial services corporation was known for her impeccable analytic style and ability to pinpoint research flaws. Her well-respected status, however, did not fill the emotional void she felt. The emptiness of her personal life was overwhelming. Eventually she became extremely ill. Forced to reevaluate, she began to study psychology and now has her own private practice.

Aloof/Independent Thinker. Freed from the need to remain an outsider, Aloofs access deep inner intuitive resources to bring wisdom and creativity to their life's work, such as being a priest, healer, or artist.

A former minister, who literally hid behind his pulpit, made a major transformation to college teaching. In the beginning, he saw himself in the position as "the preacher," creating an artificial separation from his congregation. After a devastating personal review by parishioners, he was shocked into an awareness of his all-too-human nature. Humbled, he could no longer live isolated by his rigid beliefs.

Poor Me/Reformer. Having experienced true nurturing and unity, the Poor Me is able to stay grounded in his or her own inner source and becomes a compassionate reformer, social worker, or healer.

> Our willingness to surrender and to believe in the process helps us to replace our self-will and allows our unconscious to take over. When this happens, the idea of a Higher Power becomes acceptable to us. We shift our attention away from wanting our addictive behavior to change, and we begin to understand that life is a process. *The Twelve Steps: A Way Out: A Working Guide for Adult Children of Alcoholic & Other Dysfunctional Families*[7]

An incest survivor who tried to commit suicide at fifteen spent years in therapy trying to find out the cause of her depression. After weathering several relationships with intimidators, losing a job, and discovering her brother had AIDS, she had no choice but to surrender to a greater understanding. Today her inner healing has given her the ability to help others find the truth in their pain.

In most cases the transformation these people experienced was catalyzed by what looked like a negative event, such as divorce, bankruptcy, or illness. Pain, disillusionment, humiliation, isolation, and a sense of failure were essential elements that produced healing *because each person was willing to take responsibility for what he or she needed to learn.*

Analyzing Control Dramas

One of the most asked questions from readers is, "How do I get out of my control drama? What can I do?"

Become Conscious of Your Behavior. The first step in stopping your pattern is to become very clear about the control drama you learned as a child. Review the descriptions above and begin to notice your behavior, especially when you are under stress or anxious about something.

Do you get belligerent, impatient, rigid, angry, and intimidate or dominate others? (Intimidator)

Are you suspicious of others, or feel they are not paying enough attention? Do you needle, remonstrate, or interrogate them? (Interrogator)

Do you keep your distance and play hard-to-get, avoiding situations where you must reveal yourself for fear of being judged? (Aloof)

Are you always complaining and focusing on problems, hoping that others will come to your rescue? (Poor Me)

Become Conscious of What Types You Attract. Stop matching their dramas. Notice the nature of your everyday interactions and be willing to disengage from the game.

For example, are you having a lot of encounters with Intimidators? If so, you are probably feeling out of control or disempowered. You might be trying to get energy from them by being an Intimidator yourself (because of a belief in scarcity, which leads to a perceived need for competition). Or, if you are feeling like a victim of their actions, your reaction might be to try to justify your powerlessness, rather than take responsibility for your own life. If you are being intimidated, recognize where you need to get in touch with your own feelings of anger or injustice. How do you need to take action in your *own* life? Watch for defensive statements which are a clue that you have moved into a Poor Me stance to get some energy from the other. One forty-year-old student said, "I have become aware that when I phone my mother (an Intimidator), I still tend to start the conversation with some little setback I've had, like car trouble or money problems. Unconsciously I want her to feel that I still need her support and energy. If I say something nice about myself, I feel like she'll criticize me to 'keep me in my place.'"

Are many Poor Me's lining up to tell you a sob story? Perhaps you have started taking more responsibility for yourself and this is a reminder not to fall back into blaming others. Perhaps you are feeling uncertain, depressed, or afraid yourself, but are not in touch with the source of your feelings. In that case, you have projected out your own Poor Me feelings. The advice you give to a Poor Me friend might be something you need to hear yourself.

Do you have a major Interrogator in your life? Perhaps you are hiding feelings and not telling the whole truth about something. Ask yourself how you are withdrawing energy from this other person. Do you want him or her to notice something about you that you don't want to say directly? Do you feel inadequate, but are trying to appear "on top of things"? How have you lost your connection to the universal source?

Is someone being Aloof with you? Hard to reach, distant, or mysterious? Do you find yourself wanting constant contact and wondering about their every thought, move, or motive? Perhaps you are doing to him what one of his parents did—interrogating and monitoring him. He may be being mysterious in order to keep from feeling engulfed or from having to perform.

Remember, your reactions are rooted in childhood insecurities.

Get in touch with your body; for example, notice if you freeze up under criticism or questioning. Rigidity, coldness, and fear sensations confirm that you are in competition for energy and that you have lost your center.

Naming the Drama

In *The Celestine Prophecy* Julia tells the main character that "all dramas are covert strategies to get energy. . . . covert manipulations for energy can't exist if you bring them into consciousness by pointing them out . . . the best truth about what's going on in a conversation always prevails. After that the person has to be more real and honest."[8]

Naming the drama brings the truth of the encounter out into the open. Naming the drama does not necessarily mean that you mentally analyze your encounter and are able to articulate that this is an Interrogator and you're going into an Aloof mode or any other psychological explanations. Naming the drama means that you are *able to notice that a power struggle is in progress and that you are feeling overwhelmed, stuck, browbeaten, powerless, or any number of feelings*. Naming it means staying in the truth of your feelings and taking steps to disengage. Notice when you find yourself trying to convince someone, defending yourself, feeling threatened, or feeling guilty because someone is making you responsible for their problems. When you feel stuck, frozen, and confused, you are in a power struggle. The very process of becoming aware allows you to make a choice about continuing it or transforming it.

Remember that naming the drama might not be very easy to accomplish if emotions are running high or there is a lot of fear. The point is to get the truth out in the open. Always project love and understanding toward the other person and trust yourself to know when to speak. Try different approaches:

With Intimidators:
- "Why are you so angry?"
- "You seem to want to make me afraid of you."

With Interrogators:
- "I like you, but when I'm with you I feel criticized."
- "Is there something else that's bothering you besides this issue?"

With Aloofs:
- "I feel like you are withdrawing and being distant. How are you feeling?"

With Poor Me's:
- "It feels like you're making me responsible for what's wrong in your life."
- "You may not mean to, but it feels like you're trying to make me feel guilty."

Don't be afraid to sound awkward in the beginning. You are changing a lifelong pattern, and you might not be too smooth at first in managing this energy. Often, the overt issues that people fight about are not the real issues. Look for the truth behind the obvious.

Look Beyond the Drama to the Real Person. Stay centered in your own energy and remember to send the other person as much energy as you can. As we know from the First Insight, each person we encounter has a message for us, and we for them. If we are stuck in the no-win struggle for energy, we miss the message. Therefore, after naming the drama, we must see the person without preconceived judgments and give them energy voluntarily so that they, in turn, are able to receive and give to us.

Listen for clues that people present about what is really going on with them. For example, in the heat of an argument, one Intimidator shouted, "I've had it with these people. I'm tired of being pushed around. I've been pushed around ever since I was a kid." This helped the other person, who was fast going into a Poor Me reaction, to realize that the issues were not about *her*, but something deeper and older. In further conversation, she was able to speak more candidly and compassionately with the other person. In this case, because she knew him fairly well, she was able to draw some parallels about the power of early childhood influences in both their lives.

Reflections in Your Mirror. Once you have time to reflect on a control drama that you are involved in, look at yourself and the other person as objectively as you can. How is the other person like one of your parents? How are you reacting as you did in early childhood? It might be helpful to write about the encounter in your journal and spend a few minutes writing down your feelings. Allow the situation to teach you, and avoid making judgments about what is happening.

Usually what bothers us about others is something we need to look at in ourselves, but are unwilling to do. Finger-pointing is a sign that we are trying to use blame instead of understanding. For example, an organizational development consultant said, "I was frustrated with an executive who kept accusing certain employees of being stupid, instead of seeing how his whole situation had developed out a lack of communication. Then I realized that I was doing the same thing with one of my own colleagues—calling him names in my mind, and not looking at deeper issues." Finger-pointing does not name the truth, so, as a result, nothing ever gets resolved. Everybody loses energy.

Ask yourself these questions:

- What is a control drama showing me that I most need to know right now?
- Do I need to set better limits in the beginning of encounters?
- Do I take events personally when they are not really about me?
- Do I try to press an advantage when I see weakness in the other?

Be Willing to Walk Away When You See You're Hooked. For example, Poor Me's will become hooked into their drama with an Intimidator or Interrogator by continually trying to reexplain, convince, or defend. If you do this, notice how much time you spend obsessing on how you can finally, once and for all, convince this person of something. As you release your need to gain energy by your old methods, you will be able to walk away from the temptation to keep convincing.

Intimidators get hooked on the adrenaline rush of overpowering and winning. If you do this, ask yourself, What do I most want? Do I need to get it only this way? Be willing to stay flexible and open; stop trying to control everything. Perhaps cooperation would bring even more benefits than how you now perceive the solution.

Interrogators get hooked by their illusion of self-righteousness. If you do this, be willing to look at the situation from the other point of view. What might you learn from doing this? Be willing to talk about your real feelings and do something to gain energy for yourself rather than chasing someone who is withdrawing.

Aloofs get hooked by wanting to cover up fears, self-doubts, and confusion. If you do this, be willing to ask for help. Admit that you don't have quite everything together. What support do you need right now? What are you feeling? Be willing to walk *toward* something. Walking away is the easy way out for you.

Case History. When Jane, a real estate broker, read about control dramas in *The Celestine Prophecy*, she became determined to change her own habits. This determination was a powerful statement of intention which synchronistically attracted opportunities to break through her pattern. Within a couple of months she had two encounters with very difficult people who reminded her of her domineering mother. She became increasingly aware that she habitually attempted to receive energy by becoming a self-righteous Poor Me. She recognized these encounters as opportunities to change her old habits.

In her most conflicted encounter, Jane found herself deadlocked with a very intimidating client who refused to negotiate on the price of his home. In addition, he was becoming increasingly belligerent over the time it was taking to sell the house. Jane's first reaction was to defend herself with justifications on how hard she was working and so forth (Poor Me). The situation worsened. Soon she was focusing entirely on how she could prove him wrong, and herself right.

Jane, by this time, had lost sight of her goal—which was to sell the house. She was hooked into her childhood pattern of feeling criticized by someone with an overbearing personality (like her mother), which resulted in trying to regain energy via a Poor Me stance.

First, Jane took note of how drained she felt and spent some time building up her energy on a daily basis.

Second, she remembered that the way out of a control drama is to name it—that is, call it out into the open and make it an overt, rather than covert, situation. Determined to try new behavior, she called her client. Staying with her feelings, she told him that she was feeling at a loss as to what to do next, because she was beginning to feel criticized for her decisions so far. She told him that she had tried her best to work with his price and understood that he did not want to reduce it. Her ability to bring her issues out in the open laid the groundwork for them to begin discussing various options of how they might continue to work together.

She admitted that it was hard to stay centered when he fired off his interrogatory comments, and not play the Poor Me match to his Intimidator/Interrogator. "Intellectually, I know he's under a lot of pressure to sell, and he's trying to exert control, too. Even so, I caught myself freezing up. My biggest hang-up was thinking that the house wasn't selling because of something I was doing or not doing. I really thought it was about me 'getting it right.' I've stopped feeling guilty for not solving his 'problems,' and recognize that he is working out issues which have little to do with me. What a relief I feel." Trying to solve his problem for him and "save" him was literally a replay of her early childhood role of caretaking her dysfunctional mother. In this instance, she let go of her need to feel in control of a situation that she could not control. Realizing that this sale was not going to be the only one she would ever make, she began to detach from the outcome.

What Our Dramas Can Teach Us

Using Jane's example, let's take a moment to recap the principles that were at work.

Parental Relationships Are Mirrored in Other Relationships. The parental review gave Jane greater insights about how old dramas recur. "I did my parental review, but it was kind of flat for me until I started actually working on the control drama with my client. This was a direct lesson about what I had to learn after I started reviewing my past. Once I saw the dynamic of how I went into a Poor Me mode, I really understood the effect my mother had on me. In retrospect, though, maybe she was a good trainer for my real estate practice!"

Every Situation Has a Message. With the increase of attention on her current question about parental influences, synchronicity provided Jane with a client that was a perfect reflection of her interior beliefs and judgments about herself.

Her Body Gave Her Clues. Jane realized that it's important to pay attention to intuitions and bodily sensations of discomfort. These physical cues let her know when she is falling into reactive behavior. The more she learns to trust her own impressions, the sooner she can stop reactive behavior.

She Told the Truth and Didn't Die. She realized she had to verbalize her discomfort to herself and communicate this in an appropriate way to the others even though she didn't know if she'd find the exact right words. Learning to confront and to give feedback in a friendly way is necessary if we are not going to continue covert behavior.

She Asked for Help. She realized that she didn't have to solve the situation alone. By bringing the situation into overt awareness and staying truthful, she has a chance of including the other person in the solution. She realized that she can only be responsible for herself. She doesn't have to come up with all the answers.

She Took a Broader View. Jane went back over her parental review and gained further insights. She said, "Some of my perceptions were so deeply buried that it took some time before I was ready to see even this much."

Progress Not Perfection

Life is a journey, not an end result, and it's important to accept ourselves and others the way we are. We might not like others or approve of their behavior, but life is about experience and bringing ourselves into loving unity. Blaming, judging, and comparing ourselves to others' "progress" or stage of enlightenment is not helpful. As you work with releasing your control drama, keep it in perspective and keep your sense of humor. Whenever you can, remember to bring yourself into peaceful oneness.

Be Easy on Yourself

> *Awareness is a mirror*
> *reflecting the four elements.*
> *Beauty is a heart*
> *that generates love*
> *and a mind that is open.*
> THICH NHAT HANH,
> *Present Moment*
> *Wonderful Moment*[9]

As you work on becoming more aware of control dramas, please realize that this information is a tool for transformation, not a weapon to use in "enlightening" others or frustrating yourself. Be easy on yourself as you begin to change your behavior. Remember that it is always easier to see these dramas in others. When you feel angry, self-righteous, shut down, depressed, or isolated, you have allowed yourself to look for solutions and energy in old ways.

When you can truthfully feel that your heart is open and you are peaceful with whatever is happening in your life, then you are connected to your own energy. When in doubt, breathe, look for the humor in what's happening, and do something to get your energy higher.

SUMMARY OF THE SIXTH INSIGHT

The Sixth Insight is the awareness of when we lose our inner connection with divine energy. Often we find that at these times we are resorting to our personal (and unconscious) way of manipulating others out of their energy. These manipulations are generally either passive or aggressive. Most passive can be called the victim, or the Poor Me, approach: always framing events as negative, looking to others for help, describing events in such a way as to make others feel guilty (and so to force them to give attention and energy).

Less passive is the distancing, or Aloof, strategy: giving vague answers to questions, never committing to anything, making others pursue in order to understand us. When others are pursuing, trying to figure us out, we gain their attention and thus their energy.

More aggressive than these two is the critic, or Interrogator, method: seeking to find something wrong with what others are doing, always monitoring. If we catch them in what we consider an error, we make them self-conscious, overly cautious, worried about what we might think. They watch us out of the corner of their eye and thus give us attention and energy. Most aggressive is the Intimidator style: appearing out of control, explosive, dangerous, and belligerent. Others watch us closely and thus we receive their energy.

Because we tend to repeat these manipulations with everyone we meet, and to structure life events around these devices, they can be understood as "control dramas," repeated patterns that seem to bring on the same life situations over and over. Once we bring our control dramas into consciousness, however, we begin to catch ourselves every time we revert to them, and so can stay more connected with inner energy. An analysis of our early childhood can reveal how our control dramas evolved, but once this is forgiven we can see deeper reasons why we were placed with our early family. From our parents' strengths and from particular growth issues they didn't complete, we can derive our life question and our work or "mission" in the world.

Further Reading

In addition to the excellent books listed in the notes for this chapter we suggest:

The Spectrum of Consciousness. Ken Wilber. Quest Books, 1977.

Quantum Consciousness. Stephen Wolinsky, Ph.D. Bramble Books, 1993.

Beyond Games and Scripts. Eric Berne and Claude M. Steiner. Ballantine, 1981.

Do What You Love and the Money Will Follow. Marsha Sinetar. Dell, 1989.

Codependent No More: How to Stop Controlling Others and Start Caring for Yourself. Melody Beattie. Hazelden, 1987.

Fire in the Soul: A New Psychology of Spiritual Optimism. Joan Borysenko. Warner, 1993.

INDIVIDUAL STUDY OF THE SIXTH INSIGHT

Parental Review

Purpose: The purpose of this exercise is to make a profile of your parents' achievements, attitudes, philosophy, weak points, and unfinished business as *you* saw them in childhood. If you can find the higher meaning of their lives, you will be more inclined to see how their lives prepared you for your life mission. Your best approach is to assume there was a positive intention at work in your early circumstances.

Directions: Do this exercise when you won't be interrupted for an hour or two.

Read the following questions and write the answers in your journal. Answer the questions from the viewpoint of your early childhood.

A. Observing the Masculine Teacher (Your Father)

You formed your ideas about how masculine energy works from your father or other significant male models. The role of the father in our lives is to help us connect with our power and leadership. The purpose of fathering is to make us self-sufficient. It is through the masculine side of our nature that we take action toward our goals.

If you did not relate well to your father, you might have difficulty with authority figures in your life or have trouble finding your identity. In either case, you have not completely accepted your own power.

Work Accomplishment
1. What type(s) of work did your father do when you were young?
2. Was he proud of what he did?
3. In what way did he excel?

Affirmative Self-Expression
4. List positive words that best describe your father (e.g., intelligent, adventurous, loving, etc.).
5. What one or two words *best* describe his personality?
6. What was unique about him?

Negative Self-Expression
7. List words that describe any negative traits in your father (e.g., critical, overbearing, opinionated, etc.).
8. What triggered negative behavior?
9. What one or two words describe his worst traits?

Father's Childhood
10. Describe as best you can your father's childhood.
11. Was he happy? Neglected? Went to work at an early age? Poor? Rich?
12. What control dramas do you think his parents used?
13. In what way did his childhood influence his life choices?

Father's Philosophy
14. What was most important to him?
15. What statement or credo best expresses your father's philosophy of life?

Missing Elements

16. List what you think was missing from your father's life.
17. What might he have done if he had had more time, money, or education?

B. Energy Analysis of the Masculine

Which description most accurately describes your father's general attitude toward you? If more than one is applicable, write a percentage on the descriptions that apply (e.g., Poor Me 60%; Aloof 40%).

_____ Intimidator: On the verge of exploding; threatening; gave orders; inflexible; angry; self-centered; made you feel afraid.

_____ Interrogator: Probed to see what you were doing; critical; undermining; needling; infallible logic; sarcasm; monitored you.

_____ Aloof: Tended to be distant; busy; away from home; not too interested in your life; unresponsive; secretive; preoccupied.

_____ Poor Me/Victim: Always saw the negative; looked for problems; always talking about being busy or tired; made you feel guilty for not solving his problems.

C. Your Reaction to the Masculine

How did you react when your father was in his control drama?

Choose one of these same modes that best describes *your* reaction to him as a child, or give percentages to two or more methods.

_____ Intimidator: Did you stand up to your father and take a strong or rebellious position?

_____ Interrogator: Did you try to get his attention by asking questions? Did you try to be smarter than him or find loopholes in arguments?

_____ Aloof: Did you withdraw into yourself, or hide out in your room doing some activity by yourself? Did you stay away from home a lot? Did you hide your true feelings?

_____ Poor Me/Victim: Did you try to make your father feel that you needed help, money, support, attention by focusing on your troubles so that he would pay more attention to you?

D. Analysis of What You Learned from Your Masculine Teacher

LIKE MY FATHER

Your observations of your father's life can function as either positive or negative _beliefs_ you still carry.

1. Finish this sentence with _positive_ qualities you got from your father: _Like my father, I am_ . . .
2. Finish this sentence with _negative_ qualities you got from your father: _Like my father, I am_ . . .
3. From Father, I learned that in order to succeed, I should:
   a.
   b.
   c.

These are beliefs and values that influenced many of your decisions either positively or negatively.

GROWING IN MY OWN WAY

4. From observing Father's life, I want to be more:
   a.

b.

c.

5. For what are you grateful to your father?

6. For what would you be willing to forgive your father?

7. From your list of what was missing from your father's life, what, if anything, have you chosen to develop?

a.

b.

c.

Your father's missing elements are directions you already might be working on or wish to develop. It's likely these elements will influence your choices about career, lifestyle, relationship, parenting, and spiritual contribution.

A. Observing the Feminine Teacher (Your Mother)

You formed your ideas about how feminine energy works from your mother or other significant female caretaker. The role of the feminine in our lives is to help us relate to others. Generally, but not always, it is our mother who shows us how to connect with our ability to heal, comfort, and nurture others. For example, if you did not relate well to your mother, you might have difficulty with intimate relationships or lack the ability to nurture yourself properly. A feeling of deprivation around the mother might even underlie such behavior as overspending or underearning. Feminine energy is the creator of your goals and reveals what has heart and meaning for you.

Work Accomplishment

1. What type(s) of work or activities did your mother do when you were young?

2. Do you think she felt fulfilled in her activities?

3. In what way did she excel?

Affirmative Self-Expression
  4. List positive words that best describe your mother (e.g., intelligent, creative, loving, etc.).
  5. What one or two words *best* describe her personality?
  6. What was unique about her?

Negative Self-Expression
  7. List words that describe negative traits in your mother (e.g., strict, insecure, opinionated, etc.).
  8. What triggered negative behavior?
  9. What one or two words describe her worst traits?

Mother's Childhood
  10. Describe as best you can your mother's childhood.
  11. Was she happy? Neglected? Went to work at an early age? Poor? Rich? Sheltered? Ambitious?
  12. What control dramas do you think her parents used?
  13. In what way did her childhood influence her life choices?

Mother's Philosophy
  14. What was most important to her?
  15. What statement or credo best expresses your mother's philosophy of life?

Missing Elements
  16. List what you think was missing from your mother's life.
  17. What might she have done if she had had more time, money, or education?

B. Energy Analysis of the Feminine

Which description most accurately describes your mother's general attitude toward you? If you feel more than one is applicable, write a percentage on the descriptions that apply (e.g., Poor Me 60%; Aloof 40%).

_____ Intimidator: On the verge of exploding; threatening; strict; gave orders; inflexible; angry; self-centered; made you feel afraid.

_____ Interrogator: Probed to see what you were doing; critical; undermining; needling; infallible logic; sarcasm; monitored you.

_____ Aloof: Tended to be distant; busy; away from home; not too interested in your life; unresponsive; secretive; preoccupied.

_____ Poor Me/Victim: Always saw the negative; looked for problems; always talking about being busy or tired; made you feel guilty for not solving her problems.

C. Your Reaction to the Feminine

How did you react when your mother was in her control drama?

Choose one of these same modes that best describes *your* reaction to her as a child, or give percentages to two or more methods.

_____ Intimidator: Standing up to your mother and taking a strong or rebellious position.

_____ Interrogator: Trying to get her attention by asking questions. Did you try to be smarter than her and find loopholes in arguments?

_____ Aloof: Did you withdraw into yourself? Hide out in your room doing some activity by yourself? Stay away from home? Hide your true feelings?

_____ Poor Me/Victim: Did you try to make your mother feel that you needed help, money, support, attention, by focusing on your troubles so that she would pay more attention to you?

D. Analysis of What You Learned from Your Feminine Teacher

LIKE MY MOTHER

Your observations of your mother's life can function as either positive or negative *beliefs* you still carry.

1. Finish this sentence with *positive* qualities you got from your mother: *Like my mother, I am . . .*
2. Finish this sentence with *negative* qualities you got from your mother: *Like my mother, I am . . .*
3. From Mother, I learned that in order to succeed, I should:
   a.
   b.
   c.

These are beliefs and values that influenced many of your decisions either positively or negatively.

GROWING IN MY OWN WAY

4. From observing Mother's life, I want to be more:
   a.
   b.
   c.
5. For what are you grateful to your mother?
6. For what would you be willing to forgive your mother?
7. From your list of what was missing from your mother's life, what, if anything, have you chosen to develop?
   a.
   b.
   c.

Your mother's missing elements are directions you already might be working on or wish to develop. It's likely these elements will influence your choices about career, lifestyle, relationship, parenting, and spiritual contribution.

Putting It All Together

As the product of your two parental lineages, your path will involve working through both the positive and negative aspects that shaped you during your particular upbringing. Take what you have learned from your previous analysis and synthesize it here.

FATHER'S	MOTHER'S
Personal Credo	Personal Credo
Values	Values
Primary Achievement	Primary Achievement
Disappointment	Disappointment
Missing Elements	Missing Elements
How He Wounded Me— and What That Taught Me	How She Wounded Me— and What That Taught Me
How He Inspired Me	How She Inspired Me
Gift to Me	Gift to Me

Finish these sentences:

1. The positive intention behind my early childhood and my parents' influence was . . .

2. Observing the lessons inherent in the lives of my parents (and perhaps grandparents), I can see that their lives prepared me to . . .

3. My life question has to do with . . .

Statement of Intention

I am evolving according to my own soul's needs, integrating everything I have learned from my childhood to the present.

Relating Your Early Influences to Your Personal Time Line

Be sure to answer question 3 in the above table about the life question you received from both your parents. Even if this is not totally clear to you, write down your *best guess* and answer the following questions in your journal:

- If you could have any kind of life you wanted, what would it look like? Write this in a short paragraph.
- Review your list of turning points on page 47. What interests, activities, jobs, relationships on your Personal Time Line (from Chapter 2) indicate that you have been working on your original life question?
- How would you describe where you are at present in your journey?
- What about your life do you like the best?

- What about your life would you most like to change?
- How has your control drama(s) affected your advancement?
- Have you been asking for direction from your higher intuitive guidance on how to live a more satisfying life?
- How are you staying connected to the feeling of love and peaceful oneness?
- What coincidences have happened lately?

Key People in Your Life

Construct a chart with the headings below. List the names of key people in your life in the leftmost column. Check the type of energy they predominantly exhibited to you. What were your lessons from each one?

NAME   POOR ME/REFORMER   ALOOF/TEACHER   INTERROGATOR/ADVOCATE   INTIMIDATOR/LEADER

STUDY GROUP FOR THE SIXTH INSIGHT

Session 10

2 hours 30 minutes

Session Purpose: This session allows people to discuss their parental reviews and particular control drama.

Preparation: Bring your completed Parental Review homework for discussion (from the Individual Study section).

General Discussion

Time: 15–20 minutes

Directions:

Step 1: Read aloud the recap of the Sixth Insight on page 135 (up to the case history of Albert Camus).

Step 2: Share your thoughts about the Sixth Insight in general. (Leave specifics for Exercise 1.) You might want to start the discussion with one of these questions:

- How many people think they know what their control drama is? (Show of hands)
- How many are (a) Intimidators, (b) Interrogators, (c) Aloofs, (d) Poor Me's? (Show of hands for each)
- How many people were able to find a life question from looking at early childhood influences? (Show of hands)

EXERCISE 1. Finding Purpose in Childhood Influences

Purpose: This exercise gives everyone a chance to discuss their childhood influences with other people and gain further insights about their life question.

Time: Decide how much time is available for individual stories and how much time you wish to have for general discussion.

Preparation: If you have four to eight members in your group, work together in one group. If your group is larger, it is a good idea to divide into twos or fours for discussion, reconvening as one group to share experiences.

Directions:

Step 1: In your small group, share the positive intentions in your parental influences and how they shaped a destiny for you. You might want to read directly from your completed section called "Putting It All Together."

Step 2: After the small discussions, return to the whole group. Ask for volunteers to share what they learned about themselves. As each person talks, practice giving him or her full attention. Offer insights if they occur to you and if it feels right to do so.

Closing

Requests for support, and sending loving energy.

For Next Session
- Read Chapter 7 in preparation for the next meeting.
- Bring rhythmic music and a tape recorder, and enough blank sheets of paper for each member.

CHAPTER 7

Engaging the Flow

In this chapter our character is instructed on how to keep his energy high in order to engage the flow of evolution and receive the information he needs to make decisions. Faced with a choice of where to go next, he is warned not to fall back into his Aloof drama, and encouraged to stay connected to the background emotion of love. He begins to notice thoughts and images that pop into his mind just when he feels at a loss. His current questions are how to find Marjorie and how to stay out of danger as he continues to track the Insights. Trusting his intuition as to which road to take at a crossroads, he nevertheless is captured. What looks like a disaster holds the key to more than one of his questions. A young Indian cellmate helps him understand the guiding messages in dreams and intuitions.

THE SEVENTH INSIGHT

The Seventh Insight tells us that we can evolve consciously. It points out that just as humans are evolving physically we are also evolving psychologically and spiritually. The Seventh Insight shows us how to do this by actively engaging the flow. Father Sanchez tells our character that the first step is to build energy, the second step is to remember our basic life questions, and the third step is to discover the immediate smaller questions. By observing our thoughts, our daydreams, and our dreams we can find messages for ourselves that tell us what our questions are and what we need to do next.

Building Energy

Father Sanchez gives very clear instructions on how to keep energy at its maximum level. Practice his method daily and it will become second nature. It is especially important to build energy whenever you feel fearful, confused, or overwhelmed. However, don't gloss too quickly over your feelings. You might need some "downtime" to integrate and accept what has happened. When you're ready, shift your attention from the negative feelings and practice the following steps:

- Focus on the environment or on one beautiful object.
- Remember how things looked when you were energized in the past.
- Look for beauty, unique shapes and colors, and a glow around everything.
- Take deep, conscious breaths, holding each one five seconds before exhaling.
- Breathe in the beauty around you until you feel buoyant.
- Visualize each breath filling you like a balloon.
- Feel the energy and lightness.
- Check to see if you feel love as a background emotion.
- Imagine that your body is surrounded by a vibrant halo of light.
- Imagine that you are a radiant being, inhaling and exhaling energy from the universe.
- Take an observer viewpoint and remember that there is a purpose in whatever is happening.

- Notice that thoughts feel different when you are in the higher vibration. In a control drama thoughts dwell on struggle. Connected to higher energy, you feel open to whatever comes.
- Stop as often as necessary to reconnect. "When you stay full, in a state of love, nothing nor anyone can pull more energy from you than you can replace. Energy flowing out of you creates a current that pulls energy into you at the same rate."[1]

The Right Question

Throughout our character's journey, he repeatedly comes to a point where he doesn't know what to do next. When this happens, someone usually comes into his life and asks him such questions as "Why are you here?" "What do you want to know?" "What is your question?" This centers him and helps bring his question into focus, into the forefront of his attention. Soon thereafter, messages begin to appear. For example, during his stay in prison, his cellmate, Pablo, asks him: "What were you just thinking about? What is happening in your life right now?"

One of the points that Father Sanchez makes is that the only time we do not get a hunch about our next step is when we have asked a question that is not part of our evolution. He says, "You see, the problem in life isn't in receiving answers. The problem is in identifying your current questions. Once you get the questions right, the answers always come."[2] The questions can be concrete about outward events, such as our character's question "Where are Marjorie and Wil?" or abstract, such as "Why are the priests against the Manuscript?"

When you listen to your intuition and feelings, you are plugged into a universal current that will show you *where* you are stuck, happy, sad, confused, or angry.

Probing Your Coincidences

Stay alert to any messages that a coincidence is bringing you. Learn to probe it for meaning. What ideas does it connect together for you? Why is it coming now? If it appears to be a disappointment, what positive result might there be? What action might it be suggesting?

A well-known concert pianist who lives in New York was offered a job in a foreign country. Although the offer was very attractive, he was uncertain whether to take it or not. While keeping this question in his mind he went to the post office. Coincidentally he was served by a man who was from this same small country he was thinking about. Deciding to probe this event a little, he casually mentioned the coincidence to the postal clerk, who said, "Well, you have to go where your friends are." Somehow the comment hit a relevant chord and gave him an insight as to where he really felt most at home—which was New York!

> *Feelings come and go like clouds in a windy sky. Conscious breathing is my anchor.*
> THICH NHAT HANH,
> *Present Moment Wonderful Moment*[3]

When to Take Action

You might decide that an intuition to take action is truly coming from universal intelligence. However, unless you feel in alignment, the action might not bear fruit. Sanaya Roman in her book *Spiritual Growth* says:

> Take action only when your feeling is inviting, open, and positive. Then the actions you take will be aligned with the Higher Will. You will need less effort to get positive results. For instance, after you have done your energy work to create results, you

may have an urge to call someone. Before you call this person, stop for a moment, get quiet, and imagine yourself calling. If calling feels warm, good, and inviting, then call. If you feel resistance, if your energy drops, or you have any other negative feeling when you think of doing something, wait.[4]

Doing What You Love

Your deeply held dreams and goals are part of the purpose that you brought to this lifetime. Sometimes we put aside our dreams and fantasies as if they were impossible to achieve, however tantalizing they might be. Perhaps we feel that we don't really deserve to have a life that good.

You have already found your way to the Insights, just as our character did by this point in the book. Your desire to make a difference in the world *is linked to the talents you have and the events that have influenced you so far.* As you become more open to the coincidences and willing to examine what their message is, you will find it easier to know which actions to take.

Carol Roghair, a private consultant in Mill Valley, California, told us this story: "I was in the pool at a hot springs up north when I overheard a woman talking about *The Celestine Prophecy* and *The Right Use of Will*. She and I started talking and figured we must have a message for each other. Well, I don't remember ex-

> Revelations can be simple or complex. They usually carry a special feeling with them; some of you get goosebumps, tingling, or other physical sensations. Sometimes you have no physical sensations, but you feel a mental "click," as if a piece has just fallen into place. You can receive revelations in many ways—directly into your mind as insights, from channeling, from reading a book, or by hearing something
>
> SANAYA ROMAN,
> *Spiritual Growth*[5]

actly how this came up, but I mentioned that I had always wanted to help people find their voice. Then she told me that that's what she does. Tears came into her eyes, and I got goose bumps. I feel like a huge shift happened to me when I acknowledged how important this idea had been for me when I was younger. I just assumed I couldn't really do it. Something is also happening with my meditation that is different. There is a feeling of deeper connection, but I don't know why. It's subtle, but it feels more alive."

Remember that each moment is an opportunity for you to stay present, even when it means going through physical or emotional pain. As much as we struggle to make "progress" and to "gain" enlightenment, we are often thrown back to our most human frailties, and in them we find our true nature, our true aliveness. Thomas Moore writes in *The Care of the Soul*:

> This is the "goal" of the soul path—to *feel existence;* not to overcome life's struggles and anxieties, but to know life first hand, to exist fully in context. . . . But the only thing to do is to be where you are at this moment, sometimes looking about in the full light of consciousness, other times standing comfortably in the deep shadows of mystery and the unknown. . . . It is probably not quite correct to speak of the soul's *path*. It is more a meandering and a wandering.[6]

The Difference between Impulsive Desires and Intuition

You are in the process of discerning messages that come from your own insecurity and those that come from your higher-self guidance. As you become more aware and attuned to your inner center, you will learn to distinguish between impulsive desires and intuitive knowing. Both can feel compelling. In the beginning, you might not be sure which is which. Don't be hard on yourself if you do mistake one for the other. An important rule of thumb is not to act out of a sense of urgency. According to Nancy Rosanoff, author of *Intuition Workout:* "An impulse always feels like it has to be done immediately; if you wait, you will miss your opportunity. With an impulse, we feel under pressure to act. After we act impulsively, we feel empty. It did not solve the problem. Impulses are, as the word implies, a strong burst of energy followed by quiet. Impulses come on strong, and then fade away."[7]

Inner knowing usually blossoms over time and subtly influences our direction. Although intuitive thoughts can be equally compelling, there is always time to reflect before acting. Rosanoff offers what she calls the Universal Law of Three:

> If [a thought] comes back to me three times, I do it. Intuitions are insistent and persistent. If it is important, you will not forget it. It will keep coming back to you. It will nag you. . . . I have several stock brokers as students. In their business they have to act quickly. But even under intense pressure, they can use the Law of Three. Within a few moments they can let an idea go, and wait. If it comes back right away, let it go again, and wait. They have learned to sense the difference between a panic reaction and an Intuition. Their Intuitions usually come just before a change in the stock market. A panic happens after a change has already occurred.[8]

As we move toward paying more attention to our inner center, we will notice

> Attentiveness rather than
> efficiency.
> Gentle flow rather than speed.
> KAZUAKI TANAHASHI,
> *Brush Mind*[9]

the differences between messages from our intellect and our intuition:

Intellect-centered messages might:
- be based on scarcity, fear, or guilt
- be based on protecting oneself
- be compelling, with no time to reflect
- be quick answers, and feel out of context with your flow
- be the first thing to come to mind
- feel like a desperate need

Intuitive-centered messages are:
- loving and reassuring
- persistent
- encouraging and positive
- not usually demanding immediate action
- rarely radical without smaller steps to initiate change

Handling Fear Images

The character in the novel asks, "What about negative thoughts? Those fear images of something bad happening, such as someone we love getting hurt, or of not achieving something we very much want?"[10]

Pablo answers him by saying, "The Seventh Insight says that fear images should be halted as soon as they come. Then another image, one with a good outcome, should be willed through the mind. Soon, negative images will almost never happen. Your intuitions will be about positive things. When negative images come after that, the Manuscript says they should be taken very seriously. For instance, if the idea comes to you that you're going to have a wreck in a truck and someone comes along and offers you a ride in a truck, then do not accept it."[11]

Fear is a natural part of life and is an ally when it helps you avoid danger. Learning to see how fear functions in your life could be an important piece of information. Fear, along with its derivatives of anxiety and worry, is an impediment to evolution if allowed to be the first or primary way we process new information or choices. It takes us out of the present by focusing on either past or future problems that might not be relevant. The advice of the Seventh Insight is to change our negative thought processes by stopping fear images and replacing them. However, it might be important to acknowledge the fear rather than trying to simply ignore or deny it.

Once you understand the message within the fear, practice letting those thoughts go and imagine the positive outcome you would like. For example, John, studying for his contractor's license, was dreading the exam. Remembering his high school days and the trouble he had on math exams added to his anxiety. But he was motivated by the thought of having his own business. He was determined to prepare as well as possible, and this prompted him to try some new behavior to deal with the fear. He began to take a few minutes to relax before studying each day. He imagined himself receiving his license in the mail and how proud he would feel. When the fear of failure came every now and then, he remembered that his father had always belittled his abilities and that he was now a capable adult and eager to progress in his life's work. "I told myself, 'John, people need well-built beautiful homes to live in and you're the guy to build 'em.' It helped raise my spirits again and keep me going." His work on his attitudes and beliefs paid off, and he passed his exam.

Notice when you tend to get fearful. During the day notice what brings your energy down. For example, you might feel drained after talking with someone about your past tragedies, your present woes, or your future fears.

Dealing with Fear and Doubt

The more you can sense energy, the more you will be able to distinguish between self-negating fears and actual warnings of danger.

At first you might not have much confidence or trust in the information you receive. If so, ask for more precise information.

See how your fear is related to your control drama. For example, if you have learned to attract energy by being a Poor Me, does your imagination look for trouble as a way for you to stay a Poor Me? As an Aloof, do your fears of being invaded keep you from asking for help from others? As an Intimidator, do your fears of not being taken seriously prompt you to look for resistance where none exists? As an Interrogator, do you fear that if you don't monitor everything, you will be abandoned and alone?

FINDING THE MESSAGE IN FEAR

- Acknowledge the fear.
- Sit with your fear, and really feel it. Feelings of heaviness are usually indicators of fear and worry.
- Bring the feelings into consciousness. Ask for guidance.
- Write down the specifics of what you fear.
- Talk to the fear and find out what message it has for you. Is it realistic?
- Notice the accompanying negative thoughts you have about yourself when you are fearful, such as "Everything is in a mess. I'm swamped. I wish I had never done it. I'm so slow. I'm so stupid." Negative inner dialogue ("self-talk") returns to you in negative feelings and fears as well as negative outcomes.
- Exaggerate the fears. See if any humor can be found.
- In what way do you feel inadequate?

RELEASING THE FEAR

- Focus on your breathing for a few minutes.
- Get as quiet as you can. Spend a few minutes alone.

- Clear your mind and relax.
- Ask for guidance in any form at this time.
- Broadcast love. Surround yourself and others with light.
- As fear and doubt thoughts arise, release them to the light.
- Focus on what you want. See clearly the outcome you desire.
- Remind yourself that you always have options and can make choices.
- When you have attained some measure of calmness, think back to the subtle signals you were getting before the full-blown fears started. Remind yourself that there are always messages coming in for your benefit.
- When you feel fear, shift your attention to your highest purpose. Imagine yourself at your best, surrounded by beauty and friends.

Releasing Control

If you are forcing, struggling, and overworking to make things happen, you are not following the universal flow. Practice asking yourself at times of confusion: "Why am I here [in this situation right now]?" and "What is happening in my life at this moment?" Spend time quietly with yourself. What happens when you release anxiety and control?

A businessman had worked for two years on developing a software program. Trying to establish his business in one location didn't work, so he moved to another. Problems continued to arise with the people he hired and no progress was being made on getting the product marketed. He moved again and after several more months of constant setbacks of one kind or another, he began to ask himself, "Why am I here? Is this business what I am supposed to be doing?"

In his heart he knew that he had only started the business in order to make enough money to have time to write a book. As painful as it was to admit that his struggles for two years had not brought him to his goal, he decided to

> The major obstacle to re-
> solving problems in our
> lives is that we deal with
> them as though they are
> something outside of us.
> The truth is that every prob-
> lem is an outward manifes-
> tation of our state of
> consciousness. When our
> consciousness is clear and
> at peace, the problem dis-
> appears.
>
> ARNOLD PATENT,
> *You Can Have It All*[12]

let go of his interest in the business. The relief he felt was so great that he sat down and finished his book in under three months. In this case, he had been fo-cused on a means to an end and was not really in the flow of his destiny.

Sometimes you do need perseverance to work through obstacles, but if you are fighting what feels like a losing battle, some-thing is not in alignment. Stop what you are doing, particularly if you feel you have no other option. When you feel boxed in and helpless, you are probably caught in an internal struggle that has manifested in your outer world. Let go. Ask for help. Be willing not to do anything for a while, or be willing *to not know what the answer is right now*. The most practical activity is to observe and connect with the beauty around you, so that you can be open to coinci-dences and new messages.

What Is the Missing Piece in Your Life's Puzzle?

Engaging in the flow usually means that you get what you need in order to prepare for the next step in life. An opportu-nity is presented, and then you must do the work. Staying in touch with your hopes, dreams, and needs helps them come into being. Judith O'Connor, a hypnotherapist in Rich-mond, California, tells this story:

"I was attending an evening seminar—an event that I

normally do not attend. One of the last people that I talked to that evening was a woman who asked for my business card. As we exchanged cards, I saw that she was an ortho-keratologist, specializing in treatments for the eye. For some reason, I found myself telling her how frustrated I have been in not being able to read, and how reading had been a struggle for at least fifteen years. I was so amazed when she said that the problem is definitely treatable and is the focus of her practice. I had the immediate feeling that I had come to the seminar so that I could meet this doctor. Later, I noticed that her business card has the logo of an eye. I have almost the same logo on my card!

"This issue about not being able to concentrate and read has been holding me back, and I've felt really intimidated by it. After working with her I found out that my left eye has not been working and connecting up to my brain, so my whole right brain function has been lowered. This heal-ing feels like the missing piece of my puzzle at this point in my life. Coincidentally, when I called her to make an appointment, we discovered that we'd both just finished reading *The Celestine Prophecy*. That just seemed like another incredible coincidence that helped me feel like I had found a like-minded healer."

What is the one thing that gives *you* the most problem right now? Be very specific. Now formulate a question that would help you deal with your problem. Imagine that ques-tion is right out in the forefront of your consciousness, some-where in front of your forehead. Be open to an immediate sign or message.

Attorney Jean Price Lewis has two grown daughters and a successful practice in Marin County, California. One week-end she took a seminar by Gary H. Craig, a personal perfor-mance consultant. He asked the question "What would you do if you knew you could not fail?" "This question really opened up a whole realm of new possibilities that I would never have thought of otherwise," she told us. "I just made out a list, and put on it things like I wanted to become an architect, be Secretary of State, own a tropical island, be a senior model, have a successful invention, learn to fly, own my own airplane, go around the world, and have *good* seats at the Academy Awards!" How is she doing? "Well, I think this list has been like a subconscious menu. Actually, it wasn't until I read *The Celestine Prophecy* that I really took notice of the strange coincidences that were popping up, seemingly as a result of my list. For example, I met a man who teaches flying, and I met another one who is selling an airplane. I'm not sure I'm ready to buy one yet, but the list seems to have a life of its own!"

Dream Study

Dreams are life lived on the inside without constraints of time or space or measure. How, then, can we account for this multidimensional, metamorphosing inner reality in a few pages or even a few volumes? Most of the time we get out of bed vaguely aware of last night's perplexing journey, places we've never been, and people who might or might not be alive, friendly, or who they appear to be. Once in a while we are astounded by some marvelous feeling of wonderment, joy, and searing love, or devastated by unbelievable terror and abysmal loss. There's no telling what will turn up each night. Like synchronicity, this nightly carnival of images might have a message if we look more deeply.

Usually we don't stop to really analyze a dream until it is so clear and unusual that we are captured by the dream, not the other way around. The Seventh Insight tells us that our thoughts, daydreams, and night dreams come to help us intuit our way, and tell us something about our lives that we are missing.

Dreams as Messengers

The Insight says that we should compare the dream to the story of our life. Let's review our character's current situation and questions, and how his dream spoke to them.

- He was looking for answers about the Manuscript.
- He was feeling lost.
- He was in prison, and feeling caught in spite of his best efforts to choose the right road.
- He felt his only option was to talk someone into letting him go home.
- He was struggling against being caught.

In the dream:

- He was looking for a key in the deep forest (looking for answers about the Manuscript; the forest is a symbol for Peru, spirituality, and being lost).
- He was lost and wishing for some guidance.
- During a thunderstorm (an act of God and out of his control, like his capture), he was washed down a deep ravine and into the river, which was flowing in the wrong direction and threatening to drown him (he felt he had taken the wrong road).
- Despite all his efforts to negotiate the cliffs, he was unable to proceed any further (being in prison).
- He realized the river he was fighting flowed out of the forest and up to a beautiful beach where he saw the key he had been looking for (he comes to the realization that what he needs to know will become clear exactly where he has landed—in prison).

Now, luckily, Pablo asks him a crucial question: "If you had to experience the dream again, what would you do different?" He answers, "I wouldn't resist the water, even though it looked as though it might kill me. I would know better."[13]

It is worth noting that our character feels excited after his comparison of the dream to his life, a sign that he connected to the true meaning of the dream. Instead of merely *analyzing* the elements in the dream, he made a *comparison* of these elements to what was really happening in his life. Pablo kept him on course by suggesting that he start at the beginning, notice the progression of events, and then look at the ending of the dream. You might want to try this method the next time you awaken with a dream or fragment of a dream. Details for dream comparison are given in the section for Individual Study on page 201.

Case History. During the writing of this chapter, we were told about the following dream, which later proved to be prophetic. Christy Roberts, who lives in Kansas City, Missouri, says she had this dream on April 4, 1993: "I had just gotten laid off my job in early 1993. I was trying to get another job in music promotion, when I had the following very vivid dream: I saw four dolphins swimming in a tank, like at Marine World. I said to them, 'Hey, guys, come and kiss me.' One by one they came and each dolphin kissed me on the lips. Then immediately I saw written in my dream the date May 19. Even in the dream I thought, 'What does this mean? May 19, but what year?' A few days after that dream, I was coincidentally invited to the going-away party for someone at A&M records. The rumor was that that person was not going to be replaced, but someone told me they were interviewing so I called. I was interviewed by four people, and on May 19 I got the job. It was a year later that I found out that the founder of the company, Jerry Moss, is a big advocate for the dolphins, and helped get the warning labels on tuna cans."

Roberts has since paid more attention to her dreams, and reported that another one came exactly one year from the first on April 4, 1994, that has provided her with a new perspective on how to handle a former personal relationship.

Case History. Robert K., owner of five automotive stores in the Forth Worth, Texas, area, recalls a dream that came the night before he had to make a decision about buying his first store.

"I had just quit working for a national chain of stores and was trying to decide if I should buy my own business. My dad and I were going out to Texas together to look over a store I had helped build four years earlier. The night before we reached Texas I dreamed that he and I were discussing the deal, and we walked out onto the porch of his house back home. Down the block I saw that the church that had always been there had been turned into a Kmart store. I didn't think much about the dream until we went over to the store in Fort Worth, and down the street, in the exact same position as the church in the dream, was a new Kmart, which had not been there four years earlier. I had no knowledge of this and was so amazed at the coincidence of anticipating this that I took it as a major sign that I was on the right track about starting this new business. It solidified what I wanted to do."

In this case, Robert's dream used parallel ideas (talking to his dad about the deal and the identical locations of the Kmarts) to reinforce that he was on the right track.

Checklist for
Engaging the Flow of Evolution

Keep Energy Strong
- Be open and feel love coming in.
- Observe beauty to increase energy.
- Stop as often as necessary to build energy.
- Stay in a state of love as much as possible.

Ask for Answers
- Center yourself in the present.
- Remember your core *life* question (from parents).
- State clearly what your *current* questions are.

- Keep these in the forefront of your attention. Watch your thoughts and dreams.

Stay Alert
- Take an observer point of view as if you are watching a mystery unravel (this helps you to release the need to control).
- Notice if something is brighter or more colorful as a signal to help you make a choice.
- Notice thoughts and hunches (this is information you now need to know).
- Compare your dreams to your present situation and see what they reveal that you are overlooking or missing.
- If you do not understand the information you are receiving or don't seem to be getting any, make sure you are asking the right question. Ask another question.

Probe Coincidences
- Notice how coincidences fill you with energy.
- What is the coincidence bringing into awareness?
- Is there further work to be done with this person?
- If you have a hunch about something or recurring thoughts, become alert for the next coincidence or message. It usually moves you in the direction of the thought or hunch.

Send Energy to Others
- Give your full attention and energy to those you meet because they all have a message for you, and you for them.
- Remember that you don't have to use your control drama to compete for energy.
- Remember that the energy flowing out of you creates a current that pulls energy into you at the same rate, so you are continuously replenished.

SUMMARY OF THE SEVENTH INSIGHT

The Seventh Insight is the awareness that coincidences have been leading us toward the attainment of our missions and the pursuit of our life questions all along. Day to day, however, we grow by understanding and following the smaller questions that are derived from our broader goals. Once we get the questions right, the answers always come through mysterious opportunities. Each synchronicity, no matter how growthful, always leaves us with another prime question, so our lives proceed through a process of question, answer, new question, as we evolve along our spiritual paths. Synchronistic answers come from many sources: dreams, daydreams, intuitive thoughts, and most frequently, other people who feel inspired to bring us a message.

Further Reading

In addition to the excellent books listed in the notes for this chapter, we suggest:

Personal Power through Awareness. Sanaya Roman. HJ Kramer, 1986.

Chi Kung: Cultivating Personal Energy. James MacRitchie. Element Books, 1993.

Illusions: The Adventures of a Reluctant Messiah. Richard Bach. Delacorte, 1977.

The Way of the Peaceful Warrior. Dan Millman. HJ Kramer, 1984.

Codependent No More: Beyond Codependency. Melody Beattie. Harper SF, 1989.

What Do You Say after You Say Hello? Eric Berne. Bantam, 1984.

At a Journal Workshop: Writing to Access the Power of the Unconscious and Evoke Creative Potential. Ira Progoff. J. P. Tarcher, 1992.

INDIVIDUAL STUDY OF THE SEVENTH INSIGHT

Gathering Information to Make a Decision

The next time you need to make a decision about career, home, family, personal growth, relationship, you might want to follow these simple guidelines.

1. Review the checklist above, Engaging the Flow of Evolution.
2. Formulate your current questions and write them on a 3 by 5 card to keep in your pocket or purse. Look at them during the day.
3. Ask for messages.
4. Be especially alert in the seventy-two hours following writing down your questions.
5. Record any messages or unusual happenings in your journal.
6. Notice if objects jump out at you, or if things have a special glow or iridescence.
7. Practice feeling an openness in your body, relaxing tense muscles whenever you think of it.
8. Give energy to those you meet in person or on the phone.
9. Be willing to share your questions if intuitively directed.
10. Watch your thoughts and follow through on decisions you make.

11. If you feel overwhelmed or utterly confused, stop trying to figure things out. Ask, "What do I need right now?"

Trial Runs or Question and Answer—Learning to Read the Signs

Another method you might try is to make a *trial decision* and see what kind of feedback you get. For example, if you want to change jobs, tell your friends and family of your decision to look for something new. Notice what happens. Do you get support from people? Does life flow better in small ways? Does something pertaining to your question arrive in the mail? Do you get little reinforcements from the universe that this is the right decision? Or do you experience small "misfortunes" like stubbing your toe, getting a ticket, losing your wallet, getting sick, or other events that seem to indicate a "no"?

An example of synchronistic signs signifying that something important is afoot comes from a woman who has her own business selling cosmetics. "On the day I had my first appointment with [an important client] I had been playing the opera *Tristan und Isolde* just before I left the house. When I got to her house, she was playing the same opera. There were many other similarities which really amazed me."

However, be careful not to make events more meaningful than they are. The meaningfulness of synchronistic events occur to us almost immediately, and shouldn't require belabored analysis. If you are spending a great deal of energy mentally trying to wrest a meaning from some event, let it go. If there is a meaning trying to come through, you will get other messages. Stay in the moment.

Purpose in Action

The more you integrate and practice the Insights, the more you will grow spiritually. As you increase self-awareness, it will be second nature to take a broader view of events and activities. At any time you can ask yourself:

- What is another possible meaning behind this event or activity?
- How is it related to a larger purpose?
- How am I contributing to others?
- Do I feel energized by this activity?
- How high a priority is this?

The more you exercise this type of reflective information-gathering, the more you will discover about your life purpose. The work you are here to do might not be summed up with a particular title on an office door.

Gratitude and Acknowledgment

When you have a creative breakthrough, acknowledge it and give yourself credit for whatever your part in it was. The more you believe in yourself as being whole, intact, and creative, the more you will feel you are fulfilling your life purpose.

Expressing gratitude for the large and small gifts you receive each day helps you stay tuned to the present, and helps replace habits of worry and pessimism.

Forgiveness

If you are feeling really stuck or locked into a power struggle, step back a little and try to look at the big picture. Ask yourself: Am I willing or able to forgive the people involved, including myself?

Once you make the decision to forgive, it will become clear whom you are forgiving and how to do it.

Getting It Right

Sometimes we fall into thinking that if we can just find that one big answer, or reach that one large accomplishment, miracles will happen and we will have "succeeded." Open yourself to all the weird and wonderful things of your life, and love and accept yourself exactly as you are right now—even if you have never done any of the exercises in this book, analyzed your dreams, or done any journal work!

Taking the Observer Position

Remember that the Manuscript says that daydreams and thoughts come to guide us. When a thought comes, get into the habit of asking yourself why. Why does this thought come now? How does it relate to my question? *Taking the observer position releases our need to control everything and places us in the flow of evolution.*

Attracting Messages

When we try to demand an answer or remain aloof, we create competition between ourselves and others which stops them from giving us a message. To attract more messages, remember to stay open to discovering what wants to happen now. Give others energy and assume that you met them for a reason at this moment. If a coincidence happens, spend a few minutes asking: What just happened? How does it relate to any questions I am asking myself right now? Do I need to follow through on anything from this?

Silver Lining Work

You are not necessarily *dis*engaged from the flow when you have a blowup of some kind. Don't make the assumption that being in the flow is all roses and beautiful music. The Insights tell us that each event has a purpose. To stay engaged in the flow, it will be necessary to pay close attention to events that seem negative. Setbacks, disappointments, frustrations, and even traffic tickets might have an important message for you. Anytime you experience a really unnerving situation, take a few quiet moments to write down your thoughts and feelings about it in your journal. Play around with possible silver linings. Ask yourself:

- How can this loss serve me?
- How does this setback relate to my life question?
- How can I see it in a different way?
- If there is a positive intention in everything, what is positive here?
- What am I really trying to accomplish?

If you feel absolutely stuck, get together with a friend and do your Self-Imposed Obstacles questionnaire (page 96) and come up with some new options—even if they sound ridiculous! Brainstorming for new answers helps unblock fear and usually restores your sense of humor.

Dream Work

If you are faced with a difficult decision, try asking for a clarifying dream each night as you drift off to sleep. To encourage your subconscious to respond, keep your journal and a pen near your bed so you can record dream information. Studies have also shown that meditation the day before dreaming increases dream recall.[14] The following method might be useful, but feel free to improvise in any way that works for you. Answer these questions in your journal:

DREAM COMPARISON

1. What are the main points of the dream?
2. What details seem significant? Why?
3. What is a one-sentence title for this dream?
4. What is a one-word title for this dream?
5. What happens in the beginning?
6. What actions are taken?
7. Who is in the dream?
8. If the people in the dream were parts of yourself, what would they be telling you?
9. What is the overall tone of the dream?
10. How does this dream compare to your life right now?
11. What is the dream telling you about your life that you might be overlooking?

12. What is the outcome of the dream?
13. If you were to live the dream in real life, what would you do differently?

Dreams often tell us the same message in different ways over time. Like intuition they are insistent and persistent. In times of stress or any other time when you desire more information, make a point of writing down nightly dream titles in list form on one page separate from the answers you write to the above questions. The titles alone might give you a clue as to the direction you are moving or the awareness that is breaking through.

An example of dream comparison comes from Micael McCore, who works in the computer industry, and is also a novelist. A recent dream gave him a new surge of energy to continue with his writing:

"I dreamed I held a hummingbird that was flying between my two palms. As I was holding it, it turned into a fluffy animal. There was a woman there advising me. I awoke full of hope and excitement and decided to analyze the dream." Here's what he noticed.

1. What are the main points of the dream? "The hummingbird, the animal, the transformation, and the woman."

2. What details seem significant? Why? "The hummingbird, because I had used it as a detail in my novel to express the beauty of the day. I'd also seen a couple of hummingbirds lately."

3. What is a one-sentence title for this dream? "I capture a hummingbird."

4. What is a one-word title for this dream? "Hummingbird."

5. What happens in the beginning? "I hold the bird (it flies in the space of my two hands)."

6. What actions are taken? "The bird turns into a fluffy animal."

7. Who is in the dream? "Me, a hummingbird, a fluffy

animal, which reminds me of *Star Trek* tribbles [a symbol to him of exponential reproduction], and an advising woman.''

8. If the people in the dream were parts of yourself, what would they be telling you? "That a woman is helping me with this transformation; that I have succeeded in capturing the hummingbird with my art; and that I need to work on creating exponential success (the fluffy animal)—grounding my art.''

9. What is the overall tone of the dream? "Hopeful, energized.''

10. How does this dream compare to your life right now? "I have finished my first novel and now need to publish it, and I've been stuck on this point. I could say that I have been following my 'inner woman' or feminine Muse in spite of the demands of my busy career, and that I have created a living symbol of spirit with my work (the bird) that apparently will 'fly.' ''

11. What is the dream telling you about your life that you might be overlooking? "That maybe I can sell my writing.''

12. What is the outcome of the dream? "Writing success.''

13. If you were to live the dream in real life, what would you do differently? "It seems complete as is.''

STUDY GROUP FOR THE SEVENTH INSIGHT

Session 11

2 hours 30 minutes

Session Purpose: To discuss the Seventh Insight—Engaging the Flow—and practice the concepts of this chapter

Preparation: Bring rhythmic music and a tape recorder, and enough blank sheets of paper for each member.

Check-In

At the beginning of the meeting, everyone can briefly express how they are feeling at the moment. Be brief, but everyone should contribute.

EXERCISE 1. Raise Energy

Time: 5–10 minutes for the music with movement exercise or 15–20 minutes for the Meditation on the Mountaintop

Directions: Decide which energy-raising exercise to do: Meditation on the Mountaintop on page 132 or listening to music for 10 minutes while moving in place.

EXERCISE 2. General Discussion of the Seventh Insight

Time: Keep individual shares brief and to the point of this Insight. When the discussion seems complete, move on to the next exercise.

Directions: Start by having someone read the recap of the Seventh Insight on page 177 and the Checklist for Engaging the Flow of Evolution on page 193. Remember to (1) stay focused; (2) give full attention to those speaking; and (3) speak when the energy prompts. You might want to use the following questions to prompt discussion:

- What stands out for people about this Insight?
- Has anyone experienced being in the flow lately?
- If someone feels "out of the flow," have them look for a purposeful intention or silver lining. Are they really off track or just getting another piece of their puzzle?
- Have the Insights made a significant difference lately in anyone's life?

- Any interesting coincidences or dreams? (Be brief and to the point!) If you wish to work on someone's dream in the meeting, refer to the section of Individual Study above on how to compare dreams to a life situation.

EXERCISE 3. An Intuition Game[15]

Purpose: To practice letting go of control and tuning into intuition by allowing sensations to surface regarding some-one's question

Time: 15 minutes per person and about 20 minutes for group discussion. Keep time and signal 15 minutes per person.

Directions:
Step 1: Pass out sheets of paper and ask everyone to write down one question and fold up the paper so the writing doesn't show. This question is to be some-thing that the person has a strong intention to find the answer to, such as "What can I do to improve my relationship with my husband?" or "What is the best way to look for a better job?" or "Should I repaint the house or just sell it as is?" Be sure that the question is really meaningful at this time. *No one else will see your question.*
Step 2: Choose a partner. Use your intuition.
Step 3: Working with a partner, one person (the an-swerer) will hold the folded paper and concentrate for a few minutes, allowing images, sensations, and feelings to flow into his mind and body without cen-soring what is received.
Step 4: Give feedback by communicating the sensations and impressions to the questioner as they come in. Don't be concerned about what you receive *even if it seems meaningless to you.*
Step 5: The person receiving information can take notes,

as these might be useful in later reflection on the messages. The questioner may or may not reply as he feels inclined. All information is given with the intention of prompting *inner knowing in the questioner*. Obviously the answerer does not even know what the question is, so there is no right or wrong way to do this. Be playful. Make it a game and have fun, staying in a lighthearted mood, but speak softly. Try not to disturb the concentration of others.

Step 6: Signal after 15 minutes, and change partners.

Step 7: When everyone has completed his or her 15 minutes, reconvene into the whole group and exchange impressions of the exercise.

Closing

Ask for support. Send loving energy.

For Next Session
Read the next chapter in preparation for your next meeting.

CHAPTER 8

The Interpersonal Ethic: A New Perspective on Relationships

Here our main character finds Marjorie, and together they make an amazing escape into the house of a woman named Karla, who seemed to be expecting them. Karla explains the Eighth Insight while driving our two adventurers to a safe haven. The Seventh Insight showed how to get into the flow by listening to inner and outer messages. The Eighth is about how to hasten that flow by taking a new approach to others—children, lovers, friends, and strangers.

In this chapter of the novel, our character learns how to find the answers to his current life questions from the people who cross his path. He also becomes aware of the mysterious power that Marjorie seems to hold over his life and how it can stop his evolution.

THE EIGHTH INSIGHT

At this stage of the journey, the Manuscript predicts that the evolutionary pace will increase as people begin to use energy in a new way when relating to others. Since our coincidences usually come to us through others, the Eighth Insight outlines how to enhance these encounters so that information is more readily given to one another. As we learn how to have more conscious relationships, our personal evolution and that of the next generation—our children—will accelerate because we will all be more fully functioning, whole people. This Insight talks about many kinds of relationships, including romantic ones, parent to child, and group dynamics. Some of the highlights of this Insight are:

- We can assist each other in giving and receiving messages by projecting energy. When we uplift one another, we avoid the competition of energy talked about in the Fourth Insight.
- Everyone we encounter has a message for us.
- As we spiritually evolve, we will form conscious groups where we can mutually raise ourselves to a higher vibration or consciousness and access greater wisdom and healing.
- Romantic love retards our evolution when it's used as a substitute for our connection to the universal energy.
- The roots of romantic addiction lie in not having a fully integrated relationship with our opposite-sex parent.
- Platonic relationships with the opposite sex can help us integrate this energy and become whole.
- Becoming a "full circle" with fully integrated assertive and receptive energy allows us to receive universal energy, and this helps us avoid trying to control our partners.
- It's important to take all the time we need to stabilize our channel with the universe.
- To evolve, we will have to recognize and reform our co-dependent ways of relating with others.
- Spiritual evolution will demand that we parent our children so that they become fully integrated, with an experience of constant love and attention to aid their developing connection to universal energy.

How We Can Assist Each Other in Our Evolution

The process of helping each other develop our destinies is outlined in the Eighth Insight as seeing beyond the ordinary self of those we meet. Instead of seeing only the surface personality, the Insight tells us to focus on the unique beauty of each person we encounter, seeing the deeper glory of his or her being. In doing this, we are projecting energy. With this increase of energy coming toward him, the person will be able to experience *being* his higher self. From this higher vibration, he will have more clarity about himself and will be able to tell his truth more easily. Thus messages will be exchanged that help the flow of evolution for both people.

In the novel our character is told, "When the energy goes into [others], it helps them see their truth. Then they can give this truth to you."[1] Feeling this beam of energy opens them up and enhances the possibility that they will know what to say to you. However, this mutual exchange of energy is only possible when there are no hidden agendas or attachments to specific outcomes.

This process has to be learned from your own experience. There are no rules as to how encounters will happen or how they will bear fruit. As you get into the habit of appreciating those you meet or know, you will begin to notice changes in your relationships and your life.

Everyone We Encounter Has a Message for Us

The Manuscript states that there are no chance encounters. Everyone comes into our life for a reason and has a message for us. It's vitally important to remember to stay alert for the people with whom we need to connect. We have already learned how important it is to keep our energy high and

> . . . the Divine whom he thus sees in himself, he sees equally in all others and as the same Spirit in all. Therefore too is a growing inner unity with others a necessity of his being and perfect unity the sign and condition of the perfect life.
>
> SRI AUROBINDO,
> *The Essential Aurobindo*[2]

our life questions in the forefront of our attention. In that state, we will attract those coincidences that we need to evolve.

The Manuscript tells us to watch for spontaneous eye contact with others, or a feeling of familiarity. A person might remind us of someone we know, and this intuition is a prompt to explore the meaning of the connection. What can this person tell us in regard to our current question(s)?

If we do have a conversation with someone who crosses our path and do not see a message pertinent to our current question, it doesn't mean that there was none. It only means that we were not able to bring it forth at that time. If we have repeated encounters with someone, we need to discover the reason behind the coincidence.

As we become more conscious of the opportunities in seemingly chance encounters, we will also have to practice sidestepping control dramas to avoid power struggles that stop the messages from being exchanged. Having learned how to identify (name) the drama and stay centered in the present, we will not assume the matching drama. By looking beyond the drama and sending the person as much energy as possible, we strengthen the possibility of receiving meaningful messages.

Forming Conscious Groups

As we spiritually evolve, we will begin to form conscious groups with like-minded people. Some of you are already doing that by forming your own study groups of the Insights.

Amazing things happen in groups when everyone has the intention to uplift each other. Working together raises us to a mutually higher vibration. There is even greater wisdom and healing available because we become larger than the sum of the individuals.

Becoming a Higher Person. The key to interacting in a group is to not become self-conscious. This process depends on everyone having clear, non-control-drama, energy.

In any group, keep your attention in the present moment, and when you feel the urge to speak, do so. Otherwise, focus on sending energy to those who are moved to speak. In a conscious group, each person will have a portion of the truth at different times and will know when to speak it. Ideas will arrive in an orderly fashion. It will not feel as if you are *thinking* them up, as much as waiting to have them occur.

With a goal of uplifting each other, you avoid the old ways of interacting, such as trying to sound brilliant, concentrating on your own thoughts instead of active listening, being intimidated, or trying to control the group. Everybody will have the experience of being filled with energy and *being their higher self*. They will have sharper intuition and a clearer vision of themselves.

Using Group Energy. Any group that is aligned in its purpose to uplift each other and engage the higher self can achieve amazing creativity. With an informal group of friends, you can begin to bring to the group any problem you are having for healing. *The more specific you can be, the greater chance you'll receive relevant information.* One man who had had prostate trouble for fifteen years asked, "What do I need to know about healing my prostate condition?" Members of the group, who had aligned themselves previously through a brief centering meditation, began to bring through messages such as "You have always been extremely centered on your intellectual prowess. This pain is a physical reminder of your inability to completely accept and use your body and not just your mind" and "You have never allowed yourself to express anger with people outside your family" and "You cut off your feelings, particularly your anger, and minimize everything with sarcasm." Afterward, the group collectively sent him healing energy to use as he saw fit. This brings up the point that energy must be sent as a gift, to be used for the highest good, with no specific outcome.

In your group, encourage members to give as much detail as possible to their area of concern. Think of pain as a homing beacon, pointing to a nugget of stuck energy that has a story to tell.

Certainly, we are not suggesting that you substitute group mind work for qualified medical help. This method is an enhancement to healing procedures and might illuminate supplementary information.

There is more research and literature than can be covered in this chapter to support the idea of healing with focused thought and the efficacy of prayer. Authors such as Michael Murphy, *The Future of the Body*; Deepak Chopra, M.D., *Quantum Healing*; Leonard Laskow, M.D., *Holoenergetic Healing*; Richard Gerber, M.D., *Vibrational Medicine*; and Carl and Stephanie Simonton, *Getting Well Again*, are just a few who have helped bring these ideas to public awareness.

Problems in Groups. As humans evolve, they will learn to master the techniques taught in the Eighth Insight. However, we are still working toward that evolution and might encounter problems as we work together. Remember that any group will have a combination of people with varying control drama tendencies.

If someone has Intimidator or Poor Me energy that monopolizes the group, the group will become fragmented. What to do? Even if the group has a facilitator, it's important for *each* member to stay in touch with his or her feelings. If a person is talking at great length or dwelling on personal issues for an inappropriate amount of time, others must be willing to point out in a loving way that the energy seems to have become stuck. The overall objective is to let the group energy stay fluid so that messages may be exchanged. Ask others if they feel the energy needs to start moving again, or in a new direction. Keep the issue as open and overt as possible and stay alert for a message within this "problem." There is a tendency for Aloof people not to speak up, and this might be a good opportunity for those people to practice verbalizing their thoughts.

If there is someone in the group who is not accepted by the others, there will be a tendency to focus on his or her irritating traits. Instead of seeing the deeper beauty of the person, which would give him energy, we actually drain his energy and do him harm when we dwell on the negative traits. If this person has a particular trait, such as being critical of others, then he is there to point out to the group their own potential for being critical. Each person has a message. If the group can talk about their feelings compassionately with the other person present, and process within the group, there is a chance for growth for all concerned. If, however, the person continues to bring down the energy of the group, then it is within the group's rights to ask the person to leave.

Becoming Addicted to the Energy from Romantic Love

Up to this point in the novel, our character has been steadily increasing his ability to evolve. However, because he has not yet stabilized his channel to the universal energy, he is still vulnerable to trying to get energy from the opposite sex—in this case, Marjorie. In the novel, he experiences such expanded energy as: "A ripple of passion filled my body." "I felt changed, energized, when she was around."

"My body pulsated." "I couldn't believe the amount of energy I felt in her presence and when she touched me." Think back to the last time you had that feeling!

The Eighth Insight reminds us that each of us can delay our evolution if we become addicted to getting energy from another person, instead of from our own divine connection within. For example, in the heightened state of "falling in love," we feel energized and expanded. Suddenly everything seems special. Colors are brighter. We feel smarter and more attractive. Life has new promise. Wanting more of this buoyant energy, we decide we must have this magical person in our life in order to keep the connection to this feeling.

When we limit our energy flow to this one person, we disconnect from our universal source and expect everything to be satisfied by the other person. These expectations sooner or later drain both people, and the old competition for getting energy begins again. Like hungry infants we want our needs satisfied. We focus on the other person as the source of our problem and use our control dramas to intimidate, interrogate, become aloof, or cry Poor Me. Judging and blaming, we feel that we must have chosen the wrong person. If only we had chosen a better partner—someone who would automatically notice and satisfy our every need—we would not be having this problem.

Childhood Roots of the Magical Romance

A child is archetypally both male and female energy. Ideally, he or she will be nurtured by both parents' energies until he or she is independent enough to receive energy directly from the universe, which is already a union of male and female.

Usually a child identifies more easily with the same-sex parent, whose energy is easier to integrate than that of the opposite gender. For example, a young girl will resonate with the feminine qualities in her mother and will instinctively be drawn to her father in order to complement her own sex and make her whole. Doing this makes her feel complete and euphoric. The reverse is true for the male child.

At first she sees her father as magical and omnipotent. She thinks this energy exists outside herself and wants to possess him and direct and command that wonderful energy. As she matures, and with his help, she outgrows her child's view and sees who he really is, with all his abilities and limitations. By true identification, she can find this realistic energy within herself. In the ideal world, both the child's parents give her attention and energy, which allow her to believe that she will always have enough. She does not need to develop control dramas to get it. The experience of enough energy creates the belief that she is self-sufficient and in charge of herself. This belief allows an easy transition from receiving energy from adults to receiving energy directly from the universal source. Often, however, families are not always able to provide enough attention for each child. In this case, she must compete for emotional energy. If she is further neglected or criticized, she feels drained and struggles for attention through the control dramas.

With an absent or intimidating father, she does not complete the important psychological process of integrating her male side. Mistakenly she assumes that the only way to get male energy is to sexually possess it. Therefore, this missing piece becomes the magnet for the addictive relationship. She is like one-half of a circle, stuck at the stage of looking for the other half in the outer world. This is how the addictive or codependent relationship is born.

The Match. In his book *Getting the Love You Want: A Guide for Couples* psychologist Harville Hendrix describes the process of the search for the ideal mate as a search for a certain blend of traits he calls the *imago.* He claims that each of us seeks the familiar mix of both positive and negative characteristics with which we were raised by our caretakers. Every significant detail of how we were talked to, touched, and taught, as well as the physical, emotional, and mental attributes of our parents, is recorded in our brain. As we meet people, we are drawn to those who most closely resemble this early picture in our unconscious. Hendrix says, ". . . no matter what their conscious intentions, most people are attracted to mates who have their caretakers' positive *and* negative traits, and, typically, the negative traits are more influential."[3]

The Link to Survival. The wounds we received, the negative experiences, are deeply etched into our subconscious. Because the composite pattern of traits was constructed in childhood when we depended so heavily on our parents, the deepest part of our brain connects *all* positive and negative traits to our survival. Therefore, when we meet the irresistible someone who matches our inner picture, we begin to think our life depends on her or him.

Filling the Void. Not only are we attracted to the other person because of the fit to our original caretakers, but the psyche is attempting to fill the void left by the opposite-sex parent. The drive to recover the missing, but necessary, part of our self fuels the addiction. Not only do we seek the complementary sexual half from childhood, but we tend to attract our missing complementary traits. For example, a person who is cautious and somewhat methodical might be dazzled by another who is a decisive, competitive risk-taker. Suddenly he can envision himself with more options and support in making changes. *Instead of developing these traits in himself, he links himself to another who exhibits them.* According to Hendrix, "We enter the relationship with the unconscious assumption that our partner will become a surrogate parent and make up for all the deprivation of our childhood. All we have to do to be healed is to form a close, lasting relationship."[4]

Healing the Wound. It's no secret that romantic love is not founded on logical thinking. If we were logical, we would choose people who are unlike the negative aspects of our parents and could compensate for our early wounds. However, the drive to gain energy and become whole is not a conscious choice, as much as it is an unconscious need. If we view this drive as an attempt to heal the old wounds, then our attractions might make more sense. Hendrix writes:

> The part of your brain that directed your search for a mate, however, was not your logical, orderly new brain; it was your time-locked, myopic old brain. And what your old brain was trying to do was re-create the conditions of your upbringing, in order to correct them. Having received enough nurturing to survive but not enough to feel satisfied, it was attempting to return to the scene of your original frustration so that you could resolve your unfinished business.[5]

Platonic Relationships

The Eighth Insight suggests that if we have not had positive parenting with healthy role modeling, then we must strengthen our opposite-sex energy by creating conscious, platonic relationships. Getting to know how someone of the opposite sex feels and thinks helps *us* achieve integration and wholeness. This is best done with someone who is willing to reveal himself honestly and who is conscious of his own evolution. This helps us break our own projection of what we *think* the opposite sex is all about.

Developing platonic relationships is often easier for single people, and more difficult for those in committed relationships. It is very important that any pursuit of platonic friendships be fully discussed with your spouse or partner, if you have one. Sometimes working with your partner to improve your relationship must take priority. If problems in communication arise, both members of the partnership might benefit by working with a professional counselor.

> The longer you are not in a relationship, the more intimacy deprived you become. The more intimacy deprived you become, the more vulnerable you are to the type of person that can set you off.
>
> TERENCE T. GORSKI,
> *Getting Love Right*[6]

Do you have satisfying friendships with people of the opposite sex? Or do you perhaps feel that these are a less important priority if they don't lead to a sexual relationship? Are your platonic relationships with the opposite sex limited to the spouses of your friends?

The Manuscript suggests that we should resist the romantic "fall" into love, and get to know the other person first without the sexual component. Getting to know well a person of the opposite sex helps us keep our own center. Once we've established true compatibility, we will be more likely to create a lasting relationship.

The Full Circle

The Eighth Insight also tells us that in addition to being comfortable with the opposite sex, we need to be able to experience well-being, and even euphoria, when we are alone. We already saw in the Fifth Insight how our character felt when he connected with energy on the mountaintop. When we are able to stay consciously in the flow of universal energy on our own, we have moved into the unified state of both male and female energy. We have become the whole circle—from within.

> When I am alone the flowers are really seen. I can pay attention to them. They are felt as a presence.
>
> MAY SARTON,
> *Journal of a Solitude*[7]

How do you feel when spending time alone? What do you typically do when you are alone? Do you tend to refresh your energy in solitude or in the company of others? When was the last time you felt genuinely happy when you were alone?

Stabilizing Our Connection to Our Inner Center

This part of the Insight says that as we begin to evolve we automatically receive our opposite-sex energy. However, we have to be careful. The integration process takes time to become established, and if someone comes along who seems to offer this energy directly, we are likely to shift all our attention to him. Once again cut off from our inner center, we regress to controlling behavior. Once we are stabilized, we won't be susceptible to abandoning our true source.

Have you ever lived alone for any period of time? How long? Do you have a method for keeping your inner center? Those who sew, paint, write, tinker, exercise, or meditate know how nourishing it is to spend time with oneself.

Stabilizing your channel requires listening to your inner guidance and feeling your feelings. Stabilizing is linked to self-worth and self-acceptance, and the release of constant negative thoughts. Stabilizing means that you can recognize control dramas before you are caught up in them. You are able to ask for support from the universe without expecting someone else to take care of you.

> When you love someone you do not love them all the time, in exactly the same way, from moment to moment. . . . We have so little faith in the ebb and flow of life, of love, of relationships . . . the only real security is not in owning or possessing, not in demanding or expecting, not in hoping, even.
>
> ANNE MORROW LINDBERGH,
> *Gift from the Sea*[8]

What Is Codependency?

Relationships that are based on control and unconscious drives and needs are the target of the Eighth Insight. In the late 1970s the word "codependency" first came into use to describe someone who lived with or was involved with an alcoholic. The codependent was the person who tried to manage and control an inherently out-of-control situation. Since that early definition was made, the term "codependency" is often applied to a greater range of relationships than just the chemically addictive one. Now we can say that our entire society verges on being codependent. Certainly, much has been written about how this attitude shapes our institutions and corporations.

Many people ask, "How do I know if I'm codependent? Maybe I'm just concerned about someone and want to help them."

Codependent Behavior. The main indicator of codependency is focusing more attention on the actions and feelings of another person(s) than you do on yourself, and feeling that you have to control everything that happens. When your thoughts are dominated by what other people are doing, you are not, by definition, centered in your own inner process. If your energy level fluctuates based on what others do or say, you might be codependent. If you feel you have to monitor everything and make it work, you might be codependent.

When you are struggling to control, you are not allowing the synchronicities of the universe to help you to develop. For example, one woman revealed, "My husband was always the flamboyant type and didn't have time for mundane things like paying bills and taking our dog for a walk. I felt like somehow it was more important for me to take care of these 'little' things, so that he would not feel tied down. There were many times when I felt I couldn't take the time to go out with my own friends because I knew he'd want me to be home when he got there. Now I see how I was doing these things to keep him from leaving me, and in the process I just gave over my own life. I kept waiting for the time when he would settle down, and he never did."

A man who lived with a woman for five years said, "I really became obsessed with everything she did. I wanted to know exactly when she'd be home. I hated her taking night classes and really got on her case for taking some weekend seminars. Whenever she was not with me I felt abandoned, but never would admit that. I had to make her wrong—just for living her life."

A fifty-five-year-old woman had this to say: "My mother always called me her best friend, and I kind of took care of her from the time I was about seven. She was moody, and drank in the evening until she fell asleep. It was only then I felt I could read my books or call a friend. I went through college, but I called home every day and felt very anxious when she started to have bad health. I married a man who was very much like her, and then I had two of them to worry about! All my life I've felt like something was breathing down my neck. I always just felt like I was waiting to have my life. The idea that I'm now free to do anything I want is almost threatening. I've been in therapy for a year now and have lately been intrigued by a couple of coincidences. I think they are pointing me in the direction of starting my own pet grooming business, which I've always wanted to do."

Themes of Codependency. These stories illustrate some common elements of imbalanced relationships:

- The focus is entirely on the actions of another person.
- There is need for energy from the other.
- Control is a major behavior.
- The codependent's own life is somehow on hold or stuck.
- The person has lost sight of his own goals.
- The relationship has rigid roles and expectations.
- The feeling of being drained is strong.

> . . . the surest way to make ourselves crazy is to get involved in other people's business, and the quickest way to become sane and happy is to tend to our own affairs.
>
> MELODY BEATTIE,
> *Codependent No More*[9]

The Eighth Insight is very clear in stating that in order for us to move ahead in our evolution we have to be willing to recognize where we have these codependencies and be willing to change our connection to these people. For more suggestions on how to recognize and work through codependency in relationships, please review the Individual Study section later in this chapter.

True Romance

What will it feel like when we're ready to have a romantic relationship? As the Insight has told us, we have no hope of having one that will not sooner or later turn into a power struggle until we have done our psychological healing work and live from our spiritual connection. You will be much closer to having the relationship you want if you:

- can live satisfactorily without a relationship
- don't try to fill yourself up with energy from another person
- don't need to control the actions of the other person
- know how to stay centered in your own energy
- honestly know what you are feeling
- communicate without blaming and manipulating
- don't use your control drama
- can stay detached from your lover's problems
- are open to the messages of coincidences
- feel comfortable being both assertive and receptive
- can work toward your own goals

Parenting

"Boy, I love my new paint set." Six-year-old.

"And I just love this big mess you made. Get to your room this minute, and don't leave till I tell you to leave." Mom.

The Need for Unconditional, Available Energy. The Eighth Insight stresses that children, as the end points in evolution, need unconditional energy flowing toward them in order to evolve. In order to thrive, they need to be around adults who can give them physical, emotional, and mental nourishment. As

> A good relationship has a pattern like a dance and is built on some of the same rules. The partners do not need to hold on tightly, because they move confidently in the same pattern, intricate but gay and swift and free . . . to touch heavily would be to arrest the pattern and freeze the movement, to check the endlessly changing beauty of its unfolding. . . . they know they are partners moving to the same rhythm, creating a pattern together, and being invisibly nourished by it.
> ANNE MORROW LINDBERGH, *Gift from the Sea*[10]

the Insight points out, draining their energy while correcting them creates control dramas. To develop into successful adults themselves, they require one-on-one interactions with people of higher levels of maturity. Children learn to trust the world and their own place in it when they are spoken to honestly and included in conversations and decision-making appropriate to their level of understanding.

The problems that children are experiencing today are the outgrowth of a profound change in parenting. In the past six decades, the urbanization of our society has completely altered the foundation of how children learn to become adults. Up until the 1930s, children were predominantly raised in families with a range of adults at various stages of life—uncles, aunts, cousins, parents, and grandparents—

spending as much time as three to four hours together. About 70 percent of children were raised in the country. They worked alongside parents and participated in the daily matters of life. Today the interaction between child and parent has been reduced to a few minutes, and this is often mainly spent in assigning tasks or negative and accusative dialogue ("Where have you been?" "Why don't you do your homework?" "Put away your clothes"). In many cases, the child does not feel unconditional love or acceptance, and, at best, must compete for his harried parents' attention.

In the book *Raising Self-Reliant Children in a Self-Indulgent World* authors H. Stephen Glenn and Jane Nelsen help identify the roots of our current dilemma: "Research is now confirming that dialogue and collaboration form the foundations of moral and ethical development, critical thinking, judgmental maturity, and teaching effectiveness. Conversely, lack of dialogue and collaboration between the more mature and less mature threatens the bonds of closeness, trust, dignity, and respect that hold our society together."[11]

Echoes of the Seventh Insight, these ideas reiterate the importance that children must learn from adults, and that we must be willing to give them one-on-one attention.

Self-Worth. Not only are children often left to fend for themselves as parents work, but their self-esteem also suffers from a lack of meaningful activity. In previous times, boys and girls had jobs to do that were important contributions to the overall maintenance of the family. Gardening, tending animals, cooking, washing and hanging clothes, caring for siblings, and cutting hay were activities that had consequences if they were not done. Doing them automatically built a sense of competence and taught the value of following through.

Today's children are too often raised in a passive way with little or no opportunity to find their identity and recognize their talents before they are thrust out into a society that is increasingly more specialized and technical. Through television, films, and video games they participate in life only as spectators or consumers of entertainment. Their ideas about problem-solving and coping with life are learned from larger-than-life heroes who plunge through experiences with arrogance, violence, and magic.

In the past, with an extended family, children had more opportunities for learning about the opposite sex and integrating both sides of their nature. Without these options children turn away from inadequate adult connections toward their peers, in whose midst they feel significant and energized. However, they cannot learn how to be an adult from those who know no more than they.

In many ways it seems as if the causes of delinquency, violence, and intellectual deterioration are mysteriously beyond our control. But if we are willing to give the time and energy to the proper nurturing of children, to support their evolution toward wholeness, the Eighth Insight predicts that we will greatly reduce the dis-ease of our current society. What we must share with our children is our own spiritual process—teaching them our own understanding of the world. After that, we need to let them go on to their own path. At times, it may look as if they are going to extremes. However, if we have done our job of helping them believe in themselves and their capacity to live life according to their own values, then we need to trust them to find balance.

The Manuscript reminds us that we are bringing a whole new spiritual generation into the world and that we need to heighten our awareness of the spiritual aspects of parenting. It's important to remember that each child brings in his or her own issues to work through in this lifetime. They are not born to be simply molded by parental influences.

The Manuscript teaches that our new way of parenting is about adding the dimensions that we didn't have when we were growing up. As we learn to work with energy and accept the flow of coincidences and messages, our children will be able to grasp these insights even more quickly because we will be the role models for them. One mother in her late forties said, "I have been studying metaphysics since the sixties and always talked about different ideas with my children—particularly about positive thinking and synchronicity. It was a common thing for us to make a list of exactly the kind of house we would like whenever we had to move. My son is now in his twenties and called me the other day, jubilant about a new apartment that he found. I enjoyed his enthusiasm and asked how he found it, and he said, as if it were the most obvious thing in the world, 'Well, Mom, I just made my list, and I got everything—even a cat door for the cats.' "

According to educators Glenn and Nelsen, there are seven significant factors that are central for children to become successful, productive and capable.[12] These attributes are the *skills* and *perceptions* that a child has:

CHARACTERISTICS OF THRIVING CHILDREN

1. "I am capable."
2. "I contribute in meaningful ways and I am genuinely needed."
3. "I can influence what happens to me."
4. "My feelings are important, and I trust myself to learn from my mistakes. I have self-control and self-discipline."
5. "I can make friends. I know how to speak out, listen, cooperate, share, and negotiate for what I want."
6. "I can be counted on, and I tell the truth. Things don't always go my way, but I can adapt when I need to."
7. "I try to solve my own problems, but I know that if I need help, I'll ask for it."

With such self-perceptions, the child is tremendously advantaged—because he knows that no matter what happens, he has the resources within himself to be a creative problem-solver. These beliefs represent some of the goals of evolved parenting that are touched upon in the Manuscript. By instilling the seven beliefs above in our children we give them the greatest gift possible. When they really believe that they can make choices, learn what they need to know, and change their lives, they will naturally be able to connect with the flow of energy. As they see how energy responds to their intention, they will attract more coincidences for themselves and make decisions based on being in the flow. Filled with energy and a higher degree of trust in themselves and in the universe, they will be more likely to find and fulfill their purpose.

What Adults Can Do Today for Children

We need not wait for a particular day to dawn when we will all begin practicing these new behaviors with children. We offer the following suggestions for parents, but these ideas can be used by anyone. Even if you do not have children yourself, you will, no doubt, have special friends who have children with whom you can become involved.

Assisting Children to Become Whole Adults

• Be there for them. Plan to have only the number of children for whom you can provide consistent, quality one-on-one attention. Remember, your purpose is to give them enough energy to make the transition to wholeness on their own as adults.

• Treat these little people as spiritual beings with a destiny to fulfill. You can give them their start in life, but you cannot control their destiny.

• Give them respect. Speak to them as human beings with a higher self. "Hello, Molly. Looks like you're having fun today. How are you?"

• Acknowledge that children have rights: to know the truth, to be cared for, to be taught how to be an adult.

• Insist on certain behavior that is for their best interest, health, and safety. "We always wear our seat belts."

• Set clear boundaries while they are under your care and supervision. "If something unexpected comes up, be sure to call and let me know, no matter what."

• Be clear about where you stand on issues. For example, "I feel that it's important to remember that other people have a right to live their lives in ways that are different from ours."

• Be open to their individual needs, knowing that they were born with their own issues to work through. Although parenting is the most significant influence on the child, it is still not the only one. One mother told us, "My four-year-old's nursery school teachers think he may need special education because he's not relating to the other kids or communicating easily. I think he is even more withdrawn and shy than I was at that age. My parents were always pushing me to smile more and be more extroverted. They made me feel it wasn't ok to be *me*. I don't want to repeat that cycle."

• Share your own spiritual process as much as is appropriate to their age level. "Mommy needs about fifteen minutes of quiet time right now. I need to sit with my eyes closed and think quiet thoughts."

• Give them explanations of the choices you are currently making, as appropriate to their maturity level. For example, "We're going to be moving to a new town. Let's find it on the map and talk about what we might find there."

• Be open to them modifying your idea of reality—be willing to *learn from them*.

• Discuss family issues or problems. Keeping troubles to yourself denies your child the truth of what is going on and any wisdom you are able to share on the subject. The tone of this kind of discussion would avoid any Poor Me elements and would be appropriate to the age level. For example, "I know you've been asking for new shoes. The reason we haven't bought them yet is that we have only so much money, and most of it is going to taking care of our household. Let's sit down and see how we could save money for the shoes and how long that might take. What kind of shoes did you have in mind?" Bring children into the issue and give them the opportunity to participate in its solution.

• Give children meaningful roles and chores in running the household. Don't do everything for them. Studies have shown that children who experience themselves as capable in handling significant tasks have better health and accelerated development.

• Don't be too quick to rescue. Obviously we're not talking about life or death situations here! But in general, children are far more capable than we give them credit for. Give them a chance to learn from their mistakes, without making them feel stupid or worthless. Encourage them to ask what happened in the situation, what they felt about it or learned, and what they would do differently next time. Refrain from draining their energy and making critical remarks. Acknowledge that life depends on taking some risks and having some failures. Experience is often a better teacher than authoritarian parental explanations.

• Remember that people move ahead to new levels only in a supportive environment. Ridicule, humiliation, and corporal punishment are not acceptable parenting techniques.

• Be open to a child's point of view. Be a good listener and don't assume you know what he's talking about.

• Encourage a sense of humor in your child that is not based on the ridicule of others.

• Give specific praise and encouragement often. "You really are a dependable person. It's great that you get up every morning and get to school on time, and still are able to make your own lunch."

• Don't forget that your children will be important mirrors of your own issues, and be willing to notice how their behavior might be telling you something you need to know about yourself.

• The most important things you can do to support your own and other's children are to listen to them, take them seriously, and acknowledge their personal worth.

Creating Networks to Help Parents

Humans have traditionally been tribal beings, creating communities for survival. The Manuscript predicts that we will evolve more quickly when we connect with like-minded people who are "evolving along the same lines of interest."[13] For the past few decades the nuclear family has been disintegrating, bringing, in many cases, debilitating isolation and fragmentation. To replace the recent tendency toward single parenting, people will need to develop new avenues such as parent support groups and neighborhood systems that foster checking in with each other.

How connected do you feel to neighbors? Other parents? What could you do to increase outside support for you and your children? If childless, how do you relate to children in your neighborhood or family?

> Each day in America: 270,000 guns are carried to school by students; 1,200,000 latchkey children come home to houses in which there is a gun.[14]

SUMMARY OF THE EIGHTH INSIGHT

The Eighth Insight is the awareness that most synchronicity takes place through the messages brought to us by other people and that a new spiritual ethic toward others enhances this synchronicity. If we are not competing with others energetically, and remain connected to mystical energy within, then we can uplift others with our energy, focusing on the beauty on every face, seeing another person's higher genius. The energy we give when we speak to the higher self lifts the other person into a fuller awareness of who they are, what they are doing, and so increases the possibility that a synchronistic message can be conveyed. The uplifting of others is especially important when interacting within a group, where the entire group's energy can enter whoever is intuitively moved to speak. Also important is using this ethic when caring for and interacting with children. To uplift children, we must speak to their higher-self wisdom and treat them with integrity. In romantic relationships, care must be taken that the euphoric love connection does not replace our connection with mystical energy within. This love euphoria always degenerates into a power struggle as both people become addicted to each other for energy.

Further Reading

In addition to the excellent books listed in the notes for this chapter we suggest:

The Numerology Kit. Carol Adrienne. Plume, 1988.

Your Child's Destiny. Carol Adrienne. Plume, 1994.

Men Are from Mars, Women Are from Venus. John Gray. HarperCollins, 1992.

Conscious Loving: The Journey to Co-Commitment. Gay Hendricks, Ph.D., and Kathlyn Hendricks, Ph.D. Bantam, 1990.

The Heart of Healing. The Institute of Noetic Sciences with William Poole. Turner, 1993.

I & Thou. Walter Kaufman and S. G. Smith. Macmillan, 1978.

Love Is Letting Go of Fear. Gerald Jampolsky. Bantam, 1984.

Healing Words: The Power of Prayer and the Practice of Medicine. Larry Dossey. Harper SF, 1993.

The Art of Loving. Erich Fromm, HarperCollins, 1989.

How Can I Help? Ram Dass and Paul Gorman. Alfred A. Knopf, 1985.

INDIVIDUAL STUDY OF THE EIGHTH INSIGHT

Use a New Approach with People

You can begin to use the power of the Eighth Insight immediately. Use the following points as guidelines as you practice this new behavior. There is no one right way to be a fully energized human being, so learn from your own experience!

FEELING ENERGIZED

- Start your day with the intention of being alert for messages.
- Before you leave the house, take 5 or 10 minutes to center yourself, concentrating on your breathing. Imagine yourself filled with light radiating out for at least 1 or 2 minutes. Imagine yourself as part of a circle of incoming and outgoing energy.
- Throughout the day, connect with the beauty in your environment as often as you can.

ENERGIZING OTHERS

- As you meet and talk with people, see beyond their ordinary face, to the glory of their spiritual essence.
- Focus on their unique qualities. See beauty in their face.
- As you listen to them, give them your complete attention.
- Project energy to them as they speak.

- Remember that their higher self has a message for you, and you can assist them in giving it by filling them with energy.

RECEIVING MESSAGES

- Listen internally for any questions or remarks that occur to you to ask others . . . it could trigger an important exchange of information.
- If you feel energized around this person, you probably have an important connection.
- If you feel drained around someone, rethink what this relationship is offering you. Review the codependency themes and warning signs.
- Notice what thoughts occur to you after conversations.
- What changes do you see in your life or your relationships as you practice these new behaviors?

Handling Control Dramas

If someone uses *intimidating* tactics with you in conversation, decline to continue if you are feeling threatened. Under the circumstances there is little chance of a true message being delivered. If appropriate, ask them why they are feeling so angry and tell them they are frightening you. Give them your complete attention and look for the underlying beauty in their nature. Don't assume you have to fix anything for them, but let your intuition guide you to the most helpful action.

If someone uses a *Poor Me* tactic, acknowledge compassionately that they seem to be having a hard time. Explain that you feel they are trying to make you responsible for their situation. Don't feel you need to solve their problems.

Ask them what *they* think they need to do. Support them in finding their own answers with the resources that are available to *them*. Decline to continue the conversation if your energy is going down the drain!

If someone is *interrogating* you, let them know you feel like you're on the spot or being monitored and criticized. Tell them that it's hard for you to have the conversation under these circumstances, and it doesn't work for you. Let them know you'd be willing to continue talking, but you'd like to change the tone, or something else about the interaction. Realize that they are working from an ingrained pattern to get attention, and probably feel like you are withdrawing from their control. If you are really willing to talk to them under changed circumstances, let them know that. If not, you might have to decline talking to them at this point.

If someone is being *aloof* with you, you won't get very far if you begin interrogating them to get them to open up and give a message! However, you might let them know that you feel it's important to talk (if it really is), but you feel they are running away from you. Ask them to express how they feel and how they would like to have the conversation. Recognize that their inner need is to have your energy come toward them, and if you are connected to your own source, you probably will be able to establish a communication. If not, you might have to forfeit the conversation for the time being.

Conscious Groups

Already-Established Groups

All of us who are working with the techniques of the Eighth Insight will be able to take these practices into whatever groups we are already participating in. These could be PTA groups, women's and men's groups, homeowner associations, book clubs, and so forth. If you feel moved to bring these ideas to any group you are in, remember that you can always practice giving and receiving energy on your own, without trying to proselytize others. As it's appropriate, and your intuition will guide you here, you might want to talk with whoever is the facilitator about how you see using these ideas. Let change happen as organically as possible. If you practice appreciating others, you will be a good role model.

Starting a Support Group

If you have an inspiration to start a small group to practice using the Eighth Insight, let your intuition and coincidence guide you to those who are right for it at this time. You can be informal, but it might be helpful to establish a regular meeting day so that people can plan ahead. For example, one group of six people decided to meet every other Friday for a while. They rotated houses each time and chose to have a potluck meal before the session. After dinner they meditated together for 15 minutes, concentrating on raising their energy. Then the meeting was open to whoever felt moved to speak. They used brainstorming as a method to bring messages through on particular problems and issues.

Romantic Relationships

If you have been studying the Insights, you will view romance in a different light than you used to. If you have just fallen in love or are about to, remember that you need to keep your own inner source of energy. Enjoy the wonderful interchange of energy and let your lover know that you are working on having more conscious relationships. As power issues come up, keep in touch with your own feelings and be willing to express them in a loving way. If you are serious about this person, don't hesitate to engage professional counseling to help you clarify issues early rather than waiting for them to go away or become more complex. Be alert for messages and coincidences that will show you the next steps.

Platonic Relationships

Be open to developing deeper platonic friendships. Spend some time with a friend of the opposite sex that you'd like to know better. Suggest going somewhere in nature where you can share peacefulness and beauty. Talk to each other about how it was to be a girl or boy in your families. If you like writing in your journal, you might want to describe your feelings being with this person, any messages he or she gave you, and what surprised you about him or her.

Warning Signs of Codependency

As you evolve, particularly in the beginning, you must continually test yourself on where you are placing your focus, in order to keep your spiritual center. Ask yourself:

- Am I constantly thinking about another person?
- Am I trying to get the attention of someone else all the time?
- Do I attract needy people?
- Do I get self-worth from solving problems for others?

- Do I minimize my needs and wants?
- Do I often defer my plans?
- Am I always checking up on others?
- Does the behavior of someone else make me try to control the situation and make up for that person's problems?
- Do I feel bad because of what others do?
- Am I involved in a power struggle with someone?
- Do I feel depressed when I'm alone? Do I avoid spending much time alone?
- Can I stay clear about my own goals?
- Do I dismiss my own coincidences when I am in a relationship so that I won't upset the status quo?

There are no easy answers for making transformations. If you feel that a relationship with a parent, child, spouse, or friend is dominating your life, you can make changes no matter how long this relationship has been going on. Some of the things you can do are:

- Read some of the books on relationships we have mentioned.
- Keep the issue out on the table. Be willing to feel your feelings, such as despair, fear, anger, and resentment.
- Consider taking some time apart to get to know yourself.
  If you have been married for a long time, this might be a very charged issue. Many times, a spouse is already withdrawing into separate activities to distance him- or herself from the other partner. Since codependency is complex, it's best to work through changes with a qualified therapist.
- Practice detaching your energy from the other. This doesn't mean that you won't care about or love the other person, but you will need to experience yourself separately for a while. Remember that you cannot solve another's problems or live his or her life.
- Practice the energy-building exercises throughout this book.

- Begin to notice any coincidences that support your new sense of yourself.
- Set some goals for yourself. Start small at first.

Stopping codependency begins with recognizing it and having a willingness to grow beyond old limitations. However, breaking deep-seated patterns is best done with the help of a qualified therapist or counselor. Additionally, much support can be gained through self-help groups based on the Alcoholics Anonymous program, such as Codependents Anonymous (CODA).

Being with Children

Love and respect children, treat them as equal human beings, and tell them the truth. If you have no children of your own, ask yourself if you would sincerely enjoy spending time with kids. If you really desire this, ask for universal energy to provide the perfect opportunities. You might have friends who would love a weekend away if you are willing to be a parent for one or two days. There are many wonderful organizations that would welcome a caring adult who is willing to volunteer quality, consistent time.

STUDY GROUP FOR THE EIGHTH INSIGHT

Session 12

2 hours 30 minutes

Session Purpose: To discuss the various themes of the Eighth Insight, and to continue practicing conscious group techniques

Check-In

At the beginning of the meeting, everyone should express how they are feeling at the moment. Be brief, but everyone should contribute.

EXERCISE 1. **Raise Energy**

Time: 5–10 minutes for the music with movement exercise or 15–20 minutes for the Meditation on the Mountaintop.

Directions: Let the group decide which energy-raising exercise they would like to do: Meditation on the Mountaintop on page 132 or listening to music for 10 minutes while moving in place.

EXERCISE 2. **General Discussion of the Eighth Insight**

Purpose: To allow members to share their ideas about the themes of the Eighth Insight, and *to practice being a conscious group*

Time: The rest of the meeting. There is a wealth of topics to be discussed, and you might want to spend one or several meetings on these themes if people are interested.

Directions: Read the discussion of the Eighth Insight on pages 207–208.

Practicing Being a Conscious Group

• Speak when you feel inspired and project energy when others speak.
• In this session, it will be particularly useful to begin to

use all the Insights and create a strong, cohesive group. In order to do that, it will be necessary to stay alert for the times when someone might dominate the group. Become aware when energy is not being allowed to shift. If intuitively directed to speak, gently express how you think energy has gotten stuck. If and when this occurs, the group might want to process whatever issues this action provokes. For example, in one group, a woman was clearly using a Poor Me drama to talk at great length about a personal problem with her goddaughter. Her self-deprecating remarks and exaggerated guilt and suffering were obvious attempts to draw everyone's sympathy and elicit advice. Another member said, "Excuse me, Vera, but I'm having trouble concentrating on what you're saying. I know this situation is really hard for you, but I'd like to open up the discussion and let everyone give you some feedback, and then move on to something else." Vera's Poor Me drama, once it is overtly stated, will be defused. However, in this case, Vera's covert demand for energy was not easily resolved, and she continued to sulk throughout the meeting. Remember that others can only grow at their own pace.

• In your group, you will have many types of interactions. Stay as close as possible to the advice of the Eighth Insight about keeping issues clearly out in the open, using gentleness and compassion and setting firm boundaries within the group.

• Look at all issues as something you need to learn or pay attention to in your own life.

• Your group will bear some resemblance to all the other relationships in your life, and even mirror some old issues from your childhood. For example, someone in the group, whether male or female, might carry energy similar to that of one of your parents. Irritation with someone might mirror your own irritation with yourself in the same area.

Discussion of the Themes of the Eighth Insight

If your group has ten or more members, you can break up into smaller groups of two or four and discuss themes you are particularly interested in:

- How romantic relationships are interfering with your evolution.
- How to develop platonic relationships. Members might want to make future plans to spend time together on an "adventure."
- What is codependency? Where am I being codependent?
- How am I working on becoming a "full circle" and integrating male and female energy?
- How can I bring more consciousness to my workplace?
- Current parenting issues in my family.

Remember that no matter what group you find yourself in, each person has a message for you. Uplift them to their higher self and encourage them to find their message for you. What information relevant to your current life questions did you receive?

Creating a Healing Circle

Your group might wish to have a healing circle at a separate meeting, since there might not be enough time after the discussion of all the topics above. Healing circles can be a wonderful outgrowth of your study group on a continuing basis.

The circle is best done with groups of four to twenty. If you have more members than twenty, form separate groups. Have everyone read through the following instructions and then start the meditation:

Step 1: Center with a 5-minute silent meditation. Continue with eyes closed or open. Sometimes it is easier to bring through intuitions with closed eyes.

Step 2: Affirm that whatever information is brought forth is for the person's higher good.

Step 3: Let whoever feels so inspired start.

Step 4: State your issue with as much detail as you feel comfortable sharing. Remember, the more details, the deeper will be the group interchange.

Step 5: Everyone will focus on the person as he or she speaks and then wait for an inspiration to respond to his or her issue.

Step 6: When the intuitive flow seems to have stopped naturally, send neutral, healing energy to the person. If he or she has asked for the healing of a physical condition, visualize the area, such as an organ, and focus on sending light into that place.

Step 7: When complete, move on to the next person who is inspired to speak.

Closing

Ask for support, and send energy to each person.

For Next Session
- Read the next chapter on the Ninth Insight.
- Optional: Make appointments to get together for platonic "adventure" dates.
- Optional: Explore ways you can spend fun time with children you know, or investigate volunteer agencies who work with children.
- Write in your journal about any messages you received at this session.
- Explore any coincidences that have occurred.

CHAPTER 9

The Emerging Culture

In the last chapter of The Celestine Prophecy *the Ninth Insight of the Manuscript is discovered in the ruins of the Celestine Temple and falls into the hands of the intractable Cardinal Sebastian. Our character reunites briefly with Dobson, Phil, and Father Sanchez and eagerly absorbs the teachings of the Ninth Insight. This Insight describes how culture will change in the next millennium as a result of conscious evolution. As the tension increases with the impending destruction of this important document, our character and Father Sanchez, led by their intuition, come face-to-face with the Cardinal. However, Sanchez fails to convince him of the truth of the Manuscript. Later, at the Celestine ruins, the two men find Julia and Wil, and the group raises their vibration to a degree where they become invisible to a pursuing cadre of Peruvian soldiers. All except Wil become frightened, lose their vibration, and are then captured. Although both adventurers are released, our character is eventually captured once again. He remains a prisoner, disheartened, until he unexpectedly encounters Father Carl. With the apparent destruction of all copies of the Manuscript, Father Carl urges him to pass on the message of the Prophecies. At that moment, his captors free him, hand him a ticket back to the States, and tell him never to return.*

THE NINTH INSIGHT

The Ninth Insight is an outline of where the human race is heading in the next one thousand years—a vision of the kind of culture that will be possible as we merge all of the previous eight Insights into one conscious way of being. The role of this Insight is to help create the confidence we need to continue on our path of spiritual evolution.

The Ninth Insight underscores the point that the more we can connect with the beauty and energy around us, the more we evolve. The more we evolve, the higher we vibrate. Ultimately, our increased perception and vibration will allow us to cross over the barrier between our physical world and the unseen world from which we came and to which we will return upon physical death. The Ninth Insight inspires us whenever we doubt our own path or lose sight of the process. It tells us that we are evolving toward the day when we can reach a vibrational heaven that already exists right where we are.

How We Get There. The way to accomplish this future life is by living all eight Insights. The Manuscript began by showing us the First Insight, which is to recognize that **the universe mysteriously presents the coincidental opportunities to move us toward our destiny**. The Second Insight allows us to see the past, and recognize that **we, collectively, are becoming aware of our essentially spiritual nature**. The Third Insight shows us that **the universe is pure energy that responds to our intention**. The Fourth Insight demonstrates that **humans mistakenly try to get energy from each other**, which results in a sense of scarcity, competition, and struggle. The Fifth Insight describes **how a mystical connection with universal energy feels and how it expands our perspective of life**, giving us a sense of lightness, buoyancy, and total security. The Sixth Insight helps us to break free of **our controlling dramas** and to define our current life quest by looking at **our parental heritage**. The Seventh Insight sets in motion the evolution of our true selves by showing us

how to ask questions, receive intuitions, and find answers.
The Eighth Insight gives us the key to keeping the mystery
operating and the answers coming by showing us **how to
bring out the best in others.** These Insights, when merged
into consciousness, feel like a heightened sense of alertness
and expectation as we evolve toward our true destiny. They
reconnect us to the mystery of existence.

Where We Will Be in the Next Millennium

By living the Insights, the culture will be sustained by its
spiritual connection and will transform rapidly. The highlights of cultural evolution presented in the Ninth Insight
include:

The First Great Shift

• The core change will be the understanding that we are
here to evolve spiritually. As a result of this understanding
there will be **changes in our vibrational frequency**.
• Our **pursuit of truth** will lead us to the new way of life.
• As we reach a critical mass of those who grasp the insights, **information will come in on a global scale**.
• There will be a period of intense **introspection**.
• We have already begun to grasp **how beautiful and
precious the natural world is**, and our understanding of its
spiritual essence will grow, encouraging us to preserve and
revere forests, lakes, rivers, and sacred sites.
• We will not tolerate any **economic activity** that threatens
these treasures.

Unfolding Destiny

• Our need for **meaning and purposefulness** will be met as we thrill to the coincidences and intuitions that light our path.

• In order to listen carefully for each new truth, **we slow down** and become alert for each new meaningful encounter to come along.

• Each time we encounter another person, we exchange our questions and receive **new direction and insights**, significantly altering our vibration.

• As we receive clear intuitions about who we are, and what we're supposed to be doing, **we will begin to change our occupations** in order to continue to grow. People might have several occupations within one lifetime.

• As each individual pursues his own destiny, truth by truth, new intuitions regarding the **solution of social and environmental problems** will occur naturally.

Living on the Earth

• Outgrowing our need for dominating nature, we will **revere the natural energy sources** of mountains, deserts, forests, lakes, and rivers. Within the next five hundred years, forests will be intentionally allowed to mature, and other natural landscapes will be protected.

• Everyone will live as close as possible to the **sacred sites** but will also be within easy travel distance of urban centers of **green technology** that provide for the necessities of life such as food, clothing, and transportation.

• Gardens will be carefully cultivated to **energize plants** for consumption.

• **Guided by our intuitions**, everyone will know precisely what to do and when to do it, and this will fit harmoniously with the actions of others.

The Next Great Shift

• In the next millennium we will **voluntarily limit reproduction** to avoid overpopulation.

• As we understand the true dynamics of the universe, we will see the act of giving as a universal support for everyone. We will understand that **money is another form of energy**. We'll know that it comes into the void created by giving, in the same way that energy flows into us when we project energy out. Once we begin to give constantly, we will always have more coming in than we could possibly give away. As more people engage in this spiritual economy, we will begin a real shift into the culture of the next millennium. Eventually we will have no need for money as currency.

• The **automation of goods** will allow everyone's needs to be met completely, without the exchange of any currency, yet without overindulgence or laziness.

• Once we **release our fear of scarcity and our need to control** so that we can give to others, we will be able to save the environment, feed the poor, and democratize the planet.

• Because of the automation, **everyone's time will be freed up** so that they can pursue other endeavors. We will find ways to further cut our employment hours to pursue our own truth. Two or three people will hold what used to be one full-time job.

• **No one will consume excessively** because people will have let go of the need to possess and control for security.

• The more readily we have energy flowing into us, the more it will **accelerate the pace of our evolution,** and our personal vibrations will increase.

Evolution of Spiritual Doctrine

• Our entire **evolution will be based on spiritual principles**, but the tenets of religions will have to change to include the evolution of individuals. All religion so far has been about humankind finding relationship to one higher source. All religions speak of a perception of God within, a perception that fills us and makes us more than we were. Religion became corrupted when leaders were assigned to explain God's will to people instead of showing them **how to find this direction within themselves**.

• The Ninth Insight mentions that one individual would grasp the exact way of connecting with God's source of energy and direction and would become a lasting example that this connection is possible. Jesus was such a figure in that he opened up the energy until he was so light he could walk on water. He transcended death and was perhaps the first to publicly expand the physical world into the spiritual. **We can connect with the same source** and follow the same path.

• As humans continue to increase their vibrations to a lighter and more purely spiritual frequency, **whole groups of people who have reached a certain level will become invisible** to those who are vibrating at a lower level. It will appear to those on the lower level that the others just disappeared, but the invisible group will feel as though they are still in the same place, only lighter and in spiritual form.

• The ability to raise the frequency to become invisible signals that we are **crossing the barrier between this life and the other world** from which we came and to which we go after death.

• **Reaching heaven on earth** (raising our vibration) is the purpose of human existence and history.

The Case for an Evolutionary Leap

Our present lives and consciousness are part of the bridge to the future. Part of our work as a bridge will be to reexamine the kinds of capacities and abilities the human body has already demonstrated and to open ourselves to accelerating these developments. So far our modern disbelief in anything but the physical aspects of life has limited investigation and development of some of our transcendental capacities.

Toward this end, Michael Murphy's book *The Future of the Body* has pulled together synopses of a broad spectrum of human abilities. From the evidence that has already been reported and documented, Murphy believes that there is a strong case that humans have a huge range of paranormal abilities that, if developed on a large scale by many people, would create a new kind of life on the planet—transcending life as we know it. This idea is also central to the thinking of such evolution visionaries as Pierre Teilhard de Chardin and Sri Aurobindo, to name only two.

Murphy brings to our attention the two epochal events that have already happened that have transcended the primordial development of inorganic matter. The first event was the appearance of life itself. The second was the birth of humankind—with its unique psychosocial characteristics. He writes:

> Inorganic matter, animal and plant species, and human nature, then, can be said to comprise three levels or kinds of existence, each of which is organized according to separate principles. These three levels comprise an evolutionary triad in which the first two have transcended themselves, inorganic elements producing living species, animals giving rise to humanity . . . in each of them there arose a new order of existence.[1]

Based on extensive documentation of transformative capacities in humans and such evolutionary theories as proposed by G. Ledyard Stebbins, Murphy believes that a new level of existence has begun to appear on earth.

The Twelve Attributes Indicating Evolutionary Change in Humans

According to Murphy, there are twelve sets of human attributes that characterize this emergent level of development:

1. Extraordinary perceptions, including apprehensions of numinous beauty in familiar objects, voluntary clairvoyance, and contact with entities or events that are inaccessible to the ordinary senses
2. Extraordinary somatic awarenesses and self-regulation
3. Extraordinary communication abilities
4. Superabundant vitality
5. Extraordinary movement abilities
6. Extraordinary capacities to alter the environment
7. Self-existent delight
8. Intellectual ideas received *tout ensemble* (all at once)
9. Supraordinary will
10. Personhood that simultaneously transcends and fulfills one's ordinary sense of self while revealing one's fundamental unity with others
11. Love that reveals fundamental unity
12. Alterations in bodily structures, states, and processes that support the experiences and capacities above[2]

Many people have already experienced these states or abilities in everyday life, often triggered, involuntarily, by personal crisis. However, as our Manuscript foretells, a growing number of people will be able to manifest these extraordinary states—voluntarily. As we expand and integrate this new level of existence, human life will be drastically altered—albeit by the transcendence of certain habits, such as conflict and control, and by self-mastery. Long the domain of spiritual adepts, the development of metanormal abilities is expanding as people practice meditation, shamanism, the martial arts, movement and breathing techniques, and other inner modes of exploration.

Desert Mystics, Saints, and Shamans

A fascinating repertoire of nonordinary human capacities and abilities has been proclaimed since biblical times, from the healing miracles of Jesus to his reappearance after the Crucifixion and the subsequent phenomena in religious figures: the stigmata of Christian mystics, their luminous auras, the absence of food intake for years, the exudation of holy odors and healing fluids, and telekinesis, or the ability to move material objects without touching them. Cases of prophecy, telepathy, and clairvoyance are reported in many lives of the saints as well as Zen masters, Sufis, yogis, and shamans.

In the 1960s anthropologist Carlos Castaneda exploded the limits of our understanding of the material world with the teachings of shaman Don Juan. Shamanic feats of travel into the underworld, healing, divination, and shape shifting forced us to question and investigate the seemingly unlimited abilities that humans possess. For example, anthropologists have witnessed shamans performing ritual surgeries on their own bodies—with no evidence of pain or subsequent scarring. However, beyond the outer phenomena of shamanism lies the true nature of this ancient practice of healing.

The increasing interest in shamanism corroborates the Manuscript's recognition of the human need for personal experience of nonordinary states of consciousness, and the desire to source oneself from divine energy. Shamanism is the direct experience of spiritual communication with the earth and connects us with nature's wisdom. According to Michael Harner, an anthropologist and one of the leading authorities on shamanism, "Specific techniques long used in shamanism, such as changes in states of consciousness, stress-reduction, visualization, positive thinking, and assistance from nonordinary sources, are some of the approaches now widely employed in contemporary holistic practice."[3] In his book *The Way of the Shaman* Harner describes shamanic methods of healing—no longer limited to a few initiates— that can be learned by anyone interested in pursuing these techniques. Through direct knowledge, a person learns to maintain personal power and move between states of consciousness at will. These ancient worldwide spiritual practices could be vitally important in helping us reclaim a balance with nature.

Strikingly similar phenomena sometimes appear in widely varying disciplines. For example, Catholic saints, Tibetan lamas, and Eskimo shamans have all demonstrated the ability to produce such phenomena as intense internal heat (generating high temperatures in below-freezing weather or in icy seas). Taoist masters and other religious adepts have been seen to shoot straight up in the air or levitate, although as yet there has been no scientific recording of feats of levitation. Hindu saints, able to exist in a catatonic state, have even survived burial for long periods of time. The bodies of other religious figures, such as Paramahansa Yogananda and many Catholic saints, are known to have been incorruptible following death and interment. Religious masters have been observed in two places at the same time (bilocation). Telepathic communication with aboriginal peoples and Amazon tribes speaking only their native language has been experienced by English-speaking explorers.[4,5]

In the past, the Catholic church has conducted extraordinarily thorough investigations and documentation of metanormal capacities and events for the canonization of saints. Since the beginning of this century, there has also been much scientific investigation into the physiological effects of spiritual practices as well as metanormal abilities and conditions. A full treatment of these studies is impossible here, but for those who are interested in specific information, there is no better compendium than *The Future of the Body*, by Murphy, and its reference sources. The data presented, the philosophies and theories explored, all support a thesis congruent with the Manuscript, which is that something beyond the ordinary self influences and energizes us and that the development of various mental, physical, and intuitive capacities "projects a future in which humans might realize extraordinary life upon earth."[6]

Supermind and the Spiritual Age

A major figure in the convergence of Eastern and Western methods, political activist and spiritual leader Sri Aurobindo, shows a profound comprehension of the scope of human evolution. "Man is a transitional being; he is not final. . . . Man in himself is little more than an ambitious nothing."[7]

He describes the upward psychospiritual ascent of humankind as a widening expression, richer, finer, more complex, and luminous with the spark of the divine. He believes that evolution is inherent within nature and unfolds through individual minds, translating the latent unconscious collective thought into awareness and creation of new forms of psychological and social organization. The individual is clearly, in his thinking, the instrument of Spirit. "All great changes therefore find their first clear and effective power and their direct shaping force in the mind and spirit of an individual or of a limited number of individuals."[8]

The first condition for advancement is the readiness of the common mind—or perhaps, in the words of the Manuscript, a critical mass of people resonating to higher guidance. Aurobindo speaks of the heart of man that is "stirred by aspirations," much as the Manuscript describes the inner restlessness in the First Insight. Additionally, the first "essential sign must be the growth of the subjective idea of life—the idea of the soul, the inner being, its powers, its possibilities, its growth, its expression and the creation of a true, beautiful and helpful environment for it."[9] With the increasing application of subjective, or inner-directed, thinking in the world, Aurobindo also, like the Manuscript, presupposes an increase in new scientific discoveries that will "thin the walls between soul and matter."[10] His idea of Supermind is no dry linear concept, but consists of "yet undreamed-of mind-powers and life-powers" that could free humankind from the limitations of time, distance, and the material body. As early as the 1950s he held that these possibilities were not far off. In this development of psychic and spiritual mastery he saw a "profound revolution throughout the whole range of human existence."[11] However, Aurobindo was also convinced that Mind was secondary to the power of the Spirit, which is eternal and original.

As humans evolve toward less reliance on their ego, we begin to achieve a truly spiritualized society. According to Aurobindo, "A spiritualized society would live like its spiritual individuals, not in the ego, but in the spirit, not as the collective ego, but as the collective soul."[12] The first aim in all activities such as art, science, ethics, economics, politics, and education would be to find and reveal the divine Self. He taught that the most important step in our evolution is to become conscious of our inner "seat of truth," to concentrate on its presence, and to make it a living fact. For us to really know our mission on earth, we must be willing to eliminate whatever contradicts our inner truth. None of this is imposed from without—by an authority or by regulation—although self-discipline is absolutely essential if we are to advance.

In a spiritual age, Aurobindo saw the most honored law as the one of growing inner freedom combined with, paradoxically, a growing inner unity with others. Aurobindo's political and spiritual leadership, which grew out of a positive blending of Western and Indian values, exemplifies a philosophy born of his own personal spiritual experiences. A pivotal collaboration extended his views when he met

Mira Richard, a French artist and spiritual seeker who later became known as the Mother. Their work together culminated in the establishment of a nondogmatic, spiritual community founded on the pursuit of changing consciousness and the evolution of humankind. Although such an adventure is fraught with pitfalls, the goal of such a community to live a conscious life is courageous and pioneering.

A New Type of Humanity

At about the same time as Aurobindo was developing his philosophy of evolution, a Jesuit priest and distinguished paleontologist, Pierre Teilhard de Chardin, was busily formulating *his* thesis of evolution. His seminal work, *The Phenomenon of Man*, probes the past strata of physical evidence but concludes that the evolutionary phenomena are processes that can never be adequately understood simply by looking at their origins. We can most clearly understand them by observing their directions and exploring their potentialities.

According to philosopher Sir Julian Huxley, who helped introduce the work of this scientific mystic, Père Teilhard was "deeply concerned with establishing a global unification of human awareness as a necessary prerequisite for any real future progress of mankind. . . ."[13] Theorizing about the development of human consciousness, Père Teilhard visualized the surface of the earth's sphere as an organizing web that allows ideas to encounter one another, generating a high level of psychosocial energy. He saw humanity as developing into a single psychosocial unit, with a collective pool of thought, much like a common head, forging a new evolutionary path. In Huxley's introduction to *The Phenomenon of Man* he underscores Père Teilhard's conclusion: ". . . that we should consider inter-thinking humanity as a new type of organism, whose destiny it is to realize new possibilities for evolving life on this planet."[14] The conditions for this advance of human fulfillment are "global unity of mankind's noetic organization or system of awareness, but a high degree of variety within that unity; love, with goodwill and full co-operation; personal integration and internal harmony; and increasing knowledge."[15] Life "by its very structure, having once been lifted to its stage of thought, cannot go on at all without requiring to ascend ever higher."[16]

What We Are Learning about Other Dimensions

The Manuscript tells us that in the late twentieth century, humans will achieve a new *experiential* understanding of what has traditionally been called mystical consciousness. In Chapter 5 we described some of the altered states reported by athletes as well as spiritual practitioners. From these states of higher consciousness, extraordinary achievements and insights became possible. Murphy describes reports of metanormal occurrences, and although they appear to be spontaneous, they seem to be "(1) triggered by intense discipline; (2) involve a new kind of functioning (a 'new dimension'); and (3) require a focused surrender."[17]

The idea of an afterlife has been part of human culture since antiquity. According to researchers in the realms of near-death and out-of-body experiences, personal consciousness survives the transition that we call physical death. These reports seem to represent a strong case that our consciousness continues to exist without the necessity of a physical body.

The Fifth Insight points out that the ability to reach this expanded consciousness and understanding will become publicized as a way of being that is actually attainable voluntarily. Such pioneers as Robert Monroe, founder of the Monroe Institute in Virginia, apparently have already developed this ability to explore nonphysical dimensions. Over a period of months in 1958, Monroe, a successful businessman, involuntarily began to leave his physical body while remaining conscious. His initial reaction, not surprisingly, was a fear that he was mentally or physically ill. The continued experience of out-of-body activity, however, eventually convinced him that consciousness exists as a continuum, and is the essence of who we are—that the physical body is only the current vehicle of our spirit as it lives and learns in the earth dimension. Subsequently, Monroe wrote three books detailing his experiences and methods for turning speculation and belief into known data that can be verified empirically.

Monroe reports in his latest book, *Ultimate Journey*, that what he calls "the second body" of the out-of-body experience is "part of another energy system that commingles with the Earth Life System but is out of phase with it."[18] This plane of existence is beyond time and space limitations. In this other system, a person's thought creates instantaneous action, whereas our thoughts take longer to manifest in this denser atmosphere of physical matter. As the Manuscript predicts, methods for accessing and entering these other dimensions are already being developed as we begin the twenty-first century. This type of scientific exploration offers virtually unlimited adventure and new perspectives on the nature and purpose of human life, although at this historical point in time, humans are able to understand, or translate, only the portion of this other plane as it relates to our earthly concepts. As information continues to be brought back by many different people, this knowledge will add to the quickening of the evolutionary pace. As the Manuscript says in the First Insight, when we reach a critical mass of humans who realize that we are more than our physical bodies, life will take a very different shape than we know it today.

In Monroe's book he sees consciousness as a continuum, not just arising out of our human physical body, but "a spectrum [which] ranges, seemingly endlessly, beyond time and space into other energy systems. It also continues 'downward' through animal and plant life, possibly into the subatomic level. Everyday human consciousness is active commonly in only a small segment of the consciousness continuum."[19]

According to the information that he and others have received during out-of-body excursions, a human lifetime is exceedingly precious and is undertaken for the purpose of gaining knowledge and experiences that can only be acquired from living in a physical body. Monroe writes: "Every single thing we learn, no matter how small or seemingly inconsequential, is of immense value There—beyond time-space. This is fully understood only when one encounters a graduate of the Earth Life System process of being human who 'resides' in the There. You then know, not just believe, that it is worth any price to be human, and to learn."[20] In our human bodies we learn to direct energy, to make decisions, to know and love others—even to laugh. Through the development of our analytical, linear left brain we further the evolution of knowledge and bring into being the inspirations of the right brain.

If we compare the tremendous changes that have happened in less than a century—for example, in the field of transportation (from the development of the horse and buggy to interplanetary rocketry)—what could we expect of the development of our paranormal abilities? How far can we range within our consciousness?

Research in other dimensions seems to suggest that we cycle through a variety of different lives, gaining more and more experience in our quest for soul development. Therefore, in most cases we might have a life purpose, a goal or mission. It is possible that we receive guidance from a cluster of influences selected from our previous (and future?) lifetimes that appear as intuitions, coincidences, or minor miracles. Usually we have but a vague awareness of our "gifts," talents, and predilections, not realizing any link to a past life.

As foreign as these ideas are to some of us, they might

be part of the evolutionary potential that exists for humanity. How much more could be actualized if we worked directly to access these deeper layers of experience? As with the near-death experiencers, Monroe and his colleagues and students report that their explorations of these nonordinary states directly change their perceptions of themselves and expand the limits of their beliefs. Continued direct communication with other levels of existence is sure to be a new frontier of development—much like outer space—as humans evolve. As more of us turn our attention to the principles of higher consciousness, the richer will be the soil of consciousness in which we can all grow.

> Don't worry about saving
>   these songs.
> And if one of our instruments
>   breaks
> It doesn't matter.
> We have fallen into the place
>   where everything is music.
> — RUMI, 13th-century
>   Sufi poet

In *Heading toward Omega* Kenneth Ring quotes from a speech given in Chicago in 1980 by John White, a primary spokesman for the view that a new form of life is appearing on the planet:

> *Homo noeticus* is the name I give to the emerging form of humanity. "Noetics" is a term meaning the study of consciousness, and that activity is a primary characteristic of . . . the new breed. Because of their deepened awareness and self-understanding, they do not allow the traditionally imposed forms, controls, and institutions of society to be barriers to their full development. Their changed psychology is based on expression of feeling, not suppression. The motivation is cooperative and loving, not competitive and aggressive. Their logic is multilevel/integrated/simultaneous, not linear/sequential/either-or. Their sense of identity is embracing-collective, not isolated-individual. . . . [21]

Since antiquity, humankind has been tapping into the deeper layers of consciousness for the purpose of healing, divination, contacting departed loved ones, and searching for the meaning of life. Although, as the Manuscript tells us, our culture is becoming more and more interested in exploring all realms of the universe, the ancients also had their "technology" for spiritual connection and investigation. One such technique, called mirror gazing, has been described by physician Raymond Moody, who is the author of several books on near-death experiences. Research on ancient Greek spiritual practices and methods of divination and visionary encounters with departed loved ones led to his latest book, *Reunions*. His contemporary work based on these contemplative practices appears to re-create the same results of accessing other realms of consciousness, as achieved by ancient cultures. This type of work, while of great value in helping people with grief-related issues, might also offer another opportunity to experience and study consciousness beyond the physical body. The popularity and increasing acceptance of such research and books as Murphy's, Monroe's, Moody's, and many others suggest that our culture might be approaching a new evolutionary juncture.

What, Where, When, and How Do We Reach Heaven on Earth?

The Ninth Insight reminds us that we are here to reach heaven on earth. From this historical perspective of planetary crisis, the idea of heaven might seem more like a fairy tale beneath which lurk disease, crime, poverty, war, and despair—a despair that deep-ecology author Joanna Macy describes in *World as Lover, World as Self*: "We are bombarded by signals of distress—ecological destruction, social breakdown, and uncontrolled nuclear proliferation. Not surprisingly, we are feeling despair . . . what is surprising is the extent to which we continue to hide this despair from ourselves and each other."[22] According to Macy, our religious and social taboos against "loss of faith," and the fear that our species might not survive, lead to psychic numbing. Paralyzed, we filter out negative information and lose our capacity to creatively address problems.

> Come, come,
> Spirits of magic,
> If ye come not,
> I shall go to you.
> Awake, awake,
> Spirits of magic,
> I am come to you.
> Arise from sleep.
> DAVID PERI and
> ROBERT WHARTON,
> "Sucking Doctor—
> Second Night"[23]

Since despair, fear, and denial happen within individuals, part of the evolutionary work to be done at this historical point will be to become aware of our own deep feelings about social problems, and work with them. In the same way that we deal with the frozen energy of our control dramas, we must perceive and accept feelings of overwhelming despair, discouragement, or hopelessness in finding solutions to our planetary problems. Naming and validating our experiences will promote a release of creative energy that is otherwise being used for denial.

Learning from Natural Systems

In a talk given in April 1994 Fritjof Capra, author of *The Tao of Physics*, defined the main challenge of our time: to create and nurture sustainable communities. Outlining the eight principles or natural laws of sustainability, he sees them as the basic living pattern by which we can design our future communities.

Natural ecosystems exist as webs, networks of interrelated parts that are multidirectional and nonlinear. They have cycles and they self-regulate by a process of feedback loops.

This feedback creates learning. For example, if we touch fire, we get burned. This is a learning process which creates growth and creativity. Thus an individual, or a community of individuals, can become self-organizing through direct experience and has no need for an outside authority to point out its mistakes. Capra takes the systems point of view: "As soon as you understand that life is networks, you understand that the key characteristic of life is self-organization."[24] This is a new operating principle for our culture, which, since the Middle Ages, has depended on the triumvirate of religion, politics, and science for guidance.

The smooth functioning of the sustained system depends on cooperation and partnership among its parts. Cyclic flow, Capra believes, is even more important than the Darwinian notion of competition. In the ecosystems of nature, species live inside one another, depending on one another for survival. Flow happens when we are centered in our own energy and able to give energy freely to others.

> A tiny mite of an insect, no bigger than the period at the end of this sentence, lives on the beak of a hummingbird. As the hummingbird approaches a flower with the right smell, this mite runs (quickly!) out to the end of the beak and hops off onto the flower, using the bird as its own little private Learjet.

Two other natural laws in the successful community are flexibility and diversity. Every living system is in constant flux. To survive, any system must respond to change. The more diversity within the system, the more chances it has to survive major change because it can draw upon these diverse resources. The First Insight reminds us of the natural role that coincidence plays in introducing diversity. Intuitive inner guidance is the epitome of flexibility and flow.

The last principle is coevolution. To sustain a community requires that it "coevolve through an interplay of creation and mutual adaptation. The creative reaching out into novelty is a fundamental property of life. . . ."[25] As creative, intuitive beings (and not paralyzed by fear or despair), we are already very well adapted to bringing forth the solutions needed by listening to inner guidance.

The eight principles of ecology, then, that are used in the design of organizations are interdependence, sustainability (seeing the long-term impact), ecological cycles, energy flow, partnership, flexibility, diversity, and coevolution.

Another leading ecology thinker, Paul Hawken, in *The Ecology of Commerce*, points out that in order to make the changes necessary to survive and sustain life on earth, we need to find a way to work with the confusion, ignorance, and revulsion that we so often feel when we become aware of the damage to our environment. Like Macy, he believes a crucial step will be to begin to find ways to introduce ecological principles and to discuss them together in a manner that draws people together and gives them hope and a chance for participation. "The salient question we need to discuss in our communities and businesses is whether humankind will participate in that restoration or be condemned by our ignorance to vanish from the planet."[26]

The Restorative Economy. The Manuscript reminds us that spiritual awareness means recognizing the interdependence of all life, and the beauty of this existence. These two perspectives lead us inevitably to the work we must do at this time—harmonizing our-

> Since evolution meanders more than it progresses, among animal species and humans alike, it is reasonable to suppose that evolutions in the metanormal domain are likely to be marked by ups and downs. The choice to cultivate our greater possibilities is ours, not God's. . . . There will be no further human development unless some of us work to realize it.
>
> MICHAEL MURPHY,
> *The Future of the Body*[27]

selves to our natural habitat, learning and living by its natural laws. New leadership is emerging. To reach the promise of the Ninth Insight requires a shift from the rapacious use of resources to what Hawken calls the restorative economy:

> The restorative economy comes down to this: We need to imagine a prosperous commercial culture that is so intelligently designed and constructed that it mimics nature at every step, a symbiosis of company and customer and ecology. . . . if we are to be effective in our lives, we have to find workable techniques and programs that can be put into practice soon, tools for change that are easily grasped and understood, and that conform naturally to the landscape of human nature.[28]

According to Hawken, the nature of business, although often exploitive and destructive in the past, is not so inherently. As we move into the next millennium, business can be—must be—redesigned for sustainability. He writes:

> Ironically, business contains our blessing. It must, because no other institution in the modern world is powerful enough to foster the necessary changes. . . . Business is the problem and it must be a part of the solution. Its power is more crucial than ever if we are to organize and efficiently meet the world's needs. . . . While commerce at its worst sometimes appears to be a shambles of defilement compared to the beauty and complexity of the natural world, the ideas and much of the technology required for the redesign of our business and the restoration of the world are already in hand. What is wanting is collective will.[29]

There is a growing trend to apply spiritual and ecological principles to commerce. Peter M. Senge, author of *The Fifth*

Discipline, believes the old view of business is hampered by *fragmentation* (lack of feedback and whole thinking), *competition* (our divisive capitalistic cornerstone), and *reactiveness* (not flexible and creative enough for the future). Dr. Senge, director of the Center for Organizational Learning at MIT's Sloan School of Management, focuses on decentralizing the role of leadership in an organization to enhance the capacity of all people to work productively toward common goals. In a recent article Senge and coauthor Fred Kofman state that changes in business, going beyond the corporate culture, "penetrate the bedrock assumptions and habits of our culture as a whole."[30] Recognizing that nothing will change without personal transformation, they believe that a corporate structure must be created to engender creativity and learning—in a safe environment. They write, "When people talk and listen to each other this way, they create a field of alignment that produces tremendous power to invent new realities in conversation, and to bring about these new realities in action."[31]

New Business. For this new vision to work, people must be committed. According to Senge, a learning organization must be grounded in three foundations: (1) a culture based on transcendent human values of love, wonder, humility, and compassion (shades of the Fifth Insight); (2) a set of practices for generative conversation and coordinated action (echoes of the new interpersonal ethics of the Eighth Insight); and (3) a capacity to see and work with the flow of life as a system (being open to coincidences and engaging the flow).

By using these principles and replacing our dysfunctional and shortsighted methods, we can move toward the automation spo-

> It is . . . love who makes the
>   mortar
> And it's love who stacked these
>   stones
> And it's love who made the
>   stage here
> Although it looks like we're
>   alone
>
>   DAVID WILCOX,
>   "Show the Way"[32]

ken of in the Ninth Insight. As it teaches, we can produce everything the culture needs for everyone, using pure energy sources and increasing durability of goods. The time will come when each individual will own equal shares in automated industries, allowing everyone to receive an income, all without a repressive central authority. The focus of life will be to let synchronicity direct our spiritual evolution. Spiritual principles—following one's inner guidance—will keep our evolution from being chaotic.

In the next millennium, perhaps even this green technology will be replaced with our own abilities. We might not need technological apparatus to produce food, to heal, travel, or communicate. We will learn to manifest what we need.

Tithing—A New Perspective on Giving

Eventually we will have no need for currency. Even now in the late twentieth century, we are not far from being able to produce the kind of automation that can free ourselves from working simply to make a living.

The Manuscript predicts that we will be paid for our insights and for our value as a human being. Class, status, power, and property will no longer be motivating factors or definitions of success. In the evolved culture, we will give to those who provide us with spiritual inspiration. The concept of tithing has traditionally meant that we give a percentage of our income to an established institution, usually a church or charity. As we increasingly value the synchronistic unfoldment of our lives, we will be inspired to give to those who give to us in energy, ideas, and opportunities. Tithing becomes a tangible exchange of energy and expression of appreciation.

Learning for the Future

In order for the future to unfold as the Manuscript predicts, we must begin to develop an enriched educational environment for the new generation so that they can more fully engage the evolutionary flow.

Not surprisingly, the same principles that govern sustainable communities have another application in education. During these years of transition there will be many new theories and programs to address the need for raising truly conscious children. As an example, one such model is being developed in Berkeley, California, at the Elmwood Institute, founded by Fritjof Capra. Termed "eco-literacy," this format uses the same eight principles for self-organizing, sustainable systems.[33]

Interdependence: "In a learning community, teachers, students, administrators, parents, business and community members are all interlinked in a network of relationships, working together to facilitate learning."

Sustainability: "Teachers see the long-term impact they have on students."

Ecological Cycles: "Everyone is both a teacher and a learner."

Energy Flow: "Learning communities are open communities where people are moving in and out, finding their own niches in the system."

Partnership: "All members work in partnership, which means democracy and empowerment because each part plays a very crucial role."

Flexibility: "There is dynamic change and fluidity. Daily schedules are fluid; each time there is a change of theme, the learning environment is recreated."

Diversity: "Students are encouraged to use diverse modes and strategies of learning . . . diverse learning styles are appreciated . . . cultural diversity is critical . . . for true community."

Coevolution: "As businesses, community groups, and parents work more in partnership with the school . . . they coevolve."

Critical Mass and Morphogenetic Fields

The central hypothesis of Kenneth Ring's work with near-death experiencers in *Heading toward Omega* is that their spiritual transformation might represent a general evolutionary drift. But, he asks, how will a change of consciousness happen fast enough to save our planet? He offers a theory that seems to resonate with the idea of critical mass taught in the First Insight.

He builds his theory on the work of Rupert Sheldrake, an English biologist, whose book *A New Science of Life: The Hypothesis of Formative Causation* was published in 1981 and is still controversial. According to Sheldrake's theory there exists an invisible organizing field which he calls the *morphogenetic field*. Sheldrake hypothesizes that this all-pervasive field, which is unbounded by time or space, determines both the form and the behavior of all systems and organisms. This means that once a change has occurred in one system or species in one part of the world, the change may affect like-systems and species in any other part of the world. Interestingly, this theory also may account for the transmission of *learned behavior*. For example, in studies conducted in 1920 by Harvard psychologist William McDougall, rats were trained to swim mazes. After several generations, the rats had learned to swim ten times faster than the first generation, indicating the retention of these learned abilities. However, even more intriguing was the discovery that rats in maze-swimming experiments in other countries were *starting out* at the same level as the advanced rats in McDougall's studies. According to Sheldrake's theory of morphic resonance, a field was established by McDougall's rats that guided later rats, allowing them to learn more quickly.

Applying this theory to the field of evolution in humans, Ring quotes science writer Peter Russell, whose commentary lays a strong foundation for the implications of the *Celestine* Manuscript:

> Applying Sheldrake's theory to the development of higher states of consciousness, we might predict that the more individuals begin to raise their own levels of consciousness, the stronger the morphogenetic field for higher states would become, and the easier it would be for others to move in that direction. Society would gather momentum toward enlightenment. Since the rate of growth would not be dependent on the achievements of those who had gone before, we would enter a phase of super-exponential growth. Ultimately, this could lead to a chain reaction, in which everyone suddenly started making the transition to a higher level of consciousness.[34]

SUMMARY OF THE NINTH INSIGHT

The Ninth Insight is the awareness of how evolution will proceed as we live the other eight Insights. As synchronicity increases, we are raised into higher and higher levels of energy vibration. Further, as we are led into our true missions, we will shift professions or vocations or invent our own business in order to work in the field that most inspires us. For many, this work will be to automate the production of basic goods and services: food (other than what is personally grown), shelter, clothing, means of travel, media access, recreation. This automation will be sanctioned because most of us will no longer be focused on these industries as our life work. Access to these goods will not be abused because we each will be synchronistically following our growth path and will consume only when necessary.

The practice of tithing, giving to others who bring us spiritual insight, will supplement incomes and free us from rigid work settings. Eventually, the need for currency will disappear altogether as free energy sources and durable goods allow the automation to be total. As the evolution continues, synchronistic growth will raise our vibrations to the point where we break through to the afterlife dimension, merging that dimension with our own and ending the birth/death cycle.

Further Reading

In addition to the excellent books listed in the notes for this chapter, we suggest:

Ishmael. Daniel Quinn. Bantam/Turner, 1993.

Coming of the Cosmic Christ. Matthew Fox. Harper & Row, 1988.

The Turning Point. Fritjof Capra. Bantam, 1992.

Autobiography of a Yogi. Paramahansa Yogananda. Self-Realization Fellowship, 1946.

Touched by Angels. Eileen Freeman. Warner, 1993.

The Mayan Factor: Path beyond Technology. Jose Arguelles. Bear & Co., 1987.

Life and Teachings of the Masters of the Far East. Bard T. Spalding. Devorss & Co., 1964.

Energy Grid: Harmonic Six Hundred Ninety-five and the Pulse of the Universe. Bruce L. Cathie. American West Publishers, 1990.

Creative Work: The Constructive Role of Business in a Transforming Society. Willis Harman and John Hormann. Knowledge Systems, 1990.

The Mind of the Cells: Or Willed Mutation of Our Species. Satprem. Institute of Evolutionary Research, 1992.

Saved by the Light. Dannion Brinkley with Paul Perry. Villard Books, 1994.

INDIVIDUAL STUDY OF THE NINTH INSIGHT

Staying in the Present

Live the Eight Insights. You are part of the evolutionary acceleration. Like so many of us, you might become excited about the vision of the future and want to be there *now*. The key is to *be here now* (to quote author and spiritual teacher Ram Dass) and to use the eight Insights in daily life.

In every workplace, in every discipline, you will encounter some resistance or fear of change as well as support and agreement. The key is to keep alert for coincidences and messages, ask questions and act from inner guidance, be willing to speak the truth in power struggles, and keep energy high through contact with nature and beauty.

Open to New Abilities

Keep Growing. Much of the focus of the Manuscript is on energy—acknowledging it, seeing it, listening to it, staying centered in it, and building it. Notice what energy disciplines attract you. Many of you might want to change careers, or simply deepen your knowledge or ability in a new field. At no time in history have there been so many new windows of wisdom available to be studied. Virtually all fields work with energy in one way or another. For example, the healing of the future might very well be focused on vibrational shifting using sound, light, movement, and mental imagery as well as shamanic methods. Nutrition and agriculture have been impacted widely by psychic energy work as well as biological and ecological principles. Psychology is widening its parameters to include hypnosis and past-life regression work to uncover deeply held experiences. Education is wide open for more self-empowering methods to help children fulfill their destiny and participate in evolution. The design of workplaces and homes is undergoing changes with the introduction of color psychology, ergonomics, and even feng shui, the ancient Chinese system of spatial energy dynamics. Spiritual groups and communities, recovery groups, and the revitalization of religious congregations all offer expanded opportunities to participate in the web of evolution. Martial arts, dance, and movement disciplines build personal well-being and power. Let your intuition show you the way, and be willing to follow through with action.

Use Imagination to Create New Opportunities

The Personal Journey. What would you rather be doing? Often we feel restless and don't know what we really want. After reading this last chapter, what were some of the ideas about the future that appealed to you personally? Describe in your journal one or more ideal lives that you would like to live. *Be really big in your thinking.* Use the following questions to help you imagine a new life:

- *Who* (Who are the people you see yourself with? Artists? Musicians? Business executives? Healers? What kind of family setting do you see?)
- *What* (What kind of occupation do you like? Adventurous? Teaching? Healing? Promoting?)

- *When* (How far away does this ideal life seem? When could you make one small step toward it?)
- *Where* (Where do you want to be? Large city? Europe? Mountains? Desert?)

Two good books to help you explore new options for yourself are Barbara Sher's *Wishcraft: How to Get What You Really Want* (Ballantine Books, 1979) and Julia Cameron's *The Artist's Way: A Spiritual Path to Higher Creativity* (Jeremy P. Tarcher/Perigee, 1992).

Shift Your Perspective

If you have a strong desire to give more meaning and breadth to your life, consider the following points that Robert Monroe gleaned from his out-of-body experiences.[35]

- Know that you are more than your physical body.
- Remember that you are here to do certain things, but don't let your need to survive make you desperate. Your ultimate goal is not physical survival.
- Understand that you are here on earth by choice. When you have satisfied your purpose in learning, you may leave.
- Perceive the world as what it really is—a place to learn.
- Participate and enjoy your life as fully as you can, but don't become addicted to it.

As you integrate these ideas into your thinking, notice any changes in your personal goals or in your interactions with others.

STUDY GROUP FOR THE NINTH INSIGHT

Session 13

2 hours 30 minutes

Purpose: To discuss the Ninth Insight

Introduction

Have volunteers read aloud the recap of the Ninth Insight on pages 244–245, up to the section "The Case for an Evolutionary Leap." Remember to speak as you feel inspired and to give energy and full attention to those who are speaking. You might want to use some of the following questions to get the discussion started:

- How has your perspective changed since studying the Insights?
- How has your behavior changed since you first read *The Celestine Prophecy* or started working on the study guide?
- What aspect of the future appeals to you the most in the Ninth Insight?
- How do you feel you are contributing to the evolutionary shift?
- What issues come up for you as you talk about the Insights with family, friends?
- What intuitions have come to you that seem related to any of the Insights, or the Ninth Insight in particular?
- How would you talk about these concepts with children?
- Intuitively, what do you feel to be the deepest truths *for you* in *The Celestine Prophecy*?

EXERCISE 1: In the Realm of Possibilities

Purpose: To open your imagination and practice expanding your limits of self-knowledge

Time: 1 hour

Directions:

Step 1: Spend 10 to 15 minutes jotting down an imaginary life for yourself—any alternative that springs to mind that is different from the one you currently live. The object here is to really be expanded!

Step 2: Choose a partner and describe your imaginary life to each other, taking turns (about 15 minutes each).

Step 3: Return to the main group and share your experiences as you feel directed.

Step 4: If you came up with imaginary lives similar to someone else's, you might want to explore what further messages are suggested by this coincidence.

EXERCISE 2. Talking about the Environment

Purpose: To mitigate some of the fear, hopelessness, or despair that we feel about environmental problems

Time: As available

Directions: You might want to use some of the following questions to start the discussion.

- What are you most afraid of in terms of planetary problems?
- What disturbs you most about the future?
- What kinds of feelings do you have about your children and their future?

- What priorities does the group feel are most pressing (someone can make a list).
- How do you cope with the stress of hearing about oil spills, the ozone layer, toxic waste, poverty, overpopulation?
- How do you try to contribute individually to understanding or resolving a specific problem?
- What books have you read that inspired you?
- Are you willing to read more books or articles and exchange information with the group at future meetings?

Closing

Requests for support, and sending loving energy.

Further Sessions

If your group wants to continue meeting, perhaps you could begin reading some of the books quoted throughout this study guide and discuss the ideas in them. Remember, your group is a good place for brainstorming and healing.

> *So now the stage is set. Feel your own heart beating*
> *In your chest. This life's not over yet.*
> DAVID WILCOX, "Show the Way"[36]

Notes

Chapter 1

1. Carlos Castaneda, *The Teachings of Don Juan* (Berkeley, Calif.: University of California Press, 1968).

2. C. G. Jung, *Collected Works*, Vol. 14, p. 464. Quoted in Aniela Jaffe, "C. G. Jung and Parapsychology," in *Science and ESP*, ed. J. R. Smythies (New York: Humanities Press, 1967), p. 280. Also quoted in Alan Vaughan, *Incredible Coincidence, The Baffling World of Synchronicity* (New York: J. B. Lippincott Co., 1979), p. 16.

3. Alan Vaughan, *Incredible Coincidence, The Baffling World of Synchronicity* (New York: J. B. Lippincott Co., 1979), p. 162.

Chapter 2

1. Michael Murphy, *The Future of the Body* (Los Angeles: Jeremy P. Tarcher, 1992), p. 173.

2. Philip Novak, Buddhist-Christian Studies, East-West Religions Project (University of Hawaii, 1984), pp. 64–65.

3. C. G. Jung, *Dreams* (Princeton: Princeton University Press, 1974), p. 36.

4. Deepak Chopra, *Ageless Body, Timeless Mind* (New York: Harmony Books, 1993), p. 4.

277

5. Ibid., p. 22.

6. Ibid., pp. 4–5.

Chapter 3

1. Peter Tompkins and Christopher Bird, *The Secret Life of Plants* (New York: Harper & Row, 1973), p. 27.

2. Ibid., p. 38.

3. Ibid., p. 27.

4. Stanislav Grof, *The Adventure of Self-Discovery* (Albany, N.Y.: State University of New York Press, 1988), p. 111.

5. George Leonard, *The Ultimate Athlete* (Berkeley, Calif.: North Atlantic Books, 1990), pp. 62–63.

6. Tompkins and Bird, p. 223.

7. Leonard Laskow, M.D., *Healing with Love: A Breakthrough Mind/Body Medical Program for Healing Yourself and Others* (New York: HarperCollins, 1992), p. 35.

8. Ibid., p. 70.

Chapter 4

1. Philip R. Kavanaugh, M.D., *Magnificent Addiction: Discovering Addiction as Gateway to Healing* (Lower Lake, Calif.: Aslan Publishing, 1992), p. 115.

2. Anne Frank, *Anne Frank: The Diary of a Young Girl*, trans. B. M. Mooyaart (Garden City, N.Y.: Doubleday & Co., 1967). Copyright 1952 by Otto H. Frank.

3. Eric Berne, M.D., *Games People Play: The Basic Handbook of Transactional Analysis* (New York: Ballantine Books, 1964), p. 46.

4. Kavanaugh, p. 187.

5. Melody Beattie, *Codependent No More: How to Stop Controlling Others and Start Caring for Yourself* (San Francisco: HarperCollins, 1987), p. 103.

6. Shakti Gawain, *Living in the Light* (New York: Bantam Books, 1993), p. xix.

7. Ibid., p. 29.

Chapter 5

1. James Redfield, *The Celestine Prophecy* (Hoover, Ala: Satori Press, 1993), p. 129.

2. Ibid., p. 129.

3. Ibid., pp. 120–21.

4. Carol Lee Flinders, *Enduring Grace: Living Portraits of Seven Women Mystics* (San Francisco: HarperSanFrancisco, 1993), p. 155.

5. Redfield, p. 121.

6. Ibid., p. 121.

7. Thich Nhat Hanh, *Present Moment Wonderful Moment: Mindfulness Verses for Daily Living* (Berkeley, Calif.: Parallax Press, 1990), p. 30.

8. Redfield, p. 122.

9. Sanaya Roman, *Spiritual Growth: Being Your Higher Self* (Tiburon, Calif.: HJ Kramer, 1989), p. 113.

10. Redfield, p. 125.

11. Roman, p. 114.

12. Michael Murphy and Rhea A. White, *The Psychic Side of Sports* (Reading, Mass.: Addison-Wesley Publishing Co., 1978), p. 21, quoted from Dick Schaap, "The Second Coming of St. Francis," *Sport*, December 1972, p. 94.

13. Ibid., p. 21, quoted from Arne Leuchs and Patricia Skalka, *Ski with Yoga* (Matteson, Ill.: Greatlakes Living Press, 1976), p. 5.

14. Ibid., p. 21, quoted from Lionel Terray, *The Borders of the Impossible* (Garden City, N.Y.: Doubleday, 1964), p. 23.

15. Ibid., p. 30, quoted from Maurice Herzog, *Annapurna* (New York: Dutton, 1952), p. 132.

16. Ibid., p. 20, quoted from George Leonard, *The Ultimate Athlete* (New York: Viking, 1975), p. 40.

17. Ibid., p. 28, quoted from Michael Novak, *The Joy of Sports* (New York: Basic Books, 1976), p. 164.

18. Ibid., pp. 30–31, quoted from Patsy Neal, *Sport and Identity* (Philadelphia: Dorrance, 1972), pp. 166–167.

19. Stanislav Grof, M.D., *The Adventure of Self-Discovery* (Albany, N.Y.: State University of New York Press, 1988), p. 113.

20. Michael Harner, *The Way of the Shaman* (San Francisco: Harper & Row, 1990), p. xv.

21. Ibid., p. 67.

22. Ibid., p. 250.

23. Paramahansa Yogananda, *Autobiography of a Yogi* (Los Angeles: Self-Realization Fellowship, 1993), pp. 166–67. First copyright 1946.

24. Robert A. Monroe, *Ultimate Journey* (New York: Doubleday, 1994), pp. 88–89.

25. Ibid., pp. 61–62.

26. Ibid., p. 62.

27. Ibid., p. 71.

28. Godfre Ray King, *Unveiled Mysteries*, 4th ed. (Schaumburg, Ill.: Saint Germain Press, 1982), pp. 3–4.

Chapter 6

1. James Redfield, *The Celestine Prophecy* (Hoover, Ala.: Satori Press, 1993), p. 142.

2. Thich Nhat Hanh, *Present Moment Wonderful Moment* (Berkeley, Calif.: Parallax Press, 1990), p. 32.

3. Joanna Macy, *World as Lover, World as Self* (Berkeley, Calif.: Parallax Press, 1991), p. 96.

4. Redfield, p. 155.

5. Glenn Gould as quoted in *Thirty-two Films about Glenn Gould*. Directed by Francois Girard. Produced by Samuel Goldwyn Company, 1994.

6. Redfield, p. 214.

7. *The Twelve Steps: A Way Out: A Working Guide for Adult Children of Alcoholic & Other Dysfunctional Families* (San Diego, Calif.: Recovery Publications, 1987), p. 13.

8. Redfield, p. 214.

9. Thich Nhat Hanh, p. 6.

Chapter 7

1. James Redfield, *The Celestine Prophecy* (Hoover, Ala.: Satori Press, 1993), p. 165.

2. Ibid.,, p. 163.

3. Thich Nhat Hanh, *Present Moment Wonderful Moment* (Berkeley, Calif.: Parallax Press, 1990), p. 29.

4. Sanaya Roman, *Spiritual Growth: Being Your Higher Self* (Tiburon, Calif.: HJ Kramer, 1987), p. 53.

5. Ibid., p. 42.

6. Thomas Moore, *The Care of the Soul* (New York: HarperCollins, 1992), p. 260.

7. Nancy Rosanoff, *Intuition Workout: A Practical Guide to Discovering and Developing Your Inner Knowing* (Boulder Creek, Calif.: Aslan Publishing, 1988), p. 121.

8. Ibid., p. 122.

9. Kazuaki Tanahashi, *Brush Mind* (Berkeley, Calif.: Parallax Press, 1990), p. 138.

10. Redfield, p. 178.

11. Ibid.

12. Arnold Patent, *You Can Have It All* (Piermont, N.Y.: Money Mastery Publishing, 1984), p. 143.

13. Redfield, p. 174.

14. Michael Murphy, *The Future of the Body* (Los Angeles: Jeremy P. Tarcher, 1992), p. 610.

15. A version of this game can be found in Rosanoff, p. 135.

Chapter 8

1. James Redfield, *The Celestine Prophecy* (Hoover, Ala.: Satori Press, 1993), p. 185.

2. Robert A. McDermott, ed., *The Essential Aurobindo* (Hudson, N.Y.: Lindisfarne Press, 1987), p. 205.

3. Harville Hendrix, Ph.D., *Getting the Love You Want: A Guide for Couples* (New York: HarperPerennial, 1990), p. 35.

4. Ibid., p. 82.

5. Ibid., p. 36.

6. Terence T. Gorski, *Getting Love Right: Learning the Choices of Healthy Intimacy* (New York: Fireside/Parkside, Simon & Schuster, 1993), p. 141.

7. May Sarton, *Journal of a Solitude* (New York: W. W. Norton & Co., 1973), p. 11.

8. Anne Morrow Lindbergh, *Gift from the Sea* (New York: Pantheon Books, 1955), p. 108.

9. Melody Beattie, *Codependent No More: How to Stop Controlling Others and Start Caring for Yourself* (New York: Hazelden Books, Harper/Collins, 1987), p. 103.

10. Lindbergh, p. 104.

11. H. Stephen Glenn and Jane Nelsen, Ed.D., *Raising Self-Reliant Children in a Self-Indulgent World* (Rocklin, Calif.: Prima Publishing & Communications, 1989), p. 29.

12. Glenn and Nelsen, p. 50.

13. Redfield, p. 217.

14. Rick DelVecchio, "Generation of Rage," *San Francisco Chronicle*, May 11, 1994, p. A8. Data from Children's Defense Fund and American Psychological Association.

Chapter 9

1. Michael Murphy, *The Future of the Body* (Los Angeles: Jeremy P. Tarcher, 1992), p. 26.

2. Ibid., pp. 27–28.

3. Michael Harner, *The Way of the Shaman* (New York: Harper & Row, 1990), p. xiii.

4. Petru Popescu, *Amazon Beaming* (New York: Viking Penguin, 1991).

5. Marlo Morgan. *Mutant Message from Downunder* (New York: HarperCollins, 1994).

6. Murphy, p. 551.

7. Robert A. McDermott, ed., *The Essential Aurobindo* (Hudson, N.Y.: Lindisfarne Press, 1987), p. 64.

8. Ibid., p. 192.

9. Ibid., p. 194.

10. Ibid., p. 195.

11. Ibid., p. 198.

12. Ibid., p. 200.

13. Pierre Teilhard de Chardin, *The Phenomenon of Man* (New York, Harper & Row, 1959), p. 15.

14. Ibid., p. 20.

15. Ibid., p. 27.

16. Ibid., p. 232.

17. Murphy, p. 66.

18. Robert A. Monroe, *Ultimate Journey* (New York: Doubleday, 1994), p. 13.

19. Ibid., p. 100.

20. Ibid., p. 84.

21. Kenneth Ring, *Heading toward Omega: In Search of the meaning of the Near-Death Experience* (New York: Quill, 1984), p. 256.

22. Joanna Macy, *World as Lover, World as Self* (Berkeley, Calif.: Parallax Press, 1991), p. 15.

23. David Peri and Robert Wharton, "Sucking Doctor—Second Night: Comments by Doctor, Patient, and Singers." Unpublished manuscript. Quoted in Michael Harner, *The Way of the Shaman* (San Francisco, Harper & Row, 1990), p. 117.

24. Fritjof Capra. Speech given at a retreat of Mill Valley School District educators at Walker Creek Ranch in Marin County, California, April 23–24, 1994.

25. Ibid.

26. Paul Hawken, *The Ecology of Commerce: A Declaration of Sustainability* (New York: HarperBusiness, 1994), p. 203.

27. Murphy, p. 198.

28. Hawken, p. 15.

29. Ibid., p. 17.

30. Peter M. Senge, Ph.D., and Fred Kofman, "Communities of Commitment: The Heart of Learning Organizations."

31. Ibid., p. 16.

32. David Wilcox, *Big Horizon*, "Show the Way." A&M Records, Los Angeles.

33. "Principles of Ecology—Principles of Education" (Berkeley, Calif.: The Elmwood Institute, 1994).

34. Ring, p. 263. From Peter Russell, *The Global Brain*, p. 129.

35. Monroe, pp. 88–89.

36. Wilcox, *Big Horizon*.

About the Authors

JAMES REDFIELD lives with his wife, Salle, in Alabama. He is the author of *The Celestine Prophecy* and *The Tenth Insight: Holding the Vision*.

For information or subscriptions to *The Celestine Journal*, a monthly newsletter, call 1-800-814-6462 9 A.M. to 5 P.M. CST (Alabama). International orders: 1-205-620-9972.

CAROL ADRIENNE, M.A., is the co-author with James Redfield of *The Celestine Prophecy: An Experiential Guide*. She is also the author of *The Numerology Kit* and *Your Child's Destiny*. Ms. Adrienne has been an intuitive counsellor, teacher, and lecturer since 1976.

For a free copy of *The Spiritual Path: Tips and Tales from the Spiritual Adventure* (a quarterly newsletter to which readers may contribute), send your name, address, and telephone number to Carol Adrienne, M.A., 12400 San Pablo Avenue, Suite 110, Richmond, CA 94805. Fax: 510-235-6727 or Tel: 415-553-2535.

Twenty-five page personal Numerological Life Charts are also available at the above address.